Wil

Suddenly I saw something back in the woods, a flash of clothing or pale skin. "There he is!" I shouted, drawing my Smith & Wesson and digging my knees into the pony's sides. The pony must have felt my urgency because it tore into the woods at a full gallop. . . .

As I burst out of the woods into a clearing, I saw a man jumping into a black truck, like a Jeep, but larger and heavier. The door slammed, and then I heard a loud crack, like something at the center of the universe had snapped in half. At that point, the world disappeared. . . .

Praise for Edgar winner Ruth Birmingham and ace Atlanta P.I. Sunny Childs

SWEET GEORGIA

RUTH BIRMINGHAM

BERKLEY PRIME CRIME, NEW YORK

This is a work of fiction. Names, characters, places, and incidents are either the product of the author's imagination or are used fictitiously, and any resemblance to actual persons, living or dead, business establishments, events, or locales is entirely coincidental.

SWEET GEORGIA

A Berkley Prime Crime Book / published by arrangement with the author

PRINTING HISTORY
Berkley Prime Crime edition / September 2000

The Penguin Putnam Inc. World Wide Web site address is http://www.penguinputnam.com

ISBN: 0-425-17671-1

Berkley Prime Crime Books are published by The Berkley Publishing Group, a division of Penguin Putnam Inc., 375 Hudson Street, New York, New York 10014.
The name BERKLEY PRIME CRIME and the BERKLEY PRIME CRIME design are trademarks belonging to Penguin Putnam Inc.

PRINTED IN THE UNITED STATES OF AMERICA

10 9 8 7 6 5 4 3 2 1

Acknowledgments

Thanks for the generous assistance provided to me by retired Atlanta Police Department homicide detective Gary Lovett and Van Pearlberg, Assistant District Attorney of Cobb County, Georgia.

To Lisa Scott, who brought Jake into our lives.
You're in our prayers forever.
Be strong, darling.

LOCKED
ROOM

CHAPTER 1

"**LOCKED ROOM MYSTERIES**," Gunnar said to his guest as I walked into the room, "only happen in books, Mr. Ratkin."

Gunnar Brushwood, my boss and the owner of Peachtree Investigations, works hard at being a man's man. And in his sanctum sanctorum, his trophy room, he is at full, hairy-knuckled bloom. On the walls of this dark, mahogany-paneled space hang the heads of at least twenty beasts that he has killed, most with a rifle, some with a bow and arrow, one with a curare-tipped blowgun dart, and one which he claims to have beaten to death with a stick. Self-defense, or so his story goes.

Gunnar himself sat in a large wingbacked chair of red leather. He is a big man of about fifty, with a square jaw, ruddy skin, and a large white mustache waxed into points, fully erumpent. He was even wearing his bush jacket, with some sort of squashy hat rolled under one epaulet like he was on home leave from a stint in the Foreign Legion. Gunnar is nothing if not theatrical.

"Ah, Sunny!" Gunnar called to me in his rich Southern accent when he noticed me entering the room. "You made good time, darling. Meet Mr. Ratkin. He's Georgia Burnett's husband."

Jeremy Ratkin didn't look like the husband of the most famous young woman in country music. Nor did he look at home among the dead beasts on the dark, paneled walls of the room.

"Sit," Jeremy Ratkin said to me, gesturing at a leather chair as though this were his house and not Gunnar's. "I was telling Gunnar a story."

I sat. Georgia Burnett's husband wore his gray hair long, and his black eyes were half hidden under heavy lids. His wide mouth turned down at the edges as though he were in a permanent state of disappointment at the world. His nose was spectacular, a long thin hook that gave him the profile of a Medici off some old Florentine coin. He wore the sort of fashionably silly black-framed glasses that I associate with movie directors, a black cashmere sweater, jeans, cowboy boots, and a close-cropped beard. Except for his clothes and his Hollywood-looking glasses, he had the look of a Talmudic scholar.

"Can we get back to your wife?" Gunnar sounded impatient. "She, what, disappeared from inside a locked room? Is that what you're saying?"

Jeremy Ratkin ignored Gunnar. "Some people know how to throw a baseball," he said. "It's instinctive. I, however, know how to make a deal. So Barry said to me, 'The back end of this deal, no, it's untenable.' Untenable, the very word. And so I stood up, and I walked out of the room. Nobody walks out of Barry's office. But *I* did. I understood his pressure points, you see? I understood. Two days later, Barry calls me up and says, 'Jeremy, can we work something out?'" Jeremy Ratkin's gaze flicked across our faces.

"Wow," I said, sucking up a little. I had no earthly idea who Barry was, but I knew Jeremy Ratkin was worth money—a commodity that had been in short supply at the firm lately—so I figured some judicious ass kissing was in order.

Strangely, however, Gunnar just sat there impassively.

When I see Gunnar—the king of bonhomie—looking impassive, I know he's pissed. What had I been missing? I wondered.

"The reason I mention this," Ratkin said, "is because I'm concerned about your fee structure."

I frowned. I had gotten a call from Gunnar half an hour earlier saying that Georgia Burnett may have been missing or murdered—the story wasn't entirely clear—and here this guy was apparently more concerned about chiseling us on our fee than telling what was going on.

"I'm sure you've already been over it with Gunnar," I said. "But before we go too far down the trail on the money issue, you think you could tell me what happened to your wife?"

Jeremy Ratkin dismissed me with a barely discernible flick of his index finger. "Fees," he said. "Fees."

Gunnar looked at me with that eerily impassive face and said, "Other than what I told you on the phone, Sunny, I don't know any more than you do. We've gotten a little bogged down on this fee issue. Since you're more involved with that than I am, I thought maybe you could address that for Mr. Ratkin."

Ratkin didn't look at me. "Gunnar, you're wasting your time bringing in Miss Childs to negotiate. I make a rule to only deal with the principal."

"Hold on, hold on," I said. "Let me be crystal clear here first. Your wife, Georgia Burnett, big-time country singing star, is . . . what? Missing? Murdered?"

Grudgingly, as though he had to pay for every word that he let escape from his mouth, Ratkin said, "Fees first."

"Mr. Ratkin . . ." I gave him my frostiest smile. "Fees bear a direct relation to the manner of work to be done. Now are you telling us that your wife, Georgia Burnett, is . . ."

Ratkin glowered at me. "Missing," he said finally.

"For how long?"

Again the grudging pause. "Since last night."

"Are the police involved?"

"Fees," he said. "First, fees. Then, information."

I stared at the cold son of a bitch for a minute. His wife was missing and all he could think about was money? No wonder Gunnar was angry.

I stood up. "Gunnar?" I said pleasantly. I decided the frosty approach wasn't right for a guy like Jeremy Ratkin. "Let me borrow your keys, how about?"

Gunnar wasn't sure where I was heading, but he let me take the lead. All matters concerning money, Gunnar leaves strictly up to me. He fished around in his pocket, tossed me a wad of keys. I took them over to a large antique gun case sandwiched between the heads of a wildebeest and a scimitar-horned oryx, opened the glass-paned door, and took out the first weapon that came to hand. There was a box of cartridges sitting next to it. I opened the box, took out one long brass bullet.

"Would you tell Mr. Ratkin about this weapon, Gunnar?" I said. I was still smiling, the kind of light, flirty smile my mother likes to use around rich men.

Gunnar watched me with a glint in his eye. "That'd be a Purdy express rifle," he said. "Handmade London best gun, box-lock, Prince of Wales grip, burled English walnut stock, silver inlays, and a carved African hunting scene on the brightwork."

"Sure," I said. "But more to the point, it's used for killing, what?"

"Elephants." Gunnar smiled a little. "It's chambered in one of the biggest, baddest rifle calibers on the planet—.450 Nitro Express. By God, that son of a bitch'll drop a charging bull rhino in one shot."

I cracked open the breech of the rifle, slid in the huge, cigar-sized cartridge. Then I pointed the gun at Jeremy Ratkin's head and said, "Sir, get out of this house. Now."

Jeremy Ratkin's eyes didn't change expression in the slightest. Not a man you'd want to play poker against. Finally, though, he stood up and walked slowly across the room. His left foot dragged just the slightest bit, his boot making a whispering noise on Gunnar's thick Afghan rug.

After we heard the sound of an engine starting up outside, Gunnar said to me, "While I'm with you in sentiment, doll, I was under the impression that our fine firm was a little short on cash these days."

I smiled as I put the elephant gun back in the cabinet. "He's a negotiator," I said. "He'll call back."

We sat for a long time in silence, the glittering glass eyes of all those dead animals looking down at us from the walls. "I went to elementary school with Georgia Burnett," I said finally.

"That right?"

"Third grade, Mrs. Portell's homeroom. That was right after Daddy died, when we were poor as dirt, living down in West End."

"Most likely to succeed type?"

"Not even hardly. I don't even remember her that well. She wasn't fat or thin, tall or short. She had a certain, hmm, overeagerness to please. I could be wrong, but I seem to recall that her old man was a plumber or a pipefitter, and that her mother was dead."

"What about Ratkin? You're the country music fanatic—you know anything about him?"

"Sure. He's the head of ArchRival Records, which is probably the biggest independent record label in Nashville. He discovered Georgia, he groomed her, he married her, he made her into a star. Cinderella meets *Entertainment Tonight*."

Gunnar scowled, looked at his watch. "You sure this boy's gonna call back?"

Before I could answer, the phone rang.

Jeremy Ratkin complained and weaseled and bullied and threatened, but I quoted him double our usual rate, take it or leave it. First, I didn't like the guy, and second I could tell he was the kind of person that if you didn't thrash the daylights out of him up front, he'd thereafter take advantage of you forever and anon as a matter of principle—question every expense report, fight every bill, slow-pay you, and then probably sue you to boot. Who needs that shit?

It was around ten that morning when he was back in Gunnar's trophy room telling us what had happened to his wife.

"Two years ago," Jeremy Ratkin said, "my wife sold five point three million units, domestic, another million two international; her tour grossed twenty-eight million and change; merchandising brought in almost a million seven; her appearances in several television dramas brought in four hundred and seventy-five thousand. This is all confidential by the way. That made her by far the most profitable artist on the ArchRival label. In addition, she was interviewed by three hundred and forty-seven journalists, and appeared on the cover of fourteen major American magazines. She received over twelve thousand fan letters and signed countless thousands of autographs.

"ArchRival records makes certain that she gets the best songs from the best songwriters in Nashville. We hire the best studio musicians and the best producers. She has a good, though not a great voice, and she sings with great sincerity."

He let this information settle for a while.

"She is, right now, a bona fide Entertainment Phenomenon—and that phenomenon has not yet peaked." He lifted his bad leg with both hands, crossed it over his good one.

He stopped speaking for a moment, took a sip of the fresh-ground Hawaiian coffee Gunnar had poured for him, and sat there in the chair without moving. What struck me as I looked at him—just as it had when I'd walked into the room an hour earlier—was that Jeremy Ratkin seemed studied, unhurried, and not one bit nervous or frightened.

We sat for a few moments, and then I said, "Mr. Ratkin, do you love your wife?"

It was the first time I'd seen even a flash of emotion in Ratkin. Something sparked in his poker-player's eyes, but I couldn't get a read on it. Whatever the emotion, it passed quickly.

"What kind of question is that?" he said irritably.

Gunnar leaned back in his chair. Finally he said, "Maybe that answers her question, bud."

"I doubt it," Ratkin said.

"My point," I said, "is that every time we ask you what happened to your wife, you start talking about money. Why is that?"

"Look," Gunnar said quickly. "We haven't exactly gotten off on the right foot here, hoss. How about you tell us what happened to your wife."

"We have two homes," Ratkin said. "One is in Nashville, and one is here, outside Atlanta. As you know, Georgia grew up in Atlanta and wanted to live around here, so after we got married, we purchased a four hundred-acre farm in Floyd County and built a cottage there."

"How long have you been married?" I said.

"Three years," Ratkin said. "We divide our time between Nashville and Atlanta. I have a lot of business in Nashville and frankly I find Floyd County to be a fairly insipid place. Georgia likes it though. She can ride her horses, knock around in the garden, things of that nature."

Ratkin frowned, then sighed loudly. "It's probably my fault. I don't spend enough time with her. She's there all alone. I keep saying, you know, I'll be down there tomorrow, I'll be down this weekend. . . ." He shrugged. "Something always comes up."

"So what exactly happened?" Gunnar said.

"When I say 'all alone,' I don't mean that literally no one is there. She has a four-person security team. Three shifts a day, one person on each shift. The fourth security person fills in as needed and on weekends."

"She have a big need for bodyguards?" I said.

"What do you think I've been talking about all this time?" Ratkin looked at me like I was extremely naive. "According to our market research, about seventy-five million people in the United States know Georgia's name. One person in four. That may not sound like so much to you, but bear in mind that one person in five can't even name the president of the United States. My wife has a pretty face, she's personable and instinctively plays to the camera, her stomach is flat, she's on the large end of the C cup spectrum, and she works out with a personal trainer every day. She arouses desire in men and jealousy in women.

"So I don't have to tell you that among the seventy-five million people who listened to her records, or saw her videos on TNN, or looked at her more or less naked body in *Penthouse Magazine*, it's a mathematical certainty that there are tens of thousands of lunatics, murderers, flashers, obsessive-compulsives, rapists, stalkers, idiots, geeks, and other people with mental disorders.

"Inevitably some of those assholes are drawn to a woman like my wife. They are drawn to the flame." For the first time he actually looked like he might have been experiencing something other than a poker game. "Four bodyguards is just barely enough."

"She's had problems in the past?"

"It's a constant problem. I'll put you in touch with Georgia's personal protection coordinator. She can give you more detailed information than I can."

"Okay," I said. "This is all useful information. But what actually *happened*?"

"I came down last night. Flew my plane down from Nashville and landed at Charlie Brown. A driver picked me up and took me to the farm. Floyd County is, what, an hour or so from the airport, so it was really late by the time I got there. I called a couple of times on the cell phone, but no one answered.

"The car dropped me off at the farm. The lights were on in the house, and her car was in the drive. I came inside. I could hear the television in the rec room, so I went down there. A movie was playing on the VCR, but no one was there.

"I called Georgia's name several times, but no one answered. So I went up to the bedroom. The door was locked. I have to mention here that on the advice of a security consultant, the bedroom of the cottage has been fortified. Reinforced door, secondary alarm system, so on. The idea being that if someone came into the house, she could hit her alarm button and stay there in safety until her security people responded. The doors lock from the inside and can't be opened from outside.

"I kept knocking but she didn't answer. We have a second house on the property where a couple of the security people live. I buzzed them to come over and one of them battered the door down. We went in and nobody was there."

"Any sign of disturbance?" Gunnar said.

Ratkin hesitated. "Blood," he said finally. "There was some blood on the floor. Just a few drops, though."

"Anything overturned or broken?" I said.

Ratkin shook his head. "Just the blood."

"Anything else?"

"We went out and looked all over the property. We checked the barn, the stables, the pool. There was nobody there."

"So did you call the police?"

Ratkin hesitated. "No," he said finally.

"Okay, Mr. Ratkin," I said. "The sixty-four thousand dollar question. How come you came to us instead of to the cops?"

"There've been no ransom demands and, other than the blood, there's nothing to indicate foul play. I'd rather not draw publicity if she just . . . I don't know, if she just decided to fly to New York and go shopping."

"Do you think that's likely—that she'd fly up there without telling anybody?"

"No."

Gunnar and I looked at each other for a moment. "Uh, at the risk of being rude," I said, "how's your marriage?"

Ratkin just looked at me.

"My point is, do you have any reason to think your wife might have left you?"

Ratkin's dark eyes were expressionless. "Of course not."

Gunnar cleared his throat. "Alright, Mr. Ratkin, we can look into this matter. But we aren't going to piddle around on it forever. If we don't find anything, and she doesn't surface soon, you'll have to go to the police."

Ratkin shrugged. "Let's just see what develops."

CHAPTER 2

FLOYD COUNTY IS pretty country. Rolling hills, farms, pine forests. And Georgia Burnett had bought the best of it: an old farm perched at the top of a hill surrounded by pastures and forests, a pastiche of warm greens in the clear Indian summer light.

"First thing," I said, "we're going to treat this crime scene just like we were cops."

It was just after eleven o'clock and I was accompanied by my best investigator, Tawanda Flornoy, plus a former crime scene technician for the Atlanta police named Roy Nidlett.

We entered the huge lobby of Georgia Burnett's "cottage" in Floyd County, a rural county an hour to the northwest of Atlanta. It was not only an extravagant room, but it was beautiful, too: airy, warm, decorated with functional modern furniture.

I was assigning Tawanda, a retired Atlanta PD homicide detective, to supervise the processing of the scene. I figured she knew better than I did how it was done.

I went on with my instructions. "Anything you find that might be relevant, I want it preserved. Hair, fiber, fingerprints, bodily fluids, glass fragments, you name it. Every sample goes into a sealed and numbered bag, which you will sign on the seal and then log in on a log sheet. God forbid something terrible happened to this woman, and God forbid this ever ends up in a court of law, we need to preserve chain of custody, just like we were law enforcement people. If you find anything like a murder implement, anything that suggests we're dealing with a crime, don't even touch it. At that point, we back off and call the cops. Got it?"

Tawanda clapped her hands. "Let's get to it, baby." She was a large black woman who wore an extravagant red wig and earrings the size of wind chimes. Imagine a black Dolly Parton, then add eight inches of height, eighty pounds in weight—that's Tawanda Flornoy. Oh, yeah, plus she has a prosthetic foot, which she got after being run over by a pimp in a Lincoln Continental.

Roy Nidlett nodded. The crime scene guy was quiet and shy, with neatly pressed clothes. His physical movements, too, were neat and clipped in a way that at first seemed a little prissy, but that I began to suspect came from an economy of purpose. I hadn't worked with him before, but he came highly recommended.

I followed Tawanda and Roy up the stairs, through a doorway that had been smashed so badly the sheetrock had buckled, and into the bedroom.

We looked around the large, unremarkable room. Nothing seemed out of place.

"What you think about this locked room thing, Sunny?" Tawanda said.

I squinted at the battered door frame. I noticed a small, black scuff mark at the bottom of the frame. The door itself lay on the floor, still attached to one of its twisted hinges. It appeared that the bottom half of the door frame had actually been wrenched inward. "Who'd they get to knock this thing off the hinges?" I said. "He must have been a tank."

On examination I found that the door locked with two large steel bolts, one of which was still sunk into a socket in the floor. A second deadbolt at the top of the door would have been mated to a socket over the door frame.

"The top socket and bolt are still completely intact," I said. "At least one of these locks should have gotten smashed if they were both locked. Instead the door just rotated inward over this bottom bolt."

"You're right, Sunny," Tawanda said. "Looks like only the bottom deadbolt was locked."

"Roy," I said, "can you take a couple photos, then give me a hand?"

Nidlett's flashbulb went off a couple of times as he photographed the position of the fallen door. I pulled on a pair of latex gloves so as not to leave fingerprints, then Nidlett and I hoisted the door back up into its normal position.

I examined the bottom bolt. There was no spring to keep it in the unlocked position. Rather, there was a catch that required you to push a small thumb release sideways, rotating a pin into a slot that kept the bolt from sliding down. I slid the thumb release to the left so the bolt teetered between the open and closed position.

"Did you see that scuff mark on the outside of the door frame?" I said.

"I was wondering about that, too," Tawanda said.

"Watch." I kicked the door frame hard. The bolt slipped sideways a tenth of an inch and dropped into the socket.

"Voila, locked room mystery solved," Tawanda said.

"Yeah," I said. "But what's it mean?"

"One thing I learned long ago," Tawanda said. "No point drawing conclusions at the beginning of a crime scene investigation. Right, Mr. Nidlett?"

"You the man," the technician said.

Once Tawanda and Roy had gotten started with their work in the bedroom, I walked out the back door onto a large cedar deck. It was a glorious fall day, clear and crisp. From the "cottage" the lawn sloped away down toward a large, fenced swimming pool. Beyond that stood a knot of agricultural outbuildings, including a stable, a barn, and a silo. Behind them several green pastures fenced with white railing, into a sparkling creek, which disappeared into a hardwood bottom. The leaves were still green, just the faintest ochers in the poplars hinting at their impending turn. Another week and the woods would be aflame with color. Additionally, there was a small house about fifty yards to the left of the main house.

Standing on the deck, facing away from me, was a tall, slim woman wearing jeans, ostrich-skin cowboy boots, and a Western shirt. Hanging from beneath a large fawn-colored Stetson was a long braid of carrot-red hair. The woman wore a short-barrelled Glock automatic in a nylon holster on her hip.

"Marla Jeter?" I said.

The woman's body was elegant and athletic, but when she turned around, the effect was somewhat spoiled: her face looked like it had been sculpted out of a railroad tie with a ball peen hammer. "I'm Marla," she said. "You must be Sunny Childs."

I nodded. "So you're in charge of Georgia's security detail."

She nodded sourly. "I don't know what the hell happened here. I really don't."

"I need to ask you a few questions," I said.

Marla Jeter turned away from me for a moment. "I got to be honest with you," she said in a hard voice. Her accent was pure West Texas. "I think this is bullshit. We should be calling the cops."

"Hey, you want to call the cops or the Georgia Bureau of Investigation, I'm not stopping you."

Marla didn't move. "Not my choice."

"How come?"

"My principal is Georgia Burnett. But my paycheck is signed by Jeremy Ratkin. You see what I'm saying?"

"Mm."

"You mind if I smoke?" Marla didn't wait for my response, but reached into her front pocket, took out a box of the sort of thin cigars that I've never seen smoked by anyone but small-time bookies in the movies. Tiparillos I think they're called. She fired up the cigar with a wooden match. "What do you want to know?"

"Tell me about your security operation."

Marla waved her match in the air, threw it off the deck into the azalea bushes. "First off, this is not my fault. I told Georgia we should put somebody in the house, twenty-four seven. But she wouldn't do it. So I insisted that Georgia carry a panic button with her at all times. Me and my day shift guy live over there." She pointed her skinny cigar at the small house to our left. "So if she hits the button, we've got the team inside the house within thirty seconds."

"So last night, she didn't hit the panic button?"

Marla Jeter took a long pull on her Tiparillo. "Obviously not."

"Speaking as a layman," I said, "a four-person security team seems like a lot, even for somebody like Georgia. Had she been receiving any threats recently? Anything that she had been particularly concerned about?"

"You obviously haven't worked for celebrities," Marla drawled, making full use of her height to look down at me. I'm five feet even. She was pushing six.

"Meaning?"

"Meaning an individual like Georgia is always getting hassled by somebody."

"I'm not talking about some giggling teenage girl sneaking onto the property to get her CD case autographed. I'm talking about stalkers, that sort of thing."

Marla stubbed out her cigar. "C'mere," she said. Then she walked down a concrete path over to the small, brick ranch house where she lived. The original farmhouse I'd been told by Ratkin now housed some of the staff for

the farm. The architects who designed the cottage and
its surroundings had hidden the old farmhouse away behind a fence and a small berm as though it were something shameful.

I followed Marla Jeter inside, into a cramped office
with a cheap wooden desk, a computer, and a filing cabinet in it. She opened the bottom drawer of the filing
cabinet, pulled out a stack of letters eight inches thick,
and set them on the desk. "These are the nutcases. And
this is just in the past year."

"I don't suppose you pass these by a threat assessment
specialist?" I said.

She curled her lip dismissively. "My opinion, those
people are overpriced charlatans. Anyway, even Jeremy
Ratkin doesn't have a bottomless bank account."

I picked up a few of the letters, scanned them. They
were all time- and date-stamped. "I'll need to study
these," I said.

"Knock yourself out," Marla said.

I turned and looked her in the eye. "Let's get something
straight right now," I said sharply. "I appreciate that this
is your sandbox, and you feel territorial about it. But
we're going to have to work together. So if you've got
a problem with me, we need to work it out . . . now."

Marla looked back at me coolly. "If this is a kidnapping, it should be the FBI on it. If it's a murder, we need
the county police and the Georgia Bureau of Investigation in here. I'm sure you guys are good at investigating
traffic accidents or corporate fraud or cheating husbands
or whatever. But when it comes to this kind of thing,
you guys are a bunch of goddamn amateurs and you
know it."

"Actually," I said, "my chief investigator, Tawanda
Flornoy, spent twenty years on the Atlanta PD, ten years
of it in homicide. The evidence tech in there is reputedly
the best guy in the state. If it comes down to it, we can
bring just as much investigative weight to bear on this

thing as the cops. I hope it doesn't come to that. But it's a fact."

Marla looked at me skeptically.

"So there's nobody that sticks out?" I said. "No stalkers or anything like that?"

"We had a guy kill a goat on the lawn," she said. "But that was like a year ago. He was a schizophrenic, and we made damn sure he got committed after that. He's still inside."

"Anything else?"

Marla Jeter's eyes narrowed thoughtfully. "Well, there was this guy. . . ."

"What guy?"

"There was a guy who followed her to every show on her last tour. I mean *every* show. Always tried to get backstage passes, always sat in the front row. Even showed up in restaurants where she was eating. It was pretty weird. He was always polite, easygoing, smiling, dressed up like he was going on a date. But he never spoke a word, just stared at her. We started calling him The Creepy Guy. He may have been crazy, but damnation that guy had incredible intel. It seemed like he knew where she was all the time."

"Did he ever threaten her?"

"Nope."

"Inappropriate behavior?"

"Other than staring at her, nah. The scary thing, this guy was like a damn shadow. *Always* there. She had to stop making reservations for restaurants—even under bogus names—because any time she did, she'd show up and he'd be sitting at a table in the back by himself, looking at her."

"But he never touched her, never threatened her, never approached her in any way?"

"Never." She frowned. "Well, okay, at the beginning of the tour, he got backstage passes a couple of times. Like from radio stations. He'd come backstage, eat some nachos, have a glass of gingerale. Couple times he left notes for her. Then he'd hit the road."

"Did you keep the notes?"

"No. Once we got worried about him, realized what he was doing, we stopped letting him backstage."

"Did he make a scene when you told him he couldn't come backstage?"

"Nope. He came to the show in Boise, showed up at the green room with this pass he got from a radio station, we said, 'Sorry, you've been here several times before, why don't you be nice and give some other fans a chance to meet Miss Burnett.' You don't want to antagonize these people. So this Creepy Guy dude just smiles, nods, walks away. After that, he never tried to get backstage again."

"You find out who he was?"

Marla sighed. "We hired a detective to track him down." She opened the file drawer, took out a manila folder, laid it in front of me. In addition to several typewritten reports and a credit bureau print-out, there were several telephoto shots of a thin-faced man with blond hair wearing a blazer and tie, khakis, penny loafers. He was ordinary enough, with no distinctive features besides his nose, which was long and thin as the blade of a log-splitting maul. "Robert Smith was the alias he was using. The detective ran the Social, you can see his credit report and stuff. Whole ID was bogus. The Robert Smith that went with that Social Security number turns out to have died in 1984 at age nineteen."

"So what happened to him?"

"Soon as Georgia's big tour was over, he disappeared. That was about three months ago. We ran his credit bureau a couple weeks ago to see if he's still around, but he seems to have dropped off the face of the earth. Stopped paying his bills, stopped using his credit cards. We figure either he went back to using his real identity, or else he knew we were looking for him and switched to another alias."

I stared at the surveillance photos of the Creepy Guy.

He looked like an insurance salesman from Kansas—utterly undistinguished.

"You try getting a restraining order?"

"Not worth the bother. First, it's impractical. Cost you a mint in legal fees because you have to get a new TRO in every state. Restraining orders aren't binding outside of any given state jurisdiction. Second, the guy never touched her, never threatened her, so there was nothing we could take to a judge."

"And that's it? Tour over, Robert Smith disappears."

"Poof."

"Did you ever get prints on him?"

"Yeah. Our PI lifted some latents from him at a restaurant one time. Ran them through AFIS, the big fingerprint database, but nothing came up."

"Alright. Well, I'll need to talk to your night man."

"Sure," Marla said. "He's probably down at the stables. Name's Ben Pryor."

CHAPTER 3

I HAD MEANT to ask who'd knocked Georgia's door off the hinges, but when I went out to the stables, the answer to the question became obvious. People who run personal security operations generally include at least one "heavy" in their team, a guy whose sheer bulk will intimidate potential threats. Ben Pryor was Marla's heavy.

I found the big man in the stables, currying a large bay gelding. He was at least six-six, and if he didn't tip the scales at over three hundred pounds, I'd be very surprised. And not much of it was fat, either.

"Who'd you play ball for?" I said.

The big man looked up from the horse he was grooming. "The Horned Frogs."

"You're making that up."

"Texas Christian University," he said. "You never heard of the TCU Horned Frogs?" Other than his bulk, he wasn't a scary-looking man: he had a sweet face and an open, boyish manner. He seemed strained and tired—understandable under the circumstances. Like Marla, his accent was pure West Texas. "Honorable mention All-American my senior year, year after that I was just a fat guy lying in bed with a broken pelvis that would never mend right."

"Sorry to hear it," I said.

He shrugged, then went back to combing the big horse. "The Lord had other plans for me." He didn't sound near as bitter as I probably would have if I believed that God had reached down out of the heavens for the sole purpose of smashing my pelvis. "You're Sunny Childs, right? The PI?"

"Right." I put out my hand and we shook. His fist was immense, the skin work-hardened, but he had an incongrously gentle touch. "So tell me about last night, Ben. Anything happen worth mentioning?"

He sighed and set down his currycomb, shook his head morosely. "I can't think of nothing. I mean, it was just another night, me wandering around the property with the flashlight. No cars come up the drive, no funny noises, nothing. I keep. . . ." He grunted almost inaudibly and a look of terrible regret crossed his face. "I just keep thinking and thinking, you know. What did I miss? What'd I do *wrong*?"

"Have there been any threatening calls or strange people hanging around recently?"

"Nah. Been pretty quiet." He stroked the flank of the big gelding, then stepped out of the stall, latched the gate. "Two years ago sometimes it would get a little crazy around here, but nowadays it's not so bad."

I followed Ben Pryor as he took a plastic bucket over to a spigot, started filling it with water. "How do you mean?"

"Well, you know, two years ago she was the hottest new thing in country music. But the last record didn't do as good. Things kind of slumped a little with her second album."

"Huh," I said. "I wasn't aware of that."

"She's gonna come back, though, I'm sure of it. She's put a lot of work into the new record." A look of near-panic crossed the big man's face. "Assuming she's okay, I mean. . . ."

"Well, no point assuming the worst." We watched the

thick stream of water burble into the pail for a while. "So how well do you know Georgia, Ben?"

He looked at me with slightly narrowed eyes. "Why?" Pryor turned off the spigot and carried the bucket over to the stall, poured it into the horse's trough.

"I'm just curious to know what she's like," I said.

"Oh." He seemed to relax a little. "Give you an example of the kind of lady she is." He smiled fondly. "Last year she found out I like to ride, next thing you know, Atlas shows up out here." He pointed to the massive gelding he'd been grooming. "She tells me as long as I work here, Atlas is my horse. No strings attached."

"A thoughtful person."

He stared thoughtfully across the stable for a moment. "Truthfully? It's more complicated than that. I've been doing personal security work for ten years now, and in my experience you got three kind of celebrities. You got the control freaks who want to rule the world. Then you got the moody artists who ain't got a practical bone in their body. Then you got folks like Miz Burnett. She's the type of person that if you put them on a desert island by theirself for more than fifteen minutes, they might just dry up and blow away. They live through other people. Got to have constant approval, constant affirmation, constant love." He looked a little sad for a moment. "I hope she's okay, because I think she's just starting to come into her own, just starting to live life for herself instead of for other people."

"Other people, meaning. . . ."

He jerked his head toward the house, presumably toward Jeremy Ratkin. "Him. Whoever."

"So is there any reason you can think of that she might have just left here? Marital problems, anything like that?"

He looked at me expressionlessly. "Can't really say."

"Can't? Or won't?"

"I mean I've worked for her for three years now and I think I've come to know her a little. If she was gonna leave because of something like that, I think I'd have known."

I nodded, then said, "You think you could give me a little tour of the property?"

"Do you ride?"

"I took some riding lessons when I was in high school. Why?"

"Four hundred acres is a lot of turf to cover on foot. Be a little quicker of we went on horseback."

Ten minutes later I was clinging to the back of a sweet-tempered black pony, following Pryor's huge bay down the trail leading away from the house.

When we got to the bottom of the pasture, the trail entered a stand of old second-growth hardwood—sweet gums, yellow poplars, scarlet oaks, maples. I awkwardly urged my pony up next to Pryor's horse. Either I knew a lot less about riding than I remembered, or I had lost my touch with horses. It was probably the former.

"So, Ben," I said. "This guy that followed Georgia around on the last tour, this Creepy Guy—what are your thoughts on him?"

Pryor was wearing a battered cowboy hat now. He hitched it up a little over his eyes. "Potentially? I thought he was very, very dangerous."

"What about Marla? Did she take him seriously?"

Ben Pryor's face was expressionless under his hat. He didn't say anything.

"Look, I'm not asking you to knock your boss, Ben. But I need to know what's going on around here."

Pryor sighed. "My opinion? Nah, Miss Jeter . . . she kept an eye on him, I don't mean she was negligent. But she didn't take the guy as serious as she should have. She should have been more proactive."

"What would you have done?"

"Threat assessment starts with who you're dealing with. The guy's obviously a psycho, right? But what's his history? She hired an investigator . . . but once they found out he was using a bogus ID, she could have pushed the investigator harder. Even if he wasn't in the FBI computer, they could have kept running them through state databases, private databases. Hell, he had an accent, maybe run him through some foreign databases. Eventually they would have found his real identity, his real history. Fruitcakes like that don't get to be thirty-five years old without getting booked somewhere for something. But Miz Jeter said it would be too time consuming, too expensive." He shrugged. "In retrospect, I guess it didn't really matter. As soon as the tour was over, the guy vanished into thin air."

Suddenly I thought of something. And it gave me a cold feeling. I reined in my horse.

Pryor looked around at me questioningly. "What?" he said.

"We need to go back to the house," I said. "Right now."

"Okay," Pryor said. We turned, and I started pushing the pony to go faster and faster until I didn't feel much in control. "What are you thinking, Miz Childs?" Ben Pryor called.

I slowed my horse. No point killing myself. "It's Sunny," I said. "Now think for a minute: this guy you called Creepy Guy—he was pretty determined, wasn't he?"

Pryor turned his horse. "Yeah."

"Pretty obsessive, too, right?"

"Yep."

"From what you said earlier, I'm guessing you've look into this threat assessment stuff, yes? The psychological side of it, I mean?"

"A little."

"Well, there are all kinds of psychological categories, right? But among the various brands of psycho freaks, you've got peepers, watchers. Guys like that, they're uncomfortable with personal contact. But boy do they like to watch."

"Aw—*son of bitch!*" Pryor said, suddenly angry at himself. He had figured out what I was thinking.

We crested the hill of the pasture, came up behind the big house. I looked up at the rear of the place. "Where's her bedroom, Ben?"

The big man pointed his hat at a long, uncurtained picture above the back door.

I rode the horse around until I was directly underneath the window, then I surveyed the woods. "Dammit!" I said. Then I started riding toward a small rise over at the edge of the treeline, pushing my pony into an uneasy canter.

Pryor followed. We hit the treeline and had to slow, threading through a maze of trunks and branches. Several low limbs threatened to knock me off the pony, and some nasty briars did a nice job of gouging up my left leg. I rode through a little dip and then up a steep hill. I was terrified of falling, but I was even more terrified of what I was about to find.

At the top of the hill, there it was: a tent, a blanket laid out on the bare earth, a scattering of food wrappers, and the putrid smell of rotting food.

Oh, yeah—and most of all, there was a powerful telescope on a tripod, a telescope aimed directly at the back of Georgia Burnett's house four or five hundred yards away.

Ben Pryor reined in his horse behind me. He made a groaning noise like someone had stabbed him, and then he started hitting himself in the leg with fist. "Stupid! Stupid! Stupid!" he said.

Suddenly I saw something back in the woods, a flash of clothing or pale skin. "There he is!" I shouted, drawing my Smith & Wesson and digging my knees into the pony's sides. The pony must have felt my urgency because it tore into the woods at a full gallop. All I could do was hang on.

There was a little bit of a trail, but it hadn't been designed for riding. I tried to slow my mount, but I'd scared her so badly and my horsemanship was so pathetic that I couldn't seem to slow her down. So I just clung to her neck, put my butt in the air, and kept my head low.

In front of me I saw a flash of red jacket in the trees, then nothing, then more trees. As I burst out of the woods into a clearing, I saw a man jumping into a black truck, like a Jeep, but larger and heavier. The door slammed, and then I heard a loud crack, like something at the center of the universe had snapped in half. At that point, the world disappeared.

CHAPTER 4

"**D**OG, SUNNY! YOU alright?"

I was lying on the ground wondering who the huge cowboy crouching over me was. "Don't hurt me," I said. The cowboy had a pistol nearly hidden in one of his massive hands.

"Sunny?" the man with the gun said. "Sunny, it's Ben Pryor!"

"Who?"

It had all come back to me by the time we'd returned to the house, but for a few minutes there I was kind of vague on some things. My own name, for instance.

I guess I must have hit my head on a branch. Whatever the case, I damn sure hit the ground hard. My head was throbbing, and I was in a very bad mood as I accompanied Tawanda Flornoy and Roy Nidlett back to the Creepy Guy's spy nest.

It was an ugly scene. It appeared he'd been living there for a long time. Months most likely. The green nylon tent sat in the middle of a flat surface of red clay, which had obviously been heavily trodden for a long time. Off to the side of the clay clearing was a large pile of garbage and a stinking, flyblown trench that the

Creepy Guy had apparently been using as a latrine.

The large telescope was mounted on a tripod in front of a ratty old beach chair. Two hollow impressions had been worn in the clay in front of the chair where the Creepy Guy's feet must have been resting for a great many hours and days and weeks.

"Jesus, Mary and Joseph," Nidlett said, shaking his head as he put down his tackle box full of forensic supplies.

"What you want to do, baby?" Tawanda said to me.

"Hold on," I said. I pulled out my cell phone and called the private number that Ratkin had given me. I outlined what we had found, that there was strong evidence here that the creep who'd been using the identity of Robert Smith had been watching his wife for months. I asked him for permission to call the police.

"Police?" he said. "Right now it still seems like all we've got is a trespasser."

I couldn't believe what he was saying. "For Christ's sake, Mr. Ratkin—"

He cut me off. "Look, Sunny, I appreciate your position. But frankly, the Floyd County Police are far less well equipped and experienced than you are. These redneck cops can't find their ass with both hands. Until we find enough to get the FBI or the GBI involved, I'd rather see you working on it."

"Are you absolutely sure?"

"Believe me. If I call the Floyd County Police, every redneck asshole with a badge in northwest Georgia will be stomping around contaminating the scene and looking for souvenirs to give their kids."

"You're the boss," I said dryly. Then I hung up. "Let's do it, folks. The client doesn't want the police involved yet."

Tawanda studied my face for a minute. "This is messed up. You *know* this is messed up, Sunny."

"What can I say?" My voice got a little tense. "We still don't know for certain that there's been a crime,

and the client has given me specific instructions." I'm
sure it sounded as lame to her as it did to me. I turned
to Marla Jeter who was standing next to me looking
extremely embarrassed and a little frightened. She knew
this had all happened on her watch. "Get all your guys
out here, put up some rope or ribbon or tape or whatever,
just like you were cops sealing off a crime scene. I don't
want anybody stumbling around screwing things up any
worse than they already are. I'm putting Tawanda Flornoy in charge here. She's an experienced police detective, so whatever she says, goes. Clear?"

"Hold up, Sunny!" the tall woman said, "My job—"

"Your job was to keep things like *this* from happening. You blew it. Now it's my turn."

Her eyes got hot and resentful. But she had no choice;
she had to do what I said. Marla Jeter turned to Ben
Pryor. "Whatever they want. I'm going back to keep an
eye on the house."

I watched Marla stalk away, then turned back to my
lead investigator. "Thoughts?"

"This guy had some money. That telescope, I guarantee, cost some scratch. Same with this tent. It's a
Kelty, top of the line, one hundred percent Gore-tex and
all that. Fancy-looking propane stove. This guy may be
a wacko, but he's a wacko with some resources."

"Any sign that he might have brought Georgia up
here?"

Tawanda shook her head. "Not so far. No blood, no
women's shoe prints."

"What you need me to do, Tawanda?"

"Show me and Mr. Nidlett where you saw the perp's
car," she said. "We need to process that area, too."

We threaded our way down the little path through the
woods. Part of the area must have been clear-cut half a
decade earlier, because it was tight going. What little
space wasn't taken up by dwarfish pines was jammed
with briars, chokeberry, wild blueberry, and Japanese
honeysuckle. My jeans were full of thorns by the time

I came out into the older growth area where I'd had my little run-in with the tree.

I pointed to a dusty gap in the trees. "There," I said. "That's where his truck was parked."

We approached it carefully, found two deep ruts worn in the moist, red clay that led up to a gravel road.

Tawanda stood with her hands on her hips, her large, orange wig sparkling in the sunshine. After surveying the scene for a few moments, she squatted down next to one of the dusty ruts. "Good news," she said. "We got clean tracks here. That'll help us identify the vehicle." She turned to the crime scene technician. "Let's get a casting of each of these tire tracks."

As Roy Nidlett began his work, I noticed a helicopter moving lazily through the sky. I shielded my eyes and looked up. As I gazed at the blue sky I noticed a second chopper, then a third. "What's with all the helicopters?" I said.

Tawanda Flornoy looked up and frowned.

CHAPTER 5

HALF AN HOUR later I was walking up to the big house. As I approached the front door I saw Gunnar's Lincoln tear up the gravel drive and skid to a stop, throwing up a cloud of gray dust. His face was red and angry as he jumped out of the big car, a newspaper rolled up in his hand like he wanted to hit somebody with it.

"What's up?" I said.

Gunnar looked around irritably. "Where the hell is Ratkin?"

"Why?"

Gunnar handed me the newspaper he was carrying. I sat down on the front step, smoothed it out. There at the top of the front page of the *Atlanta Journal*, the afternoon paper, was a headline that read LOCKED ROOM MYSTERY in huge letters. Underneath the banner was a story about the disappearance of Georgia Burnett. In the third paragraph it said that "celebrity private investigator Gunnar Brushwood" had been hired to pursue the case. On the jump page they had a sidebar about Gunnar, accompanied by a photo of my boss in a state of full machismo: eyes flinty, waxed mustache bristling, jaw square, the straps of a shoulder holster peeping out from underneath his bush jacket.

I looked up at him questioningly.

"There were calls coming into the office this morning from every tabloid newspaper, every tabloid TV show, ABC, CNN, NBC, Fox, CBS, and damn near every legit newspaper in the country. There's also a gang of remote broadcast trucks parked outside the gate of the farm."

"My recollection," I said, "is that the deadline for most afternoon newspapers is around nine o'clock in the morning. That means this story was filed before Ratkin had even hired us."

"You're goddamn right," Gunnar growled.

I reread the first page of the story. The details were sketchy, but the paper had gotten an accurate general picture. And one crucial detail was right on the money: "According to sources close to the Georgia Burnett organization, evidence from the scene indicated that the noted country chanteuse may have disappeared from inside a locked room."

I dialed Ratkin on my cell phone.

"What the hell is going on?" I said. "The *AJC* had a story in the paper this morning. That means they filed it before you'd even hired us."

"Welcome to the tabloid century," Ratkin said dryly.

"What's that supposed to mean?"

"Do you have any conception of how much money *The Star* or *The Globe* or *Weekly World News* is willing to pay for celebrity gossip? Tens of thousands of dollars. Every script girl and makeup artist's assistant in L.A. knows this. And I guarantee you that every music company secretary and sound engineer in Nashville knows it, too. It's a sad fact, but there's no way to keep information about famous people hidden."

"The *Atlanta Journal-Constitution* is not the *Weekly World News*. I know reporters there and I guaran-damn-tee you they don't pay their sources. So I want to know how this story got there. I want to know why there are fifty reporters trying to sneak onto your farm right now."

"Sunny, are you accusing me of something?"

"I'm asking you. Did you leak this story to the press?"

There was a long pause. "Okay, look," Ratkin said finally. "I knew this would hit eventually. Right? So I figured it's better to ride the lightning than to get struck by it."

"Ride the lightning. What the hell does that mean? This isn't some kind of presidential scandal where you have to worry about spin control. This is a missing person investigation."

"Sunny, no offense, but don't be naive. Fame changes all the rules."

"You want our help?" I said. I could hear my voice getting testy.

"That's why I wrote you a check for twenty thousand dollars this morning."

"Good. If you wish us to continue with our services, then don't talk to the press without talking to me or Gunnar first. That's not negotiable. If some maniac has kidnapped your wife, you need to be very, very careful about what information you release. We don't want to drive this guy over the edge. Do you understand me?"

"What guy?"

I realized I hadn't told him about the Creepy Guy yet. "We found a guy. Apparently he's been camped out on your farm for the past three months, staring at your wife through a telescope. Unfortunately he got away." I filled him in on the details.

There was another long silence. "Jesus *Christ*," Ratkin said finally. "I want you to fire Marla Jeter and her whole incompetent goddamn team right this minute."

"Bad idea," I said. "We need her and her people here to keep the press off your property."

"I'm going to rip her head off and stuff it down her throat. I'm going to—"

"That's nice, Jeremy. But I've got something to say. Are you listening?"

"What!" He obviously didn't like being interrupted.

"It's time to call in law enforcement."

I could hear a scratchy noise, like he was running his

fingers through his beard. "Let's see what you turn up today," he said. "I'm still hoping this isn't what it looks like."

"Eight hours," I said. "That's it."

"Eight hours." Ratkin hung up.

I turned to Gunnar. "This whole thing sucks."

Gunnar was looking through the *Atlanta Journal*. "Yeah," he said. "There is an upside, though."

"What's that?"

He tapped the paper with his index finger, grinned. "They spelled my name right."

"Not you, too. . . ." I said.

CHAPTER 6

I T WAS FIVE o'clock in the evening and Tawanda was reporting to me and Gunnar what she and Roy Nidlett had found at the crime scenes ... *if* they were crime scenes. We were sitting around the breakfast nook table eating fried chicken—our first meal of the day.

"Good news," Tawanda said. "Mr. Nidlett's been a busy, busy boy. We dusted the telescope, came up with a nice thumb print and two partials. We got a stack of fan magazines with prints all over them. He's got fibers. He's got hairs. We even got a notepad with a handwriting sample. If there's something going on here, and if the telescope guy is our man—that's a lot of ifs, I know—then we got a heck of a lot to work with."

"Assuming this is, in fact, the Creepy Guy that they ran through AFIS last year. They didn't get a hit on him," I said.

"If the prints off the telescope are the same as the ones they got during Georgia's tour," Gunnar said, "then at least we know who we're dealing with. Plus, we can run the prints through other data banks. Military, private, foreign, whatnot. Maybe we'll get a hit somewhere else."

"True."

"Anyway, here's the thing, Sunny," Tawanda said. "We got a big box of evidence. We can send the whole shebang out to private labs if we want. But in the long run it would be best if law enforcement took possession and did the lab tests themselves."

"That's assuming that law enforcement gets called at all," I said sourly.

"*Are* they gonna get called?"

I looked at my watch. "If nothing happens by about midnight, yeah."

"Who you gonna call?"

"Right now this is still a missing persons case. That means we call the Floyd County Police."

"*That's* reassuring," Tawanda said sarcastically.

"If we turn up anything to indicate it's a kidnapping, we call the FBI."

Tawanda nodded. "Okay, then my recommendation— and I think Roy will agree with me on this—is that we hold this evidence under lock and key until midnight, at which point we turn it over to the duly constituted authorities."

"Sounds reasonable. Anything else?"

Tawanda gave a secret look to Roy Nidlett. "We saved the best for last."

Roy took an eight inch long plaster of paris slab out of a box and set it on the table. "I don't want to brag," he said, smiling, "but I'm not bad at my job."

"That's why you're here, buddy," Gunnar said.

Roy smiled, flushed. "I try to keep on top of tire treads," he said. "At least the most popular models. And this right here is a Bridgestone Dueler 225 70/16. That's very interesting news."

He waited, eyes gleaming. "Tell us," I said finally.

The Bridgestone Dueler is what we call an OEM tire. Their performance is not so brilliant, but they're fairly cheap. As a result they're used mostly by original equipment manufacturers—auto makers in other words. Now it so happens that the Bridgestone Dueler has a new

tread pattern that only came out this year. This particular
tread pattern in this particular size is only sold on one
car in the entire country." He looked at us expectantly.
"That's this year's model of the Toyota Land Cruiser.

"Now the Land Cruiser is an expensive and fairly un-
usual car. If I were to guess, there weren't more than
twenty-five thousand Land Cruisers sold in this country
last year. Sunny, you said the vehicle you spotted was
black. Black is not a hugely popular color. Typically
only about five percent of all cars are black. So we've
just narrowed this car down to around a thousand people—in the whole country. I don't suppose you got a
look at the license. If it was a Georgia license, that
would narrow it even more."

I shook my head. "Sorry."

"Still. Toyota Motor Corporation keeps records of
every car buyer in the country. They could run a list for
us in about ten minutes."

"With a court order," I said.

Nidlett shrugged, smiled furtively. "I'm told there are
back-channel ways of doing this without troubling our
overburdened law enforcement system."

Tawanda said, "I might not mind taking a crack at it."

"Hold on, hold on," Gunnar said, winking broadly at
Tawanda. I thought I detected a slight elevation in his
testosterone level. "Before we get carried away, maybe
y'all might benefit by watching the master work."

I laughed loudly, nearly choked on the piece of
chicken I was eating. Gunnar had been a great bounty
hunter in his day, but investigation was something he
generally accomplished through a strong dose of dele-
gation. He looked a little hurt, so I stopped laughing.

Like most of the rooms in the house, the breakfast
nook had a fancy telephone in it. Gunnar pulled it over,
hit the speakerphone button, then dialed a number.

A voice answered, saying, "Steve Fine Ford."

"Put Steve on would you, darling," Gunnar said, in
his most hectoring, big-shot voice.

"I'm sorry he's unavail—"

"Tell him it's Gunnar Brushwood," he said, smiling genially at us.

And it worked. I don't know what it is about the guy, but Gunnar can flat-ass bust down doors when he feels like it.

There were several clicks, and then a grating voice came out of the phone. "Gunnar, my friend, how the hell you been?"

"Great!" Gunnar said. Then they talked about hunting for a while, Gunnar going on about some recent safari in Tanzania, and then the car dealer talking about shooting some kind of obscure mountain goat in Russia. Finally Gunnar said, "Look, I need a favor. You own a Toyota dealership don't you, hoss?"

"I got *two* Toyota stores," Steve Fine said.

"Terrific. Here's the thing. I'm doing some work for a certain celebrity who shall go nameless, but who I can assure you is in danger for her life. We got a line on a threat who bought himself a black Land Cruiser within the past year. You got any way of pulling something like that off the computer?"

"What? Everybody that bought a black Land Cruiser in the past year?"

"Everybody in whole U.S. of A., bud."

"That's very confidential information, Gunnar. I'd be violating my ethics giving you something like that."

Gunnar laughed, yucking it up a little. "An ethical car dealer. Ain't that an oxymoron! Tell you what, buddy, I was thinking about putting together a trip to Greenland next year. I understand the government up there is allowing a select group of hunters to buy bowhunting tags for musk ox. Invitation only, type thing. You ever taken a musk ox, Steve?"

"Musk ox?" The car dealer's voice suddenly took on the barest hint of sentimental longing.

"See, hoss, I've been invited, due to my stature in the bowhunting community. Me and one friend. Only one.

Now I got to tell you, Wally Crouch over at Crouch Lincoln-Mercury sold me a nice Continental last month, a hundred fifty below invoice, and I kinda owe him a favor."

"Wally Crouch! *That* son of a bitch?"

"I know you and him have a little bit of a hunting rivalry going on. He's awful hot to hang that musk ox head up on the wall of his lodge."

"You'd take Wally *Crouch*? That lowlife, lying, worthless, no-account piece of dogshit?"

"Every black Land Cruiser in the past twelve months," Gunnar said. "I need the buyer's address, phone, Social Security. Take a moment. Meditate on your ethical commitments as an automobile dealer, and then meditate on that big ol' trophy musk ox. Huh? Huh? See where that takes you, how 'bout?"

Ten minutes later a fax was rolling out of Georgia Burnett's machine, a fax with an alphabetical list of all six hundred and seventy-eight people who had bought black Land Cruisers in the past year.

I scanned through the list.

"Robert Smith—here he is!" I said triumphantly. "Telescope Guy is Robert Smith. Robert Smith is Creepy Guy. Now all we need to do is find out Creepy Guy's real identity."

"I got some ideas on that," Tawanda said. "Let me make a couple of calls."

As she reached for the receiver, the phone rang.

CHAPTER 7

"**W**AIT!" I SAID. The phone rang again. "Has this phone rung yet today?"

Everybody looked at me blankly. The phone kept ringing.

I dug around in my purse till I found my miniature Sony tape recorder and a small condenser microphone. The mic has a sucker on it just like on a kid's dart gun, allowing me to attach it to the phone receiver. The phone continued to ring.

I pressed the red Record button and picked up the phone. "Hello?"

"Who am I speakink to?" A man's voice demanded. He had a foreign accent. Middle Europe maybe, Russia maybe—I couldn't be sure. Then again, I'm no linguist.

"Who do you want to speak to?"

"Whoever's in charge."

"*I'm* in charge."

"What's your name?"

"Sunny."

"Okay, Sunny. Who do you work for? And don't tell me you're a friend of the family."

I hesitated. Finally I figured I might as well be honest. "I'm a private investigator."

"You work for that man in the newspaper. Brush-wood."

"Yeah." My heart was beating so hard I could barely think straight. "So, ah, what's up?"

"Tomorrow morning, six A.M., five million dollars," the man said. "A penny less, Georgia dies."

"Uh, uh, uh . . ." My mind felt frozen. Then I knew what had to be done first. "Okay, wait! You want money? Prove she's alive."

"I'll kill her!"

"I understand that." I tried to speak firmly, calmly—though I can't say how successful I was. "But for us to meet your demands, you have to show us some good faith. Prove that she's alive, or you don't get jack."

There was a pause, then a woman's panicky voice came on. "This is Georgia! Please do what he says! I'm—"

Then she was gone.

"Five million," the man said. "Six o'clock tomorrow morning. No FBI. No cops. Are we clear?"

"Yes."

"Talk to Ratkin. I'll call back in one hour."

The line went dead.

Everyone was staring at me. I hit the Stop button on my tape recorder, set down the handset.

"It's a snatch," I said.

CHAPTER 8

FIFTEEN MINUTES LATER a red helicopter with the ArchRival Records logo painted on the side landed in the middle of the front lawn. The door opened and Jeremy Ratkin climbed out, one hand clutching his long gray hair in a makeshift ponytail, the other holding a fat black briefcase.

Gunnar and I led him inside and told him about the ransom call. He sat motionless for a moment. I couldn't detect anything in his expression. Not relief, anguish, anger—nothing.

"Five, huh?"

"Five," Gunnar said.

"You taped the call?"

I nodded.

"Play it."

I took out my little Sony, cued the tape, pressed the Play button. When the recording was finished, Ratkin said. "That's definitely her voice. So at least she's alive."

"Can you raise the five million?" Gunnar asked.

"Tomorrow? Six A.M.?" Ratkin stroked his beard thoughtfully. "I'll have to call my banker." He dialed a number, and then said, "Anton. Jeremy Ratkin here, Georgia's husband. I need to speak to you about something very important." Then he started outlining the situation to the banker in a hushed but insistent tone. The conversation went on for a while, and as it did I noticed Ratkin's face going slowly gray, the color draining away. It was the first time I'd sensed the terrible strain he must have been under. He glanced up at us irritably, then waved an imperious hand in our direction, "A little space, guys? Huh?"

Gunnar and I stepped out onto the deck.

"What do you think of this bird, Sunny?"

I watched Ratkin through the window. He seemed to be shouting at his banker, though I couldn't hear a word of what was being said. "He's one seriously cold fish, Gunnar. Did you see his face when we told him she'd definitely been kidnapped? He looked like we'd told him there was a five-minute delay on the expressway."

Gunnar glanced through the window. "Seems to be sinking in finally, though."

I nodded.

"Yeah, Sunny, there's something about this sumbitch that chafes my ass."

"We need to get the FBI in here as soon as he finishes talking to his bank, then gracefully bow out and send him a nice fat bill."

Gunnar stroked his mustache. It was obvious that the case still attracted him. It was the free publicity, I suppose. I love Gunnar to death, but he's one of those guys who lives to see his face on TV. He sighed. "I expect you're right."

"You don't agree?"

He looked off toward the sun setting in the distant trees. "It's an intriguing case, Sunny. You got to admit it's intriguing as hell."

A few minutes later Jeremy Ratkin came out onto the deck, a can of Diet Coke in his hand.

"You need to make a decision about whether or not to call the FBI," I said. "The kidnapper said he would kill her if we did. But frankly I think you should do it anyway."

Ratkin nodded. "It's already done. They've got a team from Atlanta on the way."

"Is there a back way onto the property?" I said. "You don't want a bunch of Feds driving through that mob of reporters out there. If they do, it'll show up on TV, and then the kidnappers will know you've called the law. Which he expressly told me not to do."

Ratkin thought for a moment. "There's a logging road. I'll get Marla to call them and set it up."

"What's their ETA?" Gunnar said.

"Under an hour," Ratkin said.

"About the bankers," I said. "When this guy calls back I have to know what to tell him. How much can you get by morning?"

Ratkin looked out at the barn and the stables behind the house for a moment.

"I have one point nine," he said finally, his voice flat and emotionless. Then he turned and walked back into the house. I could see why he'd gone a little pale when he was talking to his banker.

When the phone rang again, I answered.

"Sunny?" The same European-inflected voice.

"Yeah."

"Ground rules. First, I talk to you and you only."

"Look, ah, Mr. Ratkin just got here. It'll be easier if—"

"No. I wouldn't know Mr. Ratkin's voice from some cop's. I'm not interested in talking to some sneaky FBI negotiator, okay?"

I hesitated. I was eager to get out of this place, eager to leave the burden of Georgia Burnett's life on some other pair of shoulders. But I didn't see any alternative. "Fair enough."

"Second, there will be no negotiation of any terms."

"Okay, but here's a question. How do we know you haven't killed her?"

"You'll have to trust me on that."

"Look, nothing personal," I said. "But you and I aren't exactly bosom buddies. Trust ain't in the bargain here. Each time we talk, I'll ask you one question. What's her birthday, something like that."

The kidnapper hesitated for a minute. "Goddammit—"

"Look," I said. "We both want the same thing. But to get from point A to point B, we have to know Georgia is alive. Failing that, we have to assume she's already dead."

The kidnapper made a sucking noise with his teeth. "Okay. You ask me a question, I ask her. But I'm not putting her on the line again."

"Deal. Ask her what her third grade teacher's name was."

"Huh?"

"Ask her! What's her third grade teacher's name?"

The kidnapper seemed a little rattled, like this wasn't working out as easily as he'd expected. "Hold on." I heard some whispering in the background. "She can't remember."

"Call me back when she does." I hung up the phone. As soon as I had set it down I got a sick feeling that maybe I'd let hubris get in the way of good sense, that maybe I'd just gotten Georgia Burnett killed. My knees were suddenly shaking so hard I had to sit down. But on the other hand, if she was already dead, what was the point? I had to trust that this man would do anything to get the money, that if he knew keeping her alive was the only way to get rich, he'd by God keep her alive.

Ratkin had been listening on a pair of headphones that Roy Nidlett had rigged up. "What the hell are you thinking, Sunny?" he said quietly.

"At some point I have to break it to this guy that he's not getting his five million," I said. "It's important that

I establish a relationship of give and take early. If he just dictates everything, he'll freak when I tell him the pot of gold is smaller than he wants. Better to piss him off over something small than over something big."

Ratkin stared at me for at least a solid minute.

"Besides, Mr. Ratkin, he's got to understand that your wife's good health is the only road to that money."

He didn't say anything in agreement—but he didn't argue with me either. With Ratkin, I got the sense that was the closest you'd ever get to having him agree that you were right and he was wrong.

"Now while we're waiting," I said, "I want to know exactly how much money you can get by tomorrow morning. Moreover, I want to know where it comes from, how you're raising it, what banks are involved, the whole nine. Down to the last penny."

"Why?"

"You're the big-time negotiator, you tell me."

"Negotiation is like poker," he said. "Never reveal your hand."

"Don't be a jerk!" I said. "This is not a game of poker."

Ratkin's black eyes locked on mine. "Everything is a game of poker."

"No. In a game of poker, the worst thing that can happen is you walk away from the table with your pockets empty. If we lose this negotiation, Georgia dies. This guy doesn't sound crazy to me. Not so far. I'm convinced trust is the key. Trust is everything. We have nothing to lose by being forthcoming. If we can't give him the money, we need to tell him why, and we need to tell him in great detail."

"No."

"Hey, look," I said. "There's the phone. Answer it yourself, Master Negotiator. But he already told me that I'm the only person he'll talk to."

Ratkin drummed on the breakfast table with his fingers for a moment, but said nothing.

After a couple of minutes the phone rang. Ratkin picked it up. "This is Jeremy Ratkin," he said. "Now you listen to me! If you—" Even from across the room I could hear the agonized screaming of a woman through the tiny telephone speaker. Ratkin stopped, his lips twitching slightly, and his face going pale. "If you think—" Again Ratkin stopped speaking. Then he took the receiver away from his ear, stared at it for a moment, set it down so softly that it made no sound at all.

"What?" I said.

Ratkin muttered something I couldn't hear, and he wouldn't meet my eyes.

We waited. I could feel my pulse thrumming. After a moment I noticed that Ratkin had taken a legal pad out of his black briefcase and started writing. I looked over his shoulder and saw that he was writing down a long row of figures. When he was done, he pushed the pad across the table to me without meeting my eyes. He hadn't referred to any notes, but I noticed that every figure was written out to the exact penny.

When the phone rang again, I didn't wait for Ratkin, I just picked it up.

"Sunny here."

"I told you," the European voice said, "I'm only talking to you."

"I understand. My client is a little headstrong."

"Next time someone else answers, I cut her fucking tongue out. Clear?"

"Yes."

"Her third grade teacher was Mrs. Portell."

"Good."

"And Sunny? Next time you hang up on me, Georgia dies. Okay?"

"I understand."

"Now, let us address the issue of money. Five million. Wire transfer. At the time of the exchange, I will give you five bank account numbers. Two banks in Panama, two in the Caymans, one in Vanuatu. The mechanics of the exchange I shall address later. But the important thing is that it will go in five stages. I do something, you do something, like that. Each stage, you transfer one million. On the final transfer, Georgia goes free."

"Hold on," I said. "We'd been assuming you were going to want cash. Let me see if it's a problem doing a wire transfer."

I put my hand over the receiver. Ratkin, listening over the headphones, said, "Not a problem. Wire transfer is good."

I spoke into the phone. "Wire transfer is fine."

"Very well. I'll call you again in an hour with details on the exchange."

"Hold on," I said. "About the money. . . ."

The kidnapper's voice rose. "Five million. That's not negotiable."

"Look," I said. "Have you ever had a hundred thousand dollars in cash before in your life?"

"Look—" the kidnapper said impatiently.

I forged on. "Well, I haven't. I haven't had a hundred grand, I haven't even had fifty. And I damn sure haven't ever put my fingers on a million dollars. Think what you can do with a million."

"Don't jerk me around goddammit, Sunny!" The kidnapper's voice rose. I noticed that sometimes his speech was very formal and sometimes it was colloquial. It seemed odd to me. "I know damn good and well he's got the money. If he tries to cheap out, I swear to Christ, Georgia is dead."

"Easy, easy," I said. "I understand. You look on some asset sheet, maybe he's good for five million, I don't know. But you're asking for him to come up with it in twelve hours. In the middle of the night."

"Dammit—"

"*Listen!* Please. Okay? Now listen to what—"

The line went dead.

"Oh man," I said, putting my face in my hands. "I don't like the sound of that at all."

"I'll tell you what I think," Gunnar said. "I think he's

moving to a new location. He knows that any fool off the street with Caller ID and a sixty-dollar CD ROM phone list can figure out where he's calling from. He's probably got her in a van or a truck, and he's going to keep calling and moving."

I felt a spurt of confidence. It made good sense. "Let's hope you're right," I said. "Because he sure sounded like he was about to lose it."

"Speaking of which," Tawanda Flornoy said, "you got Caller ID on your phone, Mr. Ratkin?"

"There's a Caller ID readout on the phone up in the bedroom," Ratkin said.

"Well, hell's bells!" Gunnar said. "Let's start tracking this sumbitch!"

"I believe we even have call tracing," Ratkin said. "You dial in some digits and then it traces the last call."

It took a couple of minutes, but together Ratkin eventually figured out how to use the tracing capability of his phone. I punched in a code number and traced the last phone number the kidnapper had used. After I wrote down the number, I dialed the home number of Earl Wickluff, one of our senior investigators. I don't especially like the guy—which was why I hadn't been using him for this assignment—but he's pretty fair with computers.

He answered the phone sounding a little drunk. "Congratulations, Earl," I said. "You just started clocking in some overtime."

"Huh?" he said.

"Jump on your computer," I said. "Use that CD ROM phone number database and find the location of this phone number."

He hesitated. "What CD ROM database?" he said innocently. The database I was talking about was property of Peachtree Investigations, and I'm sure he didn't want me to know he had a pirate copy of it on his home computer. A copy, incidentally, which he employed to do freelance work for various slimy ambulance chasers and collections agents in his spare time.

"We don't have time for you to bullshit me," I said, "I know you steal copies of all the firm's software for your home computer, so get on there and find out the location of this number."

Earl sighed loudly. I hung up.

Two minutes later he called back. "It's a pay phone," Earl said. "Located at the corner of Peachtree and Tenth Street in Atlanta."

"Great," I said. "Stand by, we're going to need you again."

I hung up and said, "Okay, Mr. Ratkin, I assume being the mogul that you are, that you've got a second line in this house? I don't want to make any of these calls on cell phones. The media assholes on the road out there will be using scanners."

Ratkin nodded. "There are two phones in the master bedroom. The one on the nightstand next to Georgia's side of the bed has the Caller ID box. The one on the other side of the bed is the other line."

"Great," I said. "Gunnar, how about you and Tawanda going upstairs. When this line rings, Tawanda, you write down the number off the caller ID box and give it to Gunnar. Gunnar, you call Earl on the second line and get him to start tracking down where the kidnapper is. By the time the FBI gets there, maybe we'll have figured out if there's a pattern to his movements."

Gunnar and Tawanda headed up the stairs. I sat down. As long as I was making decisions I was okay. But as soon as the waiting started, the shaking set in again. I looked out the big picture window at the barn and the trees and the meadows. The sun was hidden behind the ridge of oaks and everything was sinking into darkness.

A minute or so later, the phone rang again. I felt another surge of adrenaline.

"Five million," the voice said. "I told you that wasn't negotiable."

"Where did she go to elementary school?"

There was a pause. "What?"

"Ask her the question, then we talk."

"Oh. Right." I heard a door slam, cars driving by, then the kidnapper got back on the phone. "West End Elementary."

"Good. Now, you were saying. . . ."

"Five million. Non-negotiable."

"Right." I took a deep breath. "Let me ask you a couple of questions. I'm not looking for an answer. Just rhetorical questions. Is it not true that Mr. Ratkin is a wealthy man? And that he has a good job? And that his wife makes a lot of money? And that if he gave you every cent he had, wouldn't he be able to make it up fairly quickly?"

"Dammit—"

"Furthermore, don't you think this man loves his wife? Don't you think getting her home safely is the highest, in fact is the *only* priority in his mind right now?"

"I'm not interested in that man's problems."

"Of course you're not. All I'm saying is to keep that in mind when I make the following explanation to you—"

"You're stalling," he said.

Dial tone.

Gunnar came to the head of the stairs. "Earl tracked it. The call came from a payphone on Howell Mill and Collier."

"He's moving around the north side of Atlanta," I said. "Places with lots of people, lots of roads, lots of avenues of escape."

"I clocked it," Ratkin said. "He's staying on the line exactly one minute."

More waiting.

Finally the phone rang again.

"She was alive five minutes ago," the kidnapper said. "I wouldn't have killed her so quick, yes? So let's skip the questions about Georgia's elementary school career."

I figured the more I could drag this out, the better off for all of us. In an injured tone, I said, "I thought we had an agreement!"

"Hey, I'm a criminal," the kidnapper said lightly. "Sometimes I lie. But if you hang up the phone, I *will* kill her. So talk."

"Remember what I was saying? How high a priority it is for Jeremy Ratkin to get his wife back? Okay, so bear that in mind while I give you some figures."

He interrupted me. "I'm leaving now. As soon as the phone rings again, pick it up and start talking. No more elementary school questions."

"Have a pencil and paper ready."

The line went dead.

"Forty-five seconds," Ratkin said. "He's getting antsy."

Gunnar came to the stairs again. "Northside Drive, near West Paces Ferry. Earl says the phone's outside a Steak and Shake."

"Steak and Shake," Ratkin said. "That's a big help,"

"That's it!" I said.

"What's it?"

"Look! Peachtree and 10th. Howell Mill. West Paces Ferry. He's moving north along I-75!" I said. "Dammit I wish the FBI was here."

Five minutes later, one ring.

"Here's the deal," I said. "Mr. Ratkin has seventy-nine thousand four hundred and twenty-two dollars and sixty-one cents in cash. These funds were spread across seven accounts—money markets, checking, and so on. He has already consolidated that cash into one account, BankAmerica account number 0003-4885-1229. In addition, he holds liquid securities with a current market value in the amount of six hundred thousand and nine dollars. He will be able to sell these and transfer the funds to the BankAmerica account by about midnight. He has three mutual funds—the Vanguard Small Cap valued at $211,471.33, the Fidelity Pro-Growth valued at $56,444.20, and the Kemper Municipal-II valued at $141,072.65. His banker assures him that these can be liquidated and transferred to the BankAmerica account by five this morning. You might note that market value could have swung a little in that time. Moreover, he's got unsecured lines of credit in the form of various charge cards in the amount of $157,000, but there's a $61,426.99 balance, leaving only $95,573.01 of credit available. He will borrow against those lines of credit and transfer those funds to the BankAmerica account by morning. Additionally—"

Again the phone went dead.

Ratkin looked at his watch. "A minute and a quarter." Ratkin's lips twitched: it was just the barest hint of a smile. It occurred to me that this was the first time since I'd met him that I'd seen him show pleasure in anything. "He likes hearing about the money."

Gunnar called down from the stairs. "He's at another pay phone. A strip shopping center on Cobb Parkway, just south of Cumberland Mall."

I noticed four dark shapes swimming into view in the sliding glass door, black silhouettes against the last weak traces of the sky. I jumped, then realized it must be the FBI.

Ratkin stood, slid open the door. Four people slipped quickly inside the house, three men and one woman. They were all casually dressed. I guess that, in case they got spotted by the media, they didn't want to make it obvious that they were FBI.

The FBI team introduced themselves. The top guy was a Deputy Special Agent-in-Charge, a light-skinned black man whose last name was Cherry. He had a ghost of a mustache and wore a bright-colored bow tie under a green Windbreaker. His thin, ascetic face was the sort I associated with long distance runners. I didn't catch the other agents's names. I filled them in quickly on what was happening, concluding by saying, "The kidnapper has insisted that he's only going to talk with me. Said he'll kill Miss Burnett if anybody besides me gets on the phone."

Deputy SAC Cherry studied me for a very long moment. I should have felt uncomfortable under his scrutiny, but for some reason I didn't. The rest of his team looked disgusted that they were going to have to work with a private investigator, but Cherry himself seemed to take it in stride.

The phone rang and, strangely, the FBI agent smiled at me. I started to reach for the receiver. "Slowly," Deputy SAC Cherry said softly. There was nothing tense or hurried about him, and he had a whisper of something foreign in his accent that I couldn't quite place. "Four rings, Miz Childs. We're in no rush. The goal here is to keep him occupied, keep him busy, keep him calm, and keep him on the line. We've got a tactical team on alert in Atlanta. I'll get local jurisdictions involved, too, as soon as we figure out what he's doing. We slow him down, we track him, and after a few more calls we close the net. "Okay?"

I wanted to be angry at him for telling me what to do, but the truth is, there was something about the calm, unwavering gaze of his hazel eyes that I found heartening. It gave me some relief from the pressure. And anyway, he was right: I'd been rushing everything.

Still, I was a little shocked when Deputy SAC Cherry took my left hand and held it in his like I was his girl-friend.

Hastily I grabbed the receiver with my other hand. "Uh, hello?"

"What took you so damn long, Sunny?"

"If you must know? I have a nervous bladder. I was in the john."

"Oh." The kidnapper seemed mildly taken aback. "Alright, tell me about the money." I noticed that his accent seemed to be sliding around a little, his vowels sounding

Germanic one minute, French or Russian the next.

"So what's the total on the numbers I gave you so far?" I said.

"A million three and change," the kidnapper said.

I could feel the even pressure of the FBI agent's hand on mine. It was a little weird—weird but comforting. "Okay, good. Now, that's the easy part. He's got other assets, but none of them are liquid."

"What about his stock in ArchRival?"

"Hold on, hold on," I said gently. "I'm getting there."

Deputy SAC Cherry nodded very slowly, smiled, made a gentle circle in the air with his free hand. His other hand kept up a steady pressure on mine. Take your time, he was saying. I had been expecting the FBI to be starchy assholes, but I had to admit I liked this guy.

"ArchRival is a private company," I said. "I don't know how familiar you are with stocks. . . ." I let the implied question hang in the air, figuring that if he replied it might tell us something useful about him.

The kidnapper said nothing, though.

"Well, the point is," I went on, "you can't just sell a big pile of privately held stock overnight. It's not like IBM, you just hit a button and it trades IBM. Nobody even knows what this company is worth. Even an expert, an investment banker or somebody like that, it takes them *weeks* to figure out what a company like ArchRival is worth. Now Mr. Ratkin has nevertheless been able to reach an arrangement with his bankers. Because of their relationship with him, they're willing to loan him four hundred thousand dollars to be collateralized by his stock. But that's it. His shares may or may not be worth more, but no bank is going to lend to full value on ten minutes notice in the middle of the night."

"Okay, we're at a million seven."

"Mr. Ratkin owns two homes. Together they are valued at $5.2 million. But he's only got a hundred grand or so in equity. His bank's trying to figure out an exact number they can loan to him, but it won't be bigger than two hundred, absolute max."

There was quiet on the line. I could feel my heart banging. But the FBI agent's hand was calming me. I didn't feel alone anymore, didn't feel like every single ounce of pressure was resting on my shoulders anymore.

"So that's where we are," I said. "As long as you're sticking to the six a.m. deadline, you're looking at somewhere in the neighborhood of $1.8 to $1.9 million bucks."

"Bullshit!" the kidnapper said, outraged. "What about *her* money? Wait. Hold that thought."

The line went dead.

"A minute thirty-five," Ratkin said.

Deputy SAC Cherry let go of my hand. "You're doing good, Sunny," he said softly. Then, in a louder voice, "Okay, y'all can stop worrying about tracing. We got people on that now."

"Where was he?" I said.

"Parking lot of Taco Mac on Roswell Road, just off I-285," the female FBI agent said. She had set up a bunch of electronic equipment in the corner of the room—call tracing, amplifiers, headphones, tape recorders—all of it hooked into the phone lines.

"He's started moving along I-285 now," I said. "That's not City of Atlanta jurisdiction anymore. It's Fulton County Police."

Cherry nodded. To a beefy red-faced agent, he said, "I want every police department in the metro area on alert. I want their SWAT people, tactical units, snipers, the whole nine, on full alert. I'll call Fulton County PD myself. You start with Atlanta PD, then Cobb, then, shoot, who am I leaving out?"

I traced an arc in the air. "He came up 75, now he's going across the 285 Perimeter. If he keeps going on 285, he'll go through the Fulton County Police jurisdiction, then he'll hit Dunwoody, then Chamblee, then Gwinnett County, then DeKalb County, then Decatur."

"Right, right, right," Deputy SAC Cherry said. Then, to his agent. "What you waiting on, son? Get to it!"

Cherry dialed something on his cell phone, went into the other room. When he came back he said, "Okay, Sunny, this time you need to keep him at least two minutes. Can you do that?"

"Try my best."

He took out a map of the Atlanta metro area. "If you're right, he's making his way west to east on Interstate 285 right now. So his next call should be from a pay phone somewhere here." He tapped his finger along the red line that arced across the north side of the city. "Somewhere in the neighborhood of Perimeter Mall, wouldn't you guess?"

I nodded.

"Fulton County Police have a SWAT unit and three plainclothes cars heading for that area right now. I've instructed them not to take him down unless they're sure they can do it without tipping their hand. We don't want them muffing this thing and tipping the guy off that the cops are after him."

The phone rang again, and I felt another clammy burst of anxiety.

I waited the requisite four rings, then picked up. This time Cherry didn't hold my hand.

The kidnapper began speaking immediately. "Okay, Sunny, what about *Georgia's* money? She's worth millions."

"Sure. But here's the problem. I just got through talking to Mr. Ratkin, and he told me that she has recently put all of her money into some kind of trust. She gets income, but she can't touch the principle. It's a tax thing or something."

The kidnapper interrupted. "You're bloody mad! Do you think I care if she has a run-in with the IRS or not?"

"Well, see that's not the problem—"

At that moment Agent Cherry came over and hit the switch hook, disconnecting the call.

"What are you doing!" I said.

"Okay, we guessed wrong," the FBI agent said. "He wasn't at Perimeter. He got off one exit early, over by Northside Hospital. He's still moving in the right direction, though."

"Yeah but—"

Agent Cherry smiled calmly. "We need to keep him moving, that's all. He's doing us no good where he is, and let's face it, you can't string him along all night. At some point all of the issues you're discussing will get resolved. So we need to hit him before you run out of things to talk about. I still think he'll stop at Perimeter. The Fulton County guys are already there, and we've got an FBI tactical unit en route, too."

"He's gonna be pissed," I said, shaking my head.

"We're doing fine," Cherry said. "He's not irrational or out of control. Just turn it back on *him*. Say something like, 'Hey, why'd you cut the line? What are you doing? Is Georgia okay?' That type of thing. Demand that he confirm Georgia's alive again. If you sense him getting impatient, get back to the money issue again. That'll keep him on the line."

"I'll try."

We waited in silence. Cherry had a nervous tic, angling his head down so his chin touched the tip of his bow tie. He'd touch one side then the other, then back, staring out the window.

The phone rang. I picked it up on the first ring this time.

"What happened!" I shouted. "How come you disconnected? Is Georgia okay?"

"I thought it was *you*," the kidnapper said sullenly. I felt like my ear was starting to hear the outlines of some actual accent lying behind the bogus Slavic/Teutonic one. But I still couldn't make out quite what it was. It wasn't an American accent, though, I was pretty sure of that. Was it a Russian pretending to be a German? A Dutchman pretending to be a Czech? I couldn't tell.

Cherry was busy on his phone. Suddenly he grinned triumphantly. He tapped the beefy agent on the shoulder, the one who had been calling the various police agencies, whispered something in his ear.

"I want to know if Georgia's okay," I said forcefully.

"Ve haff been through zat." The kidnapper's accent had suddenly gone into full-blown movie-Nazi mode.

"Ask her, ah, ask her who her math teacher was in third grade."

"Vat's vith all this third grade shit?"

"Just ask her!"

"Shut the fuck up with third grade, or I'll put a bullet in her goddamn head and walk away!"

Cherry scrawled something on a legal pad, then held it up so I could see it. It said, HE'S NEAR PERIMETER MALL!!! DON'T LET HIM OFF THE LINE!!! He had underlined the last sentence so hard his pen had torn a hole in the paper.

"Alright, alright!" I said into the phone. "I'll trust you for now. So what were we talking about?"

"Georgia's money."

"Oh, yeah. Georgia's money. See, here's the main thing. I don't know quite how to say this, but it's like, you can't write a check if you aren't there to sign it. You see what I mean? Even if she could get at the principal—and I don't think she can—it's irrelevant anyway. Banks won't authorize fund transfers without signatures. I mean, for her to arrange for this to happen, you'd have to set her free so she could sign the documents. Catch-22."

There was a long pause. "Dammit . . ." he said finally. Then he sighed loudly. "So what you're telling me is that all Ratkin can raise is a million nine."

"Thereabouts, yeah." There was a brief pause. Cherry made a signal to me to keep talking, bringing his third and fourth fingers together with his thumb in rapid succession. He was obviously afraid the kidnapper would hang up and move to another phone. I could feel the seconds ticking away as the SWAT cops near the mall were undoubtedly rocketing toward their prey. Then again, knowing the traffic in that area, they may have just been sitting in a long line of cars beating their fists on their steering wheels.

"So, look . . ." I said, trying to think of something to say. "A million, nine. That's more money than most people see in their lives. I've been sitting here with Mr. Ratkin, watching him deal with these bankers, and believe me, the guy's working these people like musical instruments. But there's a limit. He's wrung every single, solitary dime out of them. So, look, have I been straight with you so far?"

"I wouldn't know."

Agent Cherry held up a legal pad for me to see. Scrawled on the paper: ONE MORE MINUTE.

"Okay, well just remember what I said. You think this guy would risk his wife's life just because he wants to grind you out of a few thousand dollars? This guy's *petrified*!"

"Something's not right here."

"Look, I don't know how you are with computers, but he's willing to give you passwords to all his accounts, phone numbers for his bankers, Internet access codes, you name it. Anything, anything, *anything* to prove to you that he's playing straight."

Cherry's sign: THIRTY SECONDS.

I could hear car horns and a shrill squealing sound. What the hell was that noise?

"I got to go."

"Wait!" I said. "Don't do something stupid when you got this much money in your hands. A million nine. Have we got a deal?"

FIFTEEN SECONDS!!!

"Done," the kidnapper said. "One million nine hundred thousand via wire transfer gets you Georgia Burnett, 6 A.M. tomorrow. You'll get final details via fax at 5 A.M."

The line went dead.

We sat as though paralyzed. A long, silent minute dragged by. And the whole time I was trying to figure out what that strange squealing noise was that I'd heard on the other end of the phone.

"Son of a bitch." It suddenly hit me. "He's at the Chamblee MARTA station! He's about to take off on the train."

Cherry grabbed his phone, ready to make a call. But before he could dial, the phone rang in his hand. "Yeah?" he demanded.

The FBI man listened for a few moments. Then he threw his phone up in the air. We watched it rotate slowly in the air, come down on the glass-topped breakfast table with a hollow, shimmering *thwack*.

"They missed him by ten seconds," Cherry said. "There's a black Land Cruiser sitting there next to the payphone, engine idling. Nobody inside."

"Can you stop the train?" Gunnar said.

"Gimme the number for the MARTA Police," Cherry snapped at one of his subordinates. It had to be maddening for him, having to juggle metro Atlanta's bewildering array of police jurisdictions. After some fumbling around, the female agent came up with the number. Cherry's thin, brown face was glazed with sweat. He had a long, angry conversation with somebody in the MARTA Police dispatcher's office who obviously didn't share his sense of urgency about the kidnapping of Georgia Burnett.

Finally Cherry hung up, put his forehead down gently on the breakfast table.

"What's going on?" Ratkin said.

Cherry didn't answer. No one moved for at least four minutes.

Cherry's phone rang. He picked up, listened, hung up. "They stopped the train," he announced to the room. "They're holding the doors closed until our people get on scene."

"Alright!" I said.

Cherry looked morose. "The train has already made two stops. He may have jumped by now."

Ten minutes later another call came through. The look on Deputy SAC Cherry's face said it all. "Gone," he said shortly. Then he stood up and walked out into the night air. Maybe I was wrong, but I swear there was something wet in his eyes.

CHAPTER 9

A **FEW MINUTES** later two people I didn't know walked into the room—a tall thin man, and a young woman with big hair. Jeremy Ratkin stood up. "Okay, here we go, people," he said, clapping his hands. "Seven o'clock news comes on in twenty-five minutes. That means we're going to have to do the press conference live."

Deputy SAC Cherry and Gunnar and I all looked up at him, appalled. With one voice we said, *"Press conference?"*

"No offense, Mr. Ratkin," the FBI agent said, "but are you out of your mind?"

"You know your business, I know mine. And what I'll tell you is this: Georgia Burnett's third album is scheduled for release in three days. This is the biggest story in the entire world at this exact moment. We go live at seven, we lead ABC and NBC. That's forty, fifty million households, easy."

"You're willing to risk your wife's life to sell a few *records*?" I said.

"Oh, so I look like a monster to you. Or some kind of idiot, maybe?" Ratkin's black eyes appraised me. "The story is out there, people. Right now the best thing we can do for Georgia is try to control it." Ratkin took the arm of the slim man who had just entered the room and said, "Sunny, Gunnar, this is my director of public relations, Gill Merrit."

The PR man was tall, with something slightly fey about his manner. His face was very smooth, his shoes were Italian, and his hair was exceptionally pretty.

Merrit in turn introduced the young woman with him. "This is Annette," he said. Then, turning to me: "Annette will be doing your makeup."

"*Makeup?*" My eyebrows rose slightly.

Merrit turned back to Jeremy Ratkin. "I'll run out to the gate and corral the reporters. We'll want to set up out by the stables. The barn makes a terrific visual— very folksy, very colorful."

The bottle blond makeup girl stepped over to me, accompanied by a cloud of patchouli. She pinched a fold in my blouse between her fingers, rubbed them together, wrinkled her nose. "I may have a couple thoughts on wardrobe, too, hon," she said.

"Whoa, whoa," I said sharply. "We won't be a part of this."

Ratkin looked at me, then at Gunnar. "Gunnar?" he said. "We need you in makeup pronto. You're playing the lead in this thing anyway."

I glared at Ratkin. "Hey! Jeremy! Did I not just say we aren't doing this?"

But Ratkin ignored me, the barest hint of a smile on his face. "Gunnar? Hm?"

Gunnar looked at me sheepishly, shrugged, then turned to the makeup girl. "Where you want me to squat, darling?"

I have never been part of a media feeding frenzy before, and I hope never to again. There must have been a hundred and fifty journalists and broadcasters parked on the lawn, huge mobile TV trucks idling, flashbulbs going off, photographers fighting to establish positions, bright lights trained at a podium that Ratkin's PR man had set up next to the barn behind the house. It was bedlam.

Ratkin's PR man, Gill Merrit, had his watch out, giving the seven o'clock news anchors time to do their lead-ins. At precisely 7:03, he stood up and said, "Let me introduce Jeremy Ratkin, Georgia Burnett's husband. He'll have a brief statement, and then we'll take a couple of questions."

Ratkin stood slowly, adjusted the microphone. He had changed out of his cashmere turtleneck into a plaid shirt. His eyes were mournful and dark as he looked down at the script Gill Merrit had supplied to him.

"Last night," he said, "my wife and soulmate, Georgia Burnett, was kidnapped. For obvious reasons involving her personal safety, I can't tell you very much. But we've spoken to her today, and she is safe."

I noticed Gill Merrit circling his way around the crowd toward me. "What do you think of the plaid shirt?" he said, pointing at his boss on the podium. "Too Uncle Jethro? I'm trying to country him a little. If he's not careful, Jeremy comes off a bit too . . . ah, Hebraic. If you know what I mean."

"Too Jewish for *whom*?"

"Our target audience," the PR man said without the barest trace of irony. "Working and middle-class white females, fifteen to thirty-five. Cornfed types." He turned and examined my face with clinical interest. "Shame you're not up there, Sunny." He reached up and touched the side of my face with the tips of his fingers. "You've got just the cheekbones for this kind of light."

"Get your hand off me," I said.

The PR man pursed his lips and then started making his way back toward the podium.

Ratkin continued with his statement. "I have spoken with Georgia today, and she wanted to convey thanks to all her fans who have been praying for her." He looked into the camera. "We're convinced that with your prayers and with God's help, she'll be safely returned in time for the release of her latest album, *Shades Of Me*, which is scheduled to be in stores this Tuesday."

Ratkin looked around at all the cameras. "Now I'd like to point out that we've had a lot of help and support in this terrible time. I'm sure that all of you are familiar with the world-renowned private investigator Gunnar Brushwood. I'd just like to take a moment to acknowledge his assistance. Gunnar, could you say a few words?"

World-renowned, huh? And to think I had had no idea.

Gunnar stood, surveyed the crowd. His handle-bar mustache gleamed in the halogen lights, and his weather-beaten features seemed especially chiseled and manly. "As you know, we're still in the midst of trying to assure Ms. Burnett's safe return." Gunnar's voice was a husky, commanding growl, and his beautiful Low Country accent was deeper, more ornately southern than ever. "So naturally we can't give y'all folks too much detail. Suffice it to say that we've been negotiating with the kidnappers all day, and we're going to do whatever it takes to get her back safe and sound."

A reporter called out a question. "Have the police or the FBI been notified?"

"Federal and state law enforcement are, ah, obviously aware of the situation. But they're not presently involved in any direct or indirect capacity. The kidnappers have insisted on that, and we've honored their request. Again, I want to stress that our main goal here is Georgia's safety."

Another reporter yelled, "Is there a ransom demand?"

Gunnar frowned grimly. "I can't comment on that, hoss."

"Is it your intention to apprehend the kidnapper or kidnappers?"

"Sir, a woman's life is at stake here." Gunnar bristled. "Rash comments like that can endanger lives. So let me reiterate: we desire one and only one thing. That is Georgia's safe return."

Gill Merrit stood up behind the podium again. "Folks, for those of you who are broadcasting live, I believe that's about all we can give you right now." He waited until the various lights had dimmed, then waved his hand to quiet the crowd. "Is anybody still going live? No? Okay good. A couple of housekeeping issues. My assistant has set up a table over there." He pointed over by the garage where the blond makeup girl sat behind a folding card table. "She's got copies of Miss Burnett's forthcoming video, *Shades Of Me*. This is a rough cut, which is not in rotation just yet . . . but we're prepared to let you air it as an outro on the news tonight, or in excerpts not to exceed fifteen seconds during any programming you might air tomorrow. Additionally, I'm sure many of you are aware that Mr. Brushwood was the subject of a made-for-TV movie, *Bounty Hunter*, which starred Brian Keith back in 1987. We've got copies of that available, too, along with some press kits about Miss Burnett's new album."

I noticed that Deputy Special Agent-in-Charge Cherry had sidled up next to me while Gill Merrit was talking. I felt his presence, but didn't say anything until Gill Merrit sat down.

"Holding my hand," I said. "That didn't seem like a real FBI kind of thing to do."

"Hope it didn't bother you."

"No. It was nice."

I wanted to tell him how alone I'd been feeling until he'd come into that room and taken my hand, how tired I was of bearing up under things. But I couldn't bring myself to say it. I didn't want to seem weak and girlie, I guess.

Up by the barn the glaring camera lights were winking off one by one until finally the black sky began to reveal itself again. As I was surveying the scene my gaze lit on Cherry for a moment, and our eyes met. I felt like something passed between us, some kind of odd spark jumping the gap. But I wasn't sure what to make of it.

"So what do you think of all this, Agent Cherry?" I took in the trucks, the reporters, the cameras with a sweep of my arm.

"It stinks to high heaven."

Ain't that the truth, I was thinking. But again, I didn't speak the words.

CHAPTER 10

T 5 A.M., a piece of paper began scrolling out of the fax machine in Jeremy Ratkin's living room. I grabbed it.

Gunnar and Ratkin and I had been lying around in the living room trying to sleep while the FBI guys had been going over the forensic evidence with Tawanda and Roy Nidlett.

I read the fax out loud.

TO SUNNY AND GUNNAR!!!!
1. *Get the bank authorization codes and other information necessary for making the wire transfer of the money from Mr. Ratkin. Make certain you have ALL necessary authorizations, procedures and phone numbers, contact names, etc. You will not have a chance to get them later!!!!*
2. *Once you have that information, get IMMEDIATELY into your vehicle and start driving. Bring Sunny's cell phone and nothing else.*
3. *Further instructions will follow!!!*

   YOU WILL BE OBSERVED during your mis-

*sion. Radio and cell phone frequencies will also
be monitored. Do EXACTLY as you are instructed.*

Here is a list of "Don'ts"!!!!
Don't wear a wire.
Don't carry a TRACKING device!!!!!
Don't be followed by feds, cops or choppers.
Don't use your cell phone except when instructed.
Don't stop driving except when instructed.
Don't use any radio devices.
Don't use DIGITAL ENCRYPTION.
Don't carry weapons!!!!!!!!!!!

*Failure to observe any of these warnings will
result in the IMMEDIATE EXECUTION of Georgia Burnett!!!!!!!!*

*BE IN THE CAR IN FIVE MINUTES OR
GEORGIA DIES!!!!!!!!*

"Okay, kids," Gunnar said. "Let's saddle up."

We gathered in the other room and listened as Ratkin
gave us instructions for making the wire transfer. As he
spoke, he scrawled the appropriate account numbers and
authorization codes on a piece of yellow legal pad.

"What do we know about this man?" Cherry said to
a guy with thick glasses and a brown suit, who I had
figured out was some kind of forensic psychologist.

"He likes exclamation points and capital letters," the
psychologist said.

"That's funny, Don," Cherry said. "But we don't have
time for funny right now."

The psychologist squinted. "Intelligent and organized,
but probably not highly educated. Probably a white male.
The exclamation points indicate an obsessive, perhaps
even somewhat delusional thought system, which—"

"Alright, screw it, that's enough," Cherry said waving
his hand dismissively at the psychologist. "Bottom line,

this guy's no fool. He's prepared, and he's thought this thing out and he's pissed."

"That's about it," the psychologist said.

"Big question," Gunnar said. "Do we wear wires or tracking devices or not?"

Deputy SAC Cherry looked at Ratkin. "He might be bluffing about scanning for radio transmissions or he might not. If he's sophisticated enough to be worried about us using radios or cell phones with digital encryption, then he might be sophisticated enough to actually be monitoring for them. My vote is to give you guys a U-band pulse device that we can track on—"

"No tracking devices, no radios, no choppers, no tail, none of that shit," Ratkin said sharply.

I looked at my watch. "We got two minutes, people!"

My cell phone rang.

"Hello?"

"Are you in the car?" the pseudo-German voice said. "Are you driving?"

"Uh, we're getting the bank stuff together."

"Get in the car right now." The caller hesitated. "Oh, and also I want you to take Mr. Ratkin's Range Rover, not Gunnar's Lincoln."

"Why?"

"There's some off-road driving involved."

"We haven't got all the bank—"

"One minute!"

The line went dead.

Ratkin, who was monitoring the call from a pair of headphones, fished his car keys out of his pocket and tossed them to Gunnar. "Go!" he said. We all trooped outside.

As I slammed the door to Ratkin's big 4-wheel drive vehicle, Ratkin leaned in the window. "Don't let her die out there, Sunny."

"You got the wire transfer information?" I said.

As he handed the legal pad through the window to

me, Ratkin whispered, "If you get into trouble, check the glove compartment."

"What do you mean?" I said. But Gunnar had already put the truck in gear and started driving.

CHAPTER 11

"WHAT WAS THE whispering about?" Gunnar said as we turned through the gate, plowing through the huge mob of reporters.

I opened the glove compartment. "Oh shit," I said.

Gunnar glanced over. A shiny, nickel-plated Colt Python .357 magnum lay on top of the Range Rover's operation manual. I closed the glove box sharply.

"I don't know if that makes me feel better or not," he said.

"Gun or no gun, I feel like throwing up right now."

Gunnar didn't say anything, but I could see he was nervous, too.

We drove a mile or so and then the cell phone rang. "You're driving south on Little Texas Valley," the kidnapper said. When you get to the sign that says Dangerous Curve, bear left, that'll take you to 27. Go north on 27. That's a left turn." Then he hung up.

I relayed the instructions. "You think he's really watching us?" I said.

Gunnar shrugged. "Doesn't matter. We have to assume he is."

Floyd County is pretty country—rolling hills, mixed

farms and pine forest. Not prosperous exactly—plenty of mobile homes and Primitive Baptist Churches—but not the kind of blighted, worn out land and pitiful-looking people you see downstate.

We turned left on U.S. 27 as instructed. It was a big four-lane road with a turn lane in the middle. The phone rang within thirty seconds. "Turn right onto state 140. It's coming up on your right. Then go until you hit mile marker four."

We turned right onto the little two-lane road, which ran down through forests of planted pine. Suddenly we were in an area that felt remote. After a minute we pulled up behind a battered pickup truck loaded with a huge, teetering stack of baled pine straw. Gunnar was forced to slow the Range Rover to a crawl. He started cussing, trying to pass the truck, but there was no room on the winding two lane road. After several minutes crawling along behind the pickup, the phone rang.

"See it?"

"Not there yet," I said. "We're stuck behind some geezer in a hay wagon." We passed a mile marker, a green metal tab about the size of a cigar box mounted on a small signpost, the number 2 painted on it.

"Okay, when you get there, you'll see a dirt road off to the side with an old mailbox that says Pearson on the side. Pull over. In the mailbox you'll find a cell phone. It's painted bright red. Put *your* cell phone in the box, take the red one, get back in the car and continue driving east. When we've verified that your cell phone is in the box, I'll call you back."

"We?" I said.

"We're watching you. The phone is painted red so that we can see that you're only talking on the phone we gave you."

The kidnapper hung up. Was there really a *we*? Was someone really watching?

"I don't think he's watching us," I said. "I think he timed the route out so that his calls would coincide with every move we made—as though he *were* watching. Since we got stuck behind grandpa up there, we fell behind the schedule he anticipated."

Gunnar grunted.

I explained about our next move.

"I bet the new phone's got digital encryption," Gunnar said. "The FBI can monitor a regular cell phone, but not one that's got an encryption chip built into it. That way he can finally stop hopscotching around from payphone to payphone."

I nodded.

The green tab indicating we'd reached mile 4 stood by the road in a long stretch of pine forest. A battered gray mailbox with several bullet holes in it appeared about a hundred yards later. In this part of the country, shooting mailboxes is a big sport, right up there with cow tipping. Gunnar pulled over, and I climbed out.

As the kidnapper had said, the box contained a cell phone slathered in bright red paint. I left my phone in the box, climbed back in the Range Rover.

We started driving and pretty soon the new phone rang.

"Alright, this is a safe phone." The kidnapper suddenly sounded like he was in a chatty mood. "Digital encryption/decryption, frequency jumping, all the goodies. No fun for the Feebies."

"That's nice," I said. "But before we go any further, I want to talk to Georgia."

The kidnapper said, "Here's how this is going to work. You will authorize a half million dollar transfer right now, and I will let you talk to her. Next you will transfer an additional half million, and I'll give you her physical location. When you arrive at the location, you'll be able to see her with your own eyes. At that point, you'll authorize the final transfer of nine hundred thousand, and she'll be released."

"Now look, I'm not going to—"

"This is not a debate!" The kidnapper's voice rose.

"Half a million right now, or I shoot her in the head."

"Okay, okay, okay! How do you want to make the transfer?"

"You will make the calls to accomplish the transfer. Your phone works on receive-only mode. That way you can't call out and chit-chat with the cops. Tell me the number of Mr. Ratkin's bank."

I told him the phone number, and he said, "The phone will ring again in about thirty seconds. Pick it up, and you'll be connected."

"Okay. So where do I transfer the money?"

"The funds are to be wired to ABN AMRO Bank—that's a bank in the Netherlands, Antilles." He gave me the account number.

I read the numbers back to the kidnapper and the phone went dead.

As soon as I had filled Gunnar in on what was going on, the phone rang. I picked up and arranged the first transfer.

"Well, let's see if he's going to take the money and run," Gunnar said dryly.

We kept driving. I jumped when the phone rang.

"Hello?" I said.

There was a brief clattering noise, and then a woman said, "Hello? Hello? Is someone there?"

"Georgia?"

"Yes?" I tried to gauge her mood from the sound of her voice. Was in she in pain? Had she been brutalized somehow? I couldn't tell.

"My name is Sunny Childs. I'm a private investigator working for your husband. We're going to get you released as soon as possible. How are you feeling? Are you hurt?"

"I'm okay. They've been, you know, they've been nice enough."

"Okay, now I need you to prove that you're actually Georgia."

She sang a few bars of "She Misses His Kisses," her big, shlocky hit from the last album. There was no mistaking Georgia Burnett's voice, even over the tinny little cell phone.

The bogus German accent came back on. "Okay, Sunny. So she's alive. Now, here's what happens next—"

Suddenly I heard a loud bang and the next thing I knew we were slewing across the road. The cell phone flew out of my hand, then trees and sky were spinning around us, and I felt my body yanked forward into the seat belt. The tires of the big Range Rover howled, and then there was another bang and a sickening concussion, and I had the strange impression we were facing in a very different direction than we had been just seconds earlier. We had gone down in a ditch and the nose of the Rover was sticking up in the air at about a 30-degree angle. I looked out the window and saw the car was surrounded by dead brown stalks of poke berry and pigweed.

"What the hell happened?" I said.

Gunnar was blinking and looking around with a dazed expression on his face. His airbag had gone off. "I think we hit a deer," he said finally. He reached up and felt his face. When his hand came away it was wet with blood. Gunnar looked at the blood without comment.

"What do we do now?" I said desperately.

Gunnar muttered something then pressed the gas. The engine was still running, but the wheels got no purchase. He tried reversing the car, but that was no better. Shifting into four-wheel drive didn't help.

Gunnar turned off the ignition. "Maybe we can rock her a little."

We climbed out of the car. I slogged through three or four inches of brackish water to the edge of the ditch, then turned to survey the scene. The Range Rover had left a swirl of skid marks on the road, then torn a swathe through fifty feet of weeds on the side of the road before coming to rest in the ditch, the rear wheels hanging off the ground, the belly of the truck sunk in a sheer four foot wall of red clay.

"Look," I said, pointing to a huddled shape in the middle of the road twenty yards away. It was an antlerless deer, still alive, eyes rolling. The deer was trying to struggle to its feet, but something was terribly wrong with it. Blood dripped from its mouth, and its jaw worked sideways like it was chewing its cud.

"Oh, my God, the poor thing," I said, running toward it.

"Careful," Gunnar called to me.

I stopped about fifteen feet from the deer. It was struggling to get up on its haunches, but both rear legs were apparently broken.

"We've got to help her!" I said.

Gunnar came up behind me, put a hand on my shoulder. "There ain't no helping her, darling."

"But there must be. . . ." I tried to think. "Could we call, like, a vet or something?" Even in my confused state the words sounded idiotic as soon as they left my mouth.

Gunnar shook his head. Then I saw he had the gun in his hand, the Colt from Ratkin's glove compartment. "I'm sorry, Sunny," he said. "It's the only humane thing to do."

"The gun!" I said. "What if he's watching?"

"He ain't watching. I think we know that by now."

He took two strides toward the agonized animal, pointed the gun at its head, and pulled the trigger. The gun made an appallingly loud bang and jumped in his hand. The deer however, continued to stare at Gunnar with its sweet black eyes.

"What the—" Gunnar's brow was furrowed. He stepped forward another stride, squeezed the trigger again. Again the gun bucked. The deer flinched a little, but continued to chew nervously and struggle around on the Tarmac.

Gunnar popped open the cylinder, pulled out one of the .357 cartridges. Then his head jerked slightly, and he got a hard look in his eyes.

"What?" I said.

Gunnar slammed the cylinder shut. "That goddamn lying long-haired full-of-shit sumbitch gave us a gun full of blanks."

Something cold started creeping up the back of my neck. From the car I heard the cell phone ringing.

CHAPTER 12

"**Y**OU WILL NOT believe," I said.

There was a long pause on the cell phone that I'd just pulled out of the wreck. The kidnapper finally spoke. "Do not, I repeat, do not start screwing with me. Not if you want this girl back alive."

"We hit a deer," I said. "We ran off the road. We're stuck in a goddamn ditch."

Long, long pause. "Can you get out?"

"I don't think so."

"Can you hitch a ride?"

"Are you kidding me?"

"You want Georgia back? Figure a way to get to the location. I don't give a damn how you do it. But if I think you're hitching along with some bunch of Feds, I'm goink to kill Georgia, and then I'll kill you. I won't hesitate to go out in a blaze of glory if that's the way it has to be."

"Alright, alright, it's just—"

"Look, here's a little incentive for you to get your ass in gear, Sunny. While you're standing around, let's make the second transfer. Then I'll tell you her location."

The kidnapper gave me a new bank and a new account number, this time a bank in the Caymans. Then the line clicked off.

Thirty seconds later the phone rang again. I talked to Ratkin's banker, and he said the second transfer of half a million would be made within a minute.

We waited, Gunnar and I leaning up against the car. Gunnar watched the dying deer with an odd expression on his face. I couldn't even look.

The phone rang. "Turn around and go back to 27, then head north. If you have a map, you'll see the Sloppy Floyd State Park. Turn right on 156 and go to mile marker nine, after that you will see several very rough dirt logging roads that go off into the woods. That's why I wanted you in the Rover. She's down one of those roads. I'll give you final directions when you get there."

As I hung up the phone, a jacked-up pickup truck screeched to a stop about fifty feet up the road from us, backed up sharply, screeched to a stop again right in front of us.

"Y'all folks need he'p?" The driver was a fat guy with a drooping mustache. He wore hunting camouflage from head to toe. "I got a winch."

"That'd be mighty fine, sir," Gunnar said.

Gunnar and the driver of the pickup got busy hooking up the winch on the front of the truck to the Range Rover. With Gunnar driving the Rover and the pickup revving loudly on the road, they had the truck hauled out of the weeds within a couple of minutes. Surprisingly the Range Rover didn't look much the worse for wear.

"I thank you, my friend," Gunnar said heartily.

"You gonna keep it?" the man in camouflage said as I opened the door of Ratkin's vehicle.

"Keep what?" I said.

He wiped his face on his sleeve, then pointed back toward the deer.

"She's all yours," Gunnar said, smiling.

As we drove off, the man in the pickup was getting

out of the cab of his truck with a baseball bat, walking purposefully back toward the dying deer.

"Oh God," I said.

We drove for a while in silence, turning north on 27 again. I was so mad and so ashamed at getting sucked into this mess that I felt like throwing up.

"Okay, Sunny," Gunnar said finally. "Go ahead and say it."

"What?"

"Go ahead. Say: 'Gunnar, you've been blinded by your craven desire for publicity. Gunnar, you've let yourself be used. Gunnar, I knew this was all a setup and a load of horseshit from the very beginning. Gunnar, I told you so.' Something like that."

"No, no," I said. "I'm no more to blame than you. I knew something wasn't right, but. . . . Hell, I don't know, maybe I was just star struck. Or maybe I was just thinking about all the money we were going to bill this guy for." I rubbed my elbow. Something was hurting. I must have banged it when we hit the deer. "So are you thinking the same thing I'm thinking?"

"This whole goddamn thing is a publicity stunt."

"Yep."

We were silent for a moment. Then Gunnar said, "Her last album wasn't selling too great; Ratkin's not getting much advance excitement on the new one; so he arranges this bogus kidnapping. I reckon when we show up at the exchange site the supposed kidnapper is gonna drag out a shotgun or something and pretend he's trying to shoot us. Then we're supposed to blast away at him with this here cap gun. The bad guy gets away, Georgia gets home safe and sound, and you and me come off looking like ass-whooping, gun-toting, fire-breathing heroes. Then Ratkin hires us to hunt down the bad guys. Probably gets a film crew from *Hard Copy* or *Entertainment Tonight* to follow us around while we kick down doors. Every day, there'll be a new clue, a new chance for Georgia's video to get more heavy exposure on TV. Nationwide goddamn dragnet. Maybe he'll even strap a pistol around Georgia's waist, get her to follow us around while her album goes triple platinum."

He shook his head in disgust.

"Uh-huh," I said. "That's about the same scenario I had in mind. Maybe a TV mini-series. Who do you think they'll get to play me?"

"That gal off *Friends*. The bony black-haired one."

We were silent again for a while. We turned off the big U.S. highway onto another dinky two-lane road.

"What do you think?" Gunnar said. "Do we go through with the charade?"

I stared at him. "Are you shitting me?" I said, offended that he'd even suggest the thought.

Gunnar took the Range Rover through a long sweeping turn past a knot of abandoned barns and a collapsing silo. Kudzu had half buried the place. I could see him working through something in his mind.

"Here's the thing, Sunny. S'pose we bail right now. We'll be a laughingstock. We'll look like cretins and nobody will ever hire us on a high-profile case again."

"Don't play that one on me, Gunnar. It's beneath you."

"Aw, come on, we're already in it up to our necks. We might as well play the hand and keep our mouths shut."

"I can't believe you're saying this, Gunnar!"

Long pause.

"I mean, Sunny, you got to admit, if this thing works out the way Ratkin wants it to, this is gonna be some hellacious publicity. The firm'll be set for years."

"And if it goes wrong?"

"Shoot, it can't go any by-God worse than it already has."

"Suppose the FBI figures out what's going on. That guy Cherry is smart. They'll assume we were in cahoots with Ratkin from the very beginning. You want to get indicted?"

"Aw, Sunny. . . ." Gunnar grinned good-naturedly. "Now you're blowing the whole thing out of proportion."

"Am I?" Ever since that blank-shooting gun had gone off, I had been feeling like I'd just swallowed something rotten.

A green tab came up on our right, mile marker 2. Gunnar's eyes narrowed. He seemed to be calculating something.

"What if . . ." he finally said.

"No, Gunnar! No way. We're not going through with this."

"Hear me out. What if it's only a *halfway* fake snatch? Say for instance, what if Ratkin knows it, but Georgia doesn't? What if he hired real criminals? I mean, whoever we meet for the final exchange, odds are they ain't gonna be out-of-work choir directors. If we don't play this thing out, who knows what might go down? Hell, Sunny, they might kill her or something!"

"Gimme a break! Ratkin didn't set this up so that his wife would get hurt. We need to find a pay phone and call the FBI. Right now."

"*What if*, though? Huh? What if?"

"No! It's all a sham. We need to pull the rip cord right now. Let the FBI sort it out." I was yelling at him.

"I mean, hey, it *could* be a mistake. Maybe the blanks got in there by accident."

"I'm not even going to dignify that."

"Sunny, c'mon, I hate it when you do this, babe."

"*En. Oh.* No! End of discussion."

Gunnar peered out the window as the next mile marker post swam up in front of us.

"Pull over," I said.

"Sunny. Come on. We're almost home."

I could see it all in his head. Just like he'd admitted earlier: he was rationalizing himself a way to get on TV, to get the adulation that he craved. He was like a child that way.

I tried to calm my voice a little. "Pull over, Gunnar. Stop the car."

Gunnar just laughed.

I reached across his leg with my left foot and stomped on the brake. The Range Rover began a screeching, groaning halt.

Gunnar looked over at me angrily as I flung open the door.

At which moment the cell phone rang.

"Bye, Gunnar."

Gunnar looked at me, then at the cell phone, then at me again. "It's all yours, Gunnar," I said. "I wash my hands of this." I slammed the door.

Gunnar stared at me for a moment as the red cell phone continued to ring. Then, finally, he picked it up.

"Gunnar here!" he said heartily.

I turned and started walking up the long empty road, back the way we'd come. The breeze was fresh and filled with the tart smell of pine trees. After a moment I heard the Rover begin to accelerate, the sound of the engine dying eventually in the distance. If I'd ever felt so angry and alone and abandoned, I sure couldn't remember when it had been.

I hadn't been walking for too long before I heard the distant sound of gunfire.

THE REAL THING

CHAPTER 13

MY SISTER IS Vietnamese. But that's another story. Her name is Sue Nguyen. She's actually my half-sister. Anyway, about two months after Georgia Burnett was kidnapped, we were sitting in a bar down on Ponce de Leon Avenue watching the silent TV that hung on the wall.

"Wait! Here's the money shot," I said. "You'll love this."

Ratkin had staged everything even better than Gunnar and I had anticipated. He had paid some "documentary filmmaker" to accidently-on-purpose just *happen* to be shooting a movie about wood lice or some bullshit thing not a hundred yards from the site of the hostage exchange. So the whole episode had been captured on film, complete with wobbly *cinema verité* camera work. The footage was played relentlessly for several weeks after the Grand Rescue, as I call it. I was a little puzzled as to why they were playing the entire video again. The whole Georgia-gets-kidnapped story had pretty much died a couple months ago, preempted by a new round of revelations in the ongoing presidential sex scandal. Something must have happened with Georgia recently—

but with the sound turned down, I couldn't make out what event had triggered the story.

Sue and I stared at the screen over the bar—as did most everybody else sitting at the bar. I had to admit, it was gripping footage:

At first, the Range Rover emerges from the woods at the edge of a large clearcut, Gunnar at the helm. The bad guy is waiting for him in a white Ford van with the name of a nonexistent electrical contractor on the side. Gunnar yells something that you can't quite hear. The side door of the van opens and there's Georgia, all tied up with her hands behind her back so that her chest is thrust forward and a tasteful amount of cleavage is hanging out of her skimpy outfit. Her hair looks great, and the camera zooms in so you catch a view of the pretty bruise accenting her left cheekbone.

The kidnapper, wearing black military garb and a black ninja hood stands behind her, fancy submachine gun at the ready.

Gunnar lifts the red phone to his ear—presumably he's talking to the bank, arranging the final wire transfer. Then more yelling. This time you can make out the words. "We did our part, son! Let the girl go!"

Gunnar looks great. He's got his gut sucked in, back straight, eyes steely, jaw determined. He is Manhood Personified.

The kidnapper talks into *his* cell phone, then shoves Georgia, who stumbles forward across the clearcut, her hands still secured behind her back with duct tape.

At about this point, I couldn't help myself. I started giving a play-by-play of the event that was unfolding before us on the screen.

"Oh no!" I said in a voice full of cartoonish drama. "Look, something goes wrong! Terrrrrrribly wrong!"

On-screen the kidnapper lowers his gun and fires one shot. Georgia looks backward, her face taut with fear, then stumbles on toward Gunnar.

"Master marksman Gunnar Brushwood draws his pistol! Returns fire! Runs toward the delicate and virginal heroine!"

On the TV over the bar the villain is slamming the door, cranking up his van. As the truck circles around, throwing up a spray of dirt from one rear tire, he shoots a burst out the window with his submachine gun. Then another.

"Oh, heavens to Betsy! Despite the hail of bullets, Gunnar springs catlike toward Our Heroine, hurls her delicate and busty form to the ground, covers her delicate frame with his own virile body! He's a human shield! What bravery! What pluck! What *élan vitale*! He empties his pistol at the panicked and cowardly villain! Hooray! He's saved the day!"

I noticed that my sister, Sue, was staring at me with a puzzled expression on her face.

"Justice prevails!" I said. "Right triumphs and evil flees ignominiously into the trackless jungle!"

Sue kept looking at me. "I think it was really brave," she said. "I don't see why you're giving Gunnar so much shit."

I took a sip of my beer. "I've got my reasons."

"Just because he fired you."

On the TV over the bar, a vapidly pretty blonde with a microphone had started yammering about something. I couldn't make out what she was saying.

"Gunnar didn't *fire* me," I said, my voice sounding a little testier than I meant it to. "I quit."

"Okay, so you quit. And for the last two months you've been doing nothing but going out drinking and line dancing at all these redneck bars. I mean you haven't even *looked* for a job."

"Whatever." I don't know why I was being this way to her. Sue is a really cool person and there was no call for me to be such a surly jerk around her.

"Hey," Sue said. "Look, it's that guy."

"What guy?"

"The one they showed on TV a minute ago. The FBI

dude." Sue pointed across the room. A man was crossing purposefully toward us, a thin black man wearing jeans, cowboy boots, a black leather jacket. He stopped right in front of me and said, "How about that for a coincidence? Sunny Childs."

"Deputy Special Agent-In-Charge Cherry," I said. I reached out and poked his black motorcycle jacket with my index finger. "I see you don't go in for that buttoned-down G-man look when you're off duty."

"Call me Barrington." He smiled warmly. "Anyway, who says I'm off duty?"

"Barrington? That's your first name?"

Agent Cherry nodded.

"So, what, you staking out the yuppies here, seeing if anybody'll confess to jaywalking on federal property?"

Barrington Cherry looked at my sister. "She in some kind of a mood or what?"

Sue shrugged. "I don't know. Seems like she's been like this ever since this thing with Georgia Burnett."

Cherry raised his chin a little, studied my face. "Funny, I thought it came out fairly well, all things considered."

I snorted.

"What?" he said. "You didn't like the outcome?"

"Look, I told you two months ago, Deputy Special Agent-in-Charge Cherry, that I'm not talking to you about Georgia Burnett."

He smiled genially. "You know and I know that whole thing was a fraud, Sunny."

"Y'all making a case?" I replied. "Fine. Send me a subpoena. Otherwise, screw you." I turned back to the bar and drained the rest of my beer.

I heard him sigh. He sat down on the stool next to me. When the bartender came over, he said, "Give me what she's having."

The bartender gave him a Sam Adams, took his credit card to start running a tab.

"I just took early retirement, Sunny," Barrington

Cherry said. "I'm not with the bureau anymore."

I turned to look at him, eyebrows raised slightly. "Why'd you do that?"

"You want to know the truth? I loved being a cop. But I was never that wild about the bureau itself. The politics, the territorial fights, all those square-jawed Mormons, all those goddamn blue suits? Shucks, I don't know. . . ." He had a mildly ironic way of saying the word shucks that I found kind of amusing. Despite my recent determination to be cynical and negative about everything, I had to smile a little. "I turned forty last month, and I just said, 'Hey, is this it? Is this all there is to life?' If I work really hard, you know, maybe I'll get promoted one more time, make Special Agent-in-Charge and then spend the rest of my life shoveling paper. No thanks."

"Shucks," I said.

"You making fun of me?"

"Why would I do a thing like that?"

Cherry shrugged. "So," he said, "I guess you heard?"

"Heard what?"

"Georgia. She's dead. Beaten to death in her own home two days ago, real ugly scene."

That must have been why they were playing the old video on the TV. I set down my beer, turned to look at him.

"I haven't been watching the news much lately," I said.

Cherry looked back intently at me. "Yeah, apparently the GBI brought Ratkin in for questioning this morning. I heard from an old friend at the bureau that they anticipate making some kind of a conspiracy-to-commit case against him." He paused, gave me a significant look. "One suspects some coconspirators will go down with him."

"What the hell's that supposed to mean?" I said.

Barrington Cherry's eyes narrowed. "Hey, forget it," he said in an injured tone of voice. "I just saw you over here, thought I'd make some conversation."

My sister watched him as he stood up and stalked out of the bar. "Why'd you have to be so antagonistic? He seemed like a nice guy," she said.

"I'm not so sure," I said. "I'm not so sure at all."

CHAPTER 14

THE INDICTMENTS ALL came at once. Jeremy Ratkin was indicted for conspiracy to commit murder; Marla Jeter was indicted for obstruction of justice and conspiracy to commit murder. But the man in the hot seat, the one they fingered for the murder itself, was Gunnar Brushwood.

Due process means different things in different places. In Floyd County it means you show up in court, stand up, sit down, go to jail. Motion for bail, denied.

And that's how Gunnar Brushwood ended up sitting in jail at the Floyd County Farm, on his way toward becoming the goat in this month's trial of the century.

Gunnar's lawyer called me in for a meeting at his large office down on Peachtree the day after the preliminary hearing. The office was filled with figurines and pictures of bulldogs wearing spiked collars and old-fashioned red rat caps emblazoned with the letter *G*. University of Georgia memorabilia.

"I think it's a bad idea, Sunny," Gunnar's lawyer said, "given your peculiar proximity to the case. But Gunnar has insisted."

"Insisted on what?"

"He wants me to hire you to find out who the hell killed Georgia Burnett."

Gunnar's lawyer was a big fellow cut from the same cloth as Gunnar. Brash, bluff, physical, large. His faintly ridiculous name was Quentin Senior, Jr., if you can feature that. He had played ball for the University of Georgia Bulldogs back in the late '5Os, an All-American or something, and was much beloved by the many football maniacs of this state. I doubt that Quentin Senior, Jr. had put on a pound since he'd wrenched his knee during his first season with the Packers—or whoever it had been—and he looked tough as old shoe leather.

He's one of those old-school Southern men who smile a lot, who quote Shakespeare at great length, who are terribly gallant in that Sir-Walter-Raleigh-throwing-his-cape-in-the-mud-so-the-queen-won't-get-her-shoes-dirty sort of way, and who, if you cross them, will track you to the ends of the earth just for the pleasure of crushing your heart in their fists. I liked him a lot.

"You have to understand," I said. "Gunnar and I had a little falling out. I haven't talked to him since the day after the hostage thing."

"I realize that. He wants you because you're the best."

I sat for a while and chewed on the thing. I was still so mad at Gunnar that I could hardly stand thinking about him. But I didn't really want to see him get put in the electric chair for something that I was dead certain he didn't do. "So what's the substance of the case against him?" I said.

Quentin Senior, Jr. rocked back in his leather chair, put his hands behind his head. "Out in Floyd County they play their evidence close to the vest. But this much I *do* know. Georgia Burnett was beaten to death with a blunt instrument. And when the GBI executed a search warrant on Gunnar's home and property, they found a baseball bat covered with a substance strongly resembling blood locked in the trunk of Gunnar's Lincoln.

They haven't disclosed the fact, but it's obvious they came up with a blood match."

I was shocked. I had assumed that whatever they had on Gunnar was a lot more circumstantial than that.

"Jesus H. Christ," I said. "Somebody must have planted it."

Quentin Senior, Jr. studied my face for a moment, then smiled genially. "Right now, that's the only theory available to the defense."

"A theory that nobody in the world will believe."

"I've sold less plausible stories than that to various juries in my day." His smile faded. "But not often. And not on a case like this."

"What a nightmare!" I still couldn't believe it. There had to be something major that we didn't know, something that would explain how a murder weapon had ended up in Gunnar's car.

"So, Sunny. You gonna come on board with us?"

I really didn't have to think about it. Gunnar and I had our problems. But at a time like this, I had to help him. I owed him too much not to.

"Yes."

"A couple of ground rules then," Quentin said. "First, you have to run this as an independent operation. You can't draw on the resources of Peachtree Investigations. If you do, they'll put you in bed with Gunnar, and you're liable to get indicted for obstruction of justice or something. It opens some potential evidentiary problems, too. So if you need to hire anybody, you'll have to do it from outside Gunnar's firm."

"That's not a problem."

"Good. Now, here's the first issue I need to knock around with you. The Floyd County law enforcement world is basically run by one man—Judge Roynell Deaks. In most jurisdictions around here, the DA releases all their evidence in the case to the defense as a matter of routine. Police investigation files, witness statements, all that stuff. But not in Floyd County. Judge

Deaks thinks that's too soft on the criminal element.

"As I'm sure you know, Sunny, last year the legislature passed a law saying that prior to trial the defense can elect to *force* the DA to turn over every scrap of evidence they have. Problem is, if the defense does make that election, however, they have to reciprocate. If we see their evidence, they see ours. If they don't reveal their evidence until trial, neither do we.

"What that means is this. If we can't find enough evidence to prove Gunnar didn't do this terrible thing, then I need to elect to force production of their evidence ASAP so I can start doing my Philadelphia lawyer act, picking it all apart, throwing up smoke screens, so on, so forth. See what I'm getting at? If, on the other hand, we *can* find evidence to prove he didn't do it, we don't care what they've got. We'll bomb them to death at the trial. So we have to make a decision."

"By when?"

"Judge Deaks has given us till tomorrow."

"Tomorrow!"

"Hate to do this to you, but if you're gonna come on board, I need to know. Can you turn up the evidence that's gonna prove Gunnar innocent?"

I thought for a minute. "First off, there's no way he did it. Not Gunnar. That's a deadlock certainty."

"I'm glad you got the same faith I do. But that's not what I'm asking."

"So if he didn't do it, as a simple matter of logic, the evidence to prove his innocence must exist."

Quentin Senior, Jr. looked at me with his cool gray eyes and said, "Darling, what I'm asking is, can you *find* that evidence?"

"I think so."

The big lawyer's cool eyes didn't waver.

"What?" I said finally.

"You *think* so? Darling, no offense, but I don't give a damn what you *think*. I need to *know*."

I tapped my fingernails on the desk and didn't answer.

"Bottom line, Sunny, I might win this case with a bunch of bullshit Philadelphia lawyering." Quentin's tone had gotten gentler. "But the only reliable way of winning a murder trial—*and* restoring a man's reputation—is with hard facts."

"I don't even know what I'm up against! You're asking me to assume the entire burden of this case on nothing but faith."

"Yes, ma'am, I am."

"That's not fair!"

"Is it fair that your friend is sitting around in the county farm for something that you know with all your heart he didn't do?"

"No." I felt peevish, like a schoolgirl getting scolded by a favorite teacher.

"Then I got to know. I got to know if you have the will to prove him innocent. I got to know if you really give a shit about your friend or not."

Being manipulated, even by people I like, irks me to no end. I tried to keep my voice calm and level. "What kind of schedule are we looking at?"

"If this were a metro Atlanta jurisdiction, we'd probably have a year." Quentin Senior, Jr. smiled thinly. "Judge Deaks, however, is a big Article VI man. 'The accused shall enjoy the right to a speedy and public trial.' He has therefore instructed us to be ready for trial at 8:30 A.M. on January 1."

My eyes widened. "That's three weeks from now!"

Quentin Senior, Jr. continued to smile without humor. "Yep. Three weeks. You up to this or not, Sunny?"

Finally I felt a surge of the emotion he'd been angling to provoke out of me the whole time: I got mad.

"Hell yes!" I said. "Tell that redneck DA out there in Floyd County to go stick it. Tell them we got our own evidence."

"That a girl!"

"I'll get on it right now." I stood up and headed for the door.

As I put my hand on the knob, Gunnar's lawyer called to me. "Merry Christmas, Sunny."

"Thanks—but in case you weren't aware, Christmas is still fifteen days away."

Quentin looked up from his desk. "Yeah, but with what you got in front of you, Sunny, that's about all the Christmas cheer you're gonna get this year."

CHAPTER 15

I HE FIRST THING I needed to do was get some help. I called Rhenda Porcher, a freelance investigator I use occasionally—but she was in the middle of a big insurance fraud investigation. Then I tried Chris Peterson, but he was about to go on some European dream vacation that he and his wife had been planning for eight million years. After that, I called a bunch of other freelance investigators and struck out on every one of them.

That left me with the unwelcome alternative of hiring somebody from Kroll or Pinkerton or Wackenhut or one of the other big agencies. I don't generally like working with those kinds of firms. Nothing wrong with them, but they tend to be a little buttoned-up, a little corporate, a little inflexible. I had a hunch this investigation would require some fancy dodging and weaving before it was over.

I was thumbing desperately through my Rolodex when I stumbled across a name: Deputy Special-Agent-in-Charge Barrington Cherry, FBI. It occurred to me that since he had just left the FBI, maybe he was looking for work. I sat there tapping the card for a while, thinking, then finally called him up. He agreed to meet for dinner that evening.

• • •

"It was that obvious?" Barrington Cherry said.

"Huh?"

"The other night? That I was angling for a date?"

We were sitting in a Jamaican restaurant down on Peachtree. I rarely wear dresses, but on a whim I'd worn one on this particular night. Black, short, simple. I was trying to impress him with my professionalism and sophistication or some damn thing, but I guess you could easily have mistaken it for a date frock.

I looked at the former FBI man. "Date?" I said. "You came in that bar the other night and scared the living shit out of me in hopes of getting a *date*?"

In the parlance of our race-crazy society, Barrington Cherry is black—but as a point of physical fact, he's a freckled guy with skin just a shade or two darker than mine would be if I spent three weeks at Cancun. He's light enough, in other words, that I could see him blushing like mad.

"So. . . ." he said. "My keenly honed social radar is picking up on the idea that this isn't a date."

I laughed nervously. "Well, actually I was going to ask if you wanted some work. I need an investigator."

"Waiter?" Barrington waved his hand in the air. "I'd like a triple shot of rye." We both laughed. "Shucks! Now I surely do feel like an idiot."

Barrington was wearing more or less the same outfit as he'd worn in the bar the other night: cowboy boots, jeans, motorcycle jacket, a shirt of pale bronze silk buttoned up to the neck. He had shaved his head since the night before, though, getting rid of his neat FBI haircut. I sensed he was in this try-out-a-new-image stage that a lot of middle-aged men go through. Quitting his job, messing around, seeing which way the wind blew—it was all part of the usual pattern.

I hadn't really been thinking of him as date material. For starters, he wore a wedding band. What was up with *that*? But now that the date notion had crossed my mind. . . . He was a very attractive guy: slim, athletic, chiseled features. He reminded me a little of a favorite painting of mine, a Velasquez portrait of a man named Juan de Pareja. The same pretty lips, the same sad eyes.

"This is a fairly short-term assignment," I said. "If you're interested." I couldn't help adding. "And then, you know, if we can still tolerate each other after working in close proximity for a month or two . . ."

Barrington smiled. "Don't tell me."

I nodded. "The Georgia Burnett case."

The ex-agent's hazel eyes grew opaque, and his smile went away. "It's not that I'm not looking for work," he said. "But don't you think we're both a little close to this?"

I shrugged. "Hey, it'll save us both some time getting you up to speed."

The waiter arrived in a cloud of dreadlocks and woody-smelling cologne, and we both ordered jerk goat with rice and plantains. After the waiter left, Cherry said, "So they found the murder weapon in Mr. Brushwood's car?"

"I can't discuss the details of this thing until you've said yea or nay to working for me." I watched Cherry sipping meditatively at his wine. I sensed some kind of mental hesitation, a snag in his mind.

"I don't know, Sunny."

Suddenly I realized what it was. "You've always been on the white horse, haven't you?" I said. "Always worn the white hat?"

He raised his eyebrows slightly in acknowledgment.

"Well, let me tell you something," I said. "If you're giving any thought to being a private investigator, there's precious little opportunity to wear the white hat. You're mostly going to spend your time working for insurance companies. Or pointing four hundred millimeter lenses at sad little people who are cheating on their spouses. Frankly, the opportunity to work for an innocent man, wrongly accused—that comes along practically never."

"That's what this is?" Barrington Cherry had just a shade of challenge in his voice. "I heard they found the murder weapon in the trunk of his car."

"I've known Gunnar Brushwood for a long, long time. He's a lot of things, but he's no hired killer. This is a frame-up, sure as I'm sitting here."

Barrington Cherry gave me that slightly amused, slightly indulgent look that men give to women right before they make some asshole remark like, *Babe, you're awful sexy when you get angry.*

Only Barrington Cherry said, "Hmmmmm."

"This is a good man."

Still with the indulgent look, eyebrows raised a fraction of an inch. "*Frame*-up."

"This is a good man who's getting raped, Barrington, because he was a little stupid and a little vain and a little gullible. Maybe even a little starstruck."

Barrington Cherry's face composed itself, and he sipped some more wine. Finally he said, "Is that the party line? I mean, do I have to buy into that in order to work for you?"

"No," I said. "What you have to be is willing to do what it takes." My tone may have been a little sharper than I'd intended. And as I said it I guess I realized that I *did* want him to believe in what he was doing.

Cherry stroked the side of his face. "I'll be honest. It feels funny."

"How you feel about Gunnar, I don't give a damn. But if you're not prepared to work for him *as though he were innocent*—then I don't need you."

Cherry nodded, smiled slightly. "I guess I could, what, suspend my disbelief?"

"I'm serious, Barrington. You can't come into this like, hey, let me dip my toe in the water and see if it feels all warm and comfortable. This is not a hot tub. A good man's life is at stake."

"World Series, bottom of the ninth, down by three runs." His voice had just the barest shade of irony.

"Forget it," I said. "I don't know why I thought underwriting some dilettante FBI agent's midlife crisis was a good idea in the first place." I threw a few bills on the table, stood up, and walked out of the restaurant.

It wasn't until that moment that I felt the cold, dead weight of this thing pressing down on me, the sense that my old friend's life was in my hands. I had talked about feeling that weight when I was in Quentin Senior's office earlier that day—but at the time it had just been a phrase. Now it was real. I felt regret then, and shame, and anger, wishing things hadn't gotten so awkward and ugly between me and Gunnar, wishing he wasn't such a damn fool, wishing I had someone to help me and hold me up as I took on this burden.

I felt plain awful, felt a darkness coming down.

I was in my car, bawling like a little kid, when I heard someone rapping on the window with their ring. I looked up and there was Barrington Cherry. I looked away so he wouldn't see the tears on my face, the goddamn eyeliner running down the side of my nose. He kept rapping and rapping his wedding ring on the window until finally I rolled it down.

"What?" I demanded.

"You really believe," he said, his voice full of wonderment.

"Believe? That's not the right word. I *know*," I said, wiping my eyes. "Gunner was framed. I know this in my bones."

Barrington Cherry kept looking at me with this funny expression on his face until finally he said, "Why don't you come back inside, let's talk a little more. You caught me by surprise. Maybe hurt my pride a little when I found out you weren't . . . you know . . . looking for a date or whatever. I shouldn't have been so flip with you."

"I wasn't crying," I said. "I was just feeling funny."

"Sure," Barrington Cherry said. "I feel funny like that sometimes, too." He handed me a little packet of Kleenex, then turned away discreetly while I wiped my eyes.

I wasn't crying.

Two hours later Barrington Cherry and I were finishing our third cups of coffee, trying to get a handle on what we could do to make this case fly.

CHAPTER 16

"**D**ON'T GET MAD, okay?" Quentin Senior, Jr. said. "But I've got to ask."

"Ask what?" Gunnar said sourly.

First thing the next morning. Gunnar's lawyer and I were visiting Gunnar at the Floyd County Jail—the county farm as it was still sometimes called. Floyd County had joined the great American jail-building binge of the '90s, so the jail was less dispiriting than some. The chairs were clean, the stainless steel table looked like something out of a fancy restaurant kitchen, and the cinder block walls were freshly painted in a warm peach color. But it was still a jail, complete with the echoing corridors and the doors banging shut with an ugly finality that's like nothing you will ever hear in a civilian building.

"The district attorney has authorized me to convey a plea bargain offer to you, Gunnar," Quentin said. "If you plea to malice murder and conspiracy and testify against Jeremy Ratkin, they'll drop the assault with a deadly weapon and recommend life rather than going for the chair."

Gunnar stared angrily at his lawyer, then at me. He was wearing white convict pants and shirt, both with black stripes down the seams, orange plastic sandals, white socks, and leg irons. His arms were manacled to a wide leather belt encircling his waist.

Quentin fiddled with one of the links on Gunnar's shackles. "I want you to think about it."

Gunnar's eyes narrowed. When he spoke, his voice was rich with outrage. "Do you think I did this thing?"

Quentin took a sip of coffee out of a cup that read FLOYD COUNTY SHERIFF on the side, but he said nothing.

Gunnar glared at his lawyer. "I'm asking you a by-God question."

Quentin Senior, Jr. frowned. "I make a point not to make judgments like that. Not with friends. Not even with my own brother. Right now we don't know what they have. We know they have a baseball bat with something that looks like blood on it, and we know they took it out of your car. We believe the blood on the bat was Georgia Burnett's, but we don't know that for a fact. We know Georgia Burnett was beaten to death. This judge, Deaks, he may be a shitheel, but he ain't a *dumb* shitheel. That bat is a hell of a piece of evidence. Whatever's in your heart, be it guilt or innocence, it won't win this case. So you need to consider their offer."

"I did not do it." Gunnar's body strained against his manacles. "And if you ever suggest, even implicitly, that I did, I will fire your sorry ass on the spot."

A vein popped up in the middle of Quentin's forehead, and his voice got louder. "Yeah, well, whatever. But it's my obligation, my *ethical* obligation—"

"Spare me your goddamn ethics, okay?" Gunnar was still red in the face.

"Guys, guys!" I said, "let's go easy here. This is not helping."

"Sorry, Quent. I'm just tired as hell." Gunnar suddenly seemed to deflate, to take up less space in the room. I noticed there were big bags under his eyes, and all the wrinkles in his face seemed deeper than ever. "I can't sleep in this damn place."

Quentin took a deep breath. "Okay, here's where we're at. We need to come up with a plausible theory that somebody else did this—a theory that also explains why and how that bat got in your car. You and Ratkin are going to be tried jointly. That makes it hard for us to try putting everything on him. If he looks bad in the trial, the jury is liable to tar you with the same brush. So as a matter of trial strategy, he's out. You got any thoughts, Gunnar, who might have done the murder?"

Gunnar shook his head.

"What about that wacko?" I said. "The Telescope Guy that was camped out behind Georgia's place?"

"The Creepy Guy!" Gunnar said. "Brilliant! I didn't even think about him."

"That's assuming that he was an *actual* wacko and that he wasn't part of Ratkin's whole ransom setup."

Quentin looked puzzled.

I explained to the lawyer who Creepy Guy was.

"Okay . . ." he said. "But you said something that puzzled me. You said he might have been part of Ratkin's *setup*. What did you mean by that?"

I looked questioningly at Gunnar. "You didn't tell him?"

Gunnar looked embarrassed as he briefly met my eyes, then looked away. "We, ah, haven't had a chance to talk details yet."

My eyes must have widened a little. "You did *tell* him, Gunnar?"

"Something you need to know, Quent," Gunnar said quickly, "is that there's a little, ah, wrinkle involved in the kidnapping case we worked back in October."

"Wrinkle?" Quentin said, sounding suddenly edgy.

"The, ah . . ." Gunnar shifted around uneasily in his manacles. "I was first hired, retained, to help out when Georgia came up missing back in October. . . ."

Quentin looked at him questioningly. "And. . . ."

I cut in. "The whole kidnapping was staged. It was a publicity stunt to promote her latest album."

Quentin Senior, Jr. threw his pen up in the air. "Oh, for cripe's *sake*!"

"You got to understand," Gunnar said. "We weren't in on it. We were hired to do the job, help investigate, then assist with the ransom. By the time we got to the end of it, though, it was obvious the whole thing was bogus. That's why Sunny quit."

Quentin groaned softly.

"So this creep," I said, "he might have been part of the whole scam."

The lawyer frowned. "Well, I guess you better try to find Creepy Guy, Sunny. But if he *was* part of this stunt, he can't do anything but hurt us."

"So, any other candidates for the murder?" I said.

"Ratkin's the key. They must have good reason for thinking he hired somebody to kill Georgia. What we need is to find another plausible hired gun. So, Sunny, you're going to have to go through everything—Ratkin's finances, his phone records, dig up every scrap on him you can. We'll try to get his cooperation. But if he really did hire somebody to do this, the likelihood of him helping us is zero."

"I'll get on it immediately," I said.

"Good," the lawyer said. "Now, Gunnar, let's turn to the day of the murder. What exactly happened on that day?"

"Well, I got a message that morning at the office saying that Georgia wanted to see me at the house in Floyd County at 11:30 that morning. My secretary, Keisha, took the message before I got to the office."

"So you didn't actually talk to Georgia yourself?" I said.

He shook his head. "Nah. In fact, I asked Keisha about it, she said the person who called had identified herself as Georgia Burnett's secretary. So nobody in the office actually talked to Georgia."

"Okay, go on."

"Anyway, I drove up there and talked to Marla Jeter

over the intercom at the front gate. She buzzed me in."

"It was definitely Marla you talked to?"

"Yep. Anyway, the gate opens, I drive up to the house, knock on the door, nobody answers. I try the handle just for grins, and the door opens. I poke my head inside, *Hello hello anybody home* that type of thing. No answer."

"How far did you poke your head in?" I said.

Gunnar looked a little uncomfortable. "Oh, I might have . . ." he trailed off. "Aw, hell. . . . Yeah, okay, I walked into the living room. The kitchen, too, I think."

"Touch anything?" Quentin said. "Leave any fingerprints?"

Gunnar spread his hands as far as the manacles would let him. "Probably."

"Great," Quentin said sarcastically. "But you didn't see anything. No dead country singers, nothing like that?"

"Hell no!"

"You didn't walk upstairs, wander into the bedroom?"

"Of course not."

"Then what?"

"I walked behind the house, down to the stables to see if she was down there. She wasn't, so I went back to the car. I was a little peeved by then, so I just hopped in and drove off."

Quentin tapped his pen on the stainless steel table, then looked at me. "Alright. We've got the autopsy report and the initial police report. So we know Georgia Burnett was discovered around 2:00 or 2:30 by Marla Jeter in the bedroom of the house, beaten to death. What's that tell you, Sunny?"

"You tell me."

"Marla Jeter was offered immunity. That means she was going to be charged with something. That means she has knowledge of *something*. Probably something that incriminates both Ratkin *and* Gunnar. Bottom line, she *is* their case. We got to know what she's gonna testify about, Sunny."

"How do we do that?"

Quentin smiled coolly. "That's your job to figure out."

"I'll try," I said. "But you know they're going to tell her not to say a word."

"If we're gonna have a prayer of making this case work, Sunny, we have to destroy this woman."

"I said I'll *try*."

"Sunny?" Quentin looked at me sternly. "Trying ain't good enough."

"I can't get blood from a stone!" I said.

Quentin kept staring at me, his gray eyes skeptical. "You're already too close to this case. The only reason—the *only* reason you're here—is that Gunnar told me you're the best. Is he right about you?"

I didn't say anything.

"*Are* you the best, Sunny?"

"I'm good," I said quietly.

"I thought we already had this conversation." The lawyer smiled humorlessly at me. "See, honey, your friend's life is at stake here. Halfway sorta kinda relatively more or less pretty good—that ain't hacking it. I'm asking if you're the best."

I looked at him defiantly. "I don't trust people that make claims like that. But I'll tell you this right now. I'll figure something out."

"What's that mean, Sunny?"

My face felt hard as the bottom of a shoe. "It means I'll break that big skinny no-ass cowgirl like a nut."

Quentin Senior, Jr. smiled a fierce, dangerous smile. "That's more like it."

"See?" Gunnar said to him with the tone of a proud father. "Didn't I tell you, hoss?"

CHAPTER 17

GUNNAR'S LAWYER LEFT the jail for an appointment, but I hung around a few minutes extra to get Gunnar's thoughts on the case. We sat in the interview room silently for a few minutes.

"Well?" I said. "Got a theory on this thing?"

"Plain as day," Gunnar said. "Ratkin did it. He meant to frame me. That's why he put the baseball bat in my trunk."

"Yeah, but my understanding is that he was in Nashville when the murder happened."

"So he says." Gunnar cracked his knuckles, shrugged. "Anyway, maybe he paid one of the security guards to do it. Hell, maybe what's-her-name did it. Marla Jeter. Maybe that's why she's turning state's evidence."

"Yeah, but if she did it, then her testimony would tend to *exonerate* you, not incriminate you."

"Damn it. Seems like we're in a logical box here, Sunny. If Ratkin framed me, then why would Marla be testifying against me?"

"What if Marla framed you *and* Ratkin?"

"Why would she do that?"

I shrugged. "Maybe *she* did it. Maybe there's some evidence that incriminates her. Her fingerprint on the bat or something. And so she made up this conspiracy thing to cover her ass."

"Hmm."

"I still like Ratkin," Gunnar said. "That boy's a damn snake."

"What's his motive? I mean, assuming his alibi holds up, then he couldn't have done it himself. Which pretty much rules out crime of passion stuff."

"Money."

"The guy had enough cash in his own bank account to send a million eight to this bogus kidnapper."

Gunnar raised his eyebrows. "Did he?"

"I talked to the banker."

"How do you know the banker wasn't some out-of-work actor, Sunny? We don't know what was real and what wasn't."

I shook my head disconsolately. "This thing's a hall of mirrors isn't it?"

"Then we got this fellow, Creepy Guy. . . ."

"Who was probably a Ratkin fabrication. Hell, he could have been setting this thing up for months so that he'd be the prime suspect in the kidnapping. Remember the car that the kidnapper ditched at the Chamblee MARTA station? A Toyota Land Cruiser. Same vehicle as the one that Creepy Guy jumped into when he was hiding out behind the house. The kidnapper and Creepy Guy—they had to be the same person."

Gunnar leaned across the table. "Start digging," he said. "We don't even know what we don't know. You'll find something."

I laced my fingers through my hair, let the breath drain out of my body. "Gunnar, I don't even know where to start."

Gunnar lifted one hand as far as the manacle would let it move, started ticking things off on his fingers. "One, talk to Ratkin. Two, talk to Marla Jeter. Three, start digging into Ratkin's life. Maybe he had a girl-friend on the side. Or a boyfriend. Maybe his financial situation was worse than it looked, and he wanted to get his hands on her dough."

"And Creepy Guy?"

"Long shot," Gunnar said. "I don't think the guy exists."

At that point, a guard banged his nightstick on the scarred Plexiglas window set in the middle of the door. The key clunked in the lock and the door swung open. "Stand up, prisoner," he said genially. "Let's git to gitting."

Gunnar stood uncertainly, grunting slightly as he rose. For a moment he looked like a beaten man, but then he squared his shoulders and smiled broadly. "The baseball bat," he said. "Find out who planted it in my car, we got this thing licked."

CHAPTER 18

THAT AFTERNOON I went back to my loft and put a want ad in the employment section of the *Atlanta Journal* for a personal security coordinator. I had to pay some extra money, but they promised the ad would start running in the paper the following day.

After I'd gotten off the phone, I crawled under my desk, unhooked the wire from my fax, and plugged in an answering machine I'd just bought down at K-Mart. Barrington Cherry was sitting in a folding chair on the other side of my cavernous room watching me with a curious look on his face.

I stood up, brushed a nice menagerie of dust bunnies off my black turtleneck, then scribbled a few lines on a legal pad.

"Here," I said. "Read this into the machine."

Barrington came over and looked at the piece of paper. I pressed the Record button on the answering machine and Barrington read my message. "Thank you for calling the international recruitment office. Please leave a brief message at the tone."

I let go of the button and the machine beeped.

"Now what?" Barrington said.

"We wait."

• • •

Next, I called Ratkin's lawyer, a guy name Mike Friend, and told him I wanted to talk to his client to get a little background on the case. Friend was one of those guys with a particularly irritating nasal voice, the vocal equivalent of a permanent sneer. He laughed loudly and patronizingly when I made the request.

"Is there a problem?" I said.

"You think I'm crazy? I'll let my client talk to you about the time hell freezes over."

"Excuse me?" I said.

"You think your client's interests are even vaguely similar to mine?"

"That's your call, not mine," I said. "I'm just looking for any information that we can use to discredit the prosecutor's case. I think you'd agree that's in both our interests."

"Forget it!"

"Look," I said. "I'm not Quentin, but it seems to me there are two ways you guys can play this. You and Quentin can spend the whole trial throwing bombs at each other—in which case the jury most likely says, 'Hey, pox on both houses, let's fry both these jerks.' Or you can work together and try to beat the state's entire case on its merits. In which case, everybody walks."

Friend just laughed again.

I called Quentin immediately and told him what had happened. Gunnar's lawyer sounded a little miffed. "First off, Sunny, I don't want you calling Friend. That's my job."

"Sorry," I said. "I didn't think."

"Second off, if that little pile of dog doo thinks he can get Ratkin off by pissing on my client, he's got another think coming. Give me a few minutes, I expect you'll be hearing from me again."

When the phone rang ten minutes later, it wasn't Quentin but Mike Friend. "Had a little skull session with

Quentin," he said brightly. I could tell he was trying to put a good face on it, but I suspect Quentin probably chewed him a new one. "Based on sharing some thoughts on our trial strategies, I decided it wouldn't hurt for you and Mr. Ratkin to speak."

"Good," I said. "Can we do it tomorrow?"

"Got a conflict. Can you do it Thursday?"

"How's eleven o'clock?"

After I got off the phone, I turned to Barrington Cherry, who was watching me from a chair on the other side of my loft. "Okay," I said. "We've got until eleven o'clock the day after tomorrow to find out everything there is to know about Jeremy Ratkin. Thoughts?"

"I could probably finagle an NCIC search out of some old friends at a certain federal agency, do some of the routine background stuff. If you've got the software, I can run a credit bureau, Dun & Bradstreet, all that sort of thing."

"Good," I said. "Let's get started."

While Barrington worked my computer, I got on the phone.

The first person I called was Georgia's agent, a guy named Linc Breedlove who worked out of Nashville. It took some doing, but I finally reached him in his car on his cell phone. When I identified myself, he said, "How'd you get this number?"

I lied and told him that Jeremy Ratkin had asked me to call.

"So?" he said. He didn't sound happy.

I decided to switch course. "Uh, actually I don't work for Mr. Ratkin. I work for Gunnar Brushwood, the guy who's been charged with killing Georgia."

"Then go fuck yourself, darling," Linc Breedlove said.

The line went dead. "Well, aren't *we* pleasant?" I muttered.

I hit redial.

"He didn't do it," I said before Breedlove had a

chance to say anything. "The whole thing was a setup."

Linc Breedlove laughed. "Yeah? Who's behind it? Aliens? The CIA? The guys who killed Kennedy?"

"I don't have time to fucking argue with you," I said. In this business, you have to take somebody's measure and play them the way they'd play you. I could tell Linc Breedlove liked hardball. So hardball it was. "I've got twenty-one days to prove an innocent man is getting shafted. So give me some quick answers, and I'm done."

The line went dead.

"Asshole," I said. Barrington looked up at me from the computer. I smiled at him, then hit redial.

"Don't be a dick," I said when Linc Breedlove answered. "You represented Georgia. I assume you have a tiny bit of loyalty to her. Do you honestly want to see the person who *really* killed her walking away scot free?"

There was a brief pause. "Talk," he said.

"Georgia and Ratkin. Did they have problems?"

"Everybody has problems. Ask my four ex-wives."

"Was this a marriage of convenience then? She gets fame and fortune, he gets a trophy wife, that sort of thing?"

There was a brief pause. "Look, it was more complicated than that. She was no idiot; she knew what he could do for her career. But I don't think that's why she married him."

"Why did she marry him then?"

"How the hell would I know? I can't even tell you why I married my own wives. Maybe she needed a father figure."

"What about him? Did he love her?"

Breedlove seemed to be thinking. "Jeremy Ratkin was generally a demanding, contrary, finicky, chiselling, slippery piece of shit. But I never saw him be disrespectful to his wife. I think that says something."

"So maybe we've got a little bit of an unrequited love

thing happening? He loves her, she uses him—that kind of thing?"

I heard a squalling of tires.

"You okay?" I said.

"Just some moron pulling out in front of me," Breedlove said. He paused for a moment. "Hard to say. She wasn't one of these calculating, gold digger types. That's what always seemed strange to me. I had represented her since she first came to Nashville. Sweet kid, moderately talented, moderately good-looking. I always saw her as kind of a long shot. Then one day she calls my office, says, 'Linc? Are you sitting down?' And she tells me she's just gotten engaged to Ratkin."

"And after that her career takes off?"

"Oh my yes! After that, Ratkin gets *very* up-close-and-personal with her career. Micromanaging every detail. Her hairstyle, her producer, the pickers in her road band, the cover art on her album, you name it. And every day that meddling sumbitch is on the phone to me riding my ass about this or that, telling me how to do my goddamn job."

"I see." I decided to shift gears. "Are you aware of her having any boyfriends then? Anything that might have gotten Ratkin pissed off at her?"

"Shoot, man," Linc said. "That girl was like canned milk. No bullshit, she was the girl next door. Went to church every Sunday. I don't see her getting it on with the pool boy."

"Any motive for Ratkin to have killed her?"

"Can't think of one, nah."

"Money?"

"Hey, Ratkin's loaded. He owns a majority stake in ArchRival Records."

"They're independent then? Not owned by Sony or anything?"

"Last of the great indy labels. They have a distribution deal with BMG, the big German company. So they're really like an A and R shop."

"I don't know what that means."

"A and R stands for artists and repertory. That's the creative side of the business. Finding artists, finding songs, hiring producers, cutting records. It's the fun part of the business. The rest of it, distribution, sales, marketing—hell, it's no different from selling potato chips."

"Good company?"

"They'd be out of business if they weren't."

"Who was their big moneymaker?"

"You kidding? Georgia Burnett sold more units than anybody they've had since the '70s. Ratkin started out as a rock producer out in LA. Had a bunch of art rock bands that did well back in the '70s. I'll say this: he's smart. This is a taste business. If you can't tell what flavor the kids want, you're screwed. Ratkin was bright enough to see that his tastes had matured, that he'd lost touch with rock and roll. So he just up and moved the whole operation to Nashville back in the '80s. Caught the wave just as the country scene started taking off."

"And the company's doing okay?"

"I gather things are a little soft right now. But this is a hit business: one day it's up, the next it's down. I hear they've got some major talent in development."

I decided to shift gears. "Gut reaction. You turned on the news, Dan Rather says Georgia's been murdered. Who'd you think did it?"

"Stalker. Lunatic fan."

"And when you heard Ratkin had been arrested?"

"Honestly? Gut instinct? It didn't sound like Ratkin. He's a calculating guy. If I may be politically incorrect for a moment . . . hey, the guy's a Jew. Goddamn Jews, they get their pound of flesh, but they don't *whack* you. That's not me saying that, man, that's Shakespeare. You can look it up."

"Uh-*huh*."

"Hey, sister, you asked."

"That I did." I looked through my notes to see what else I needed. "You got any recommendations of other people to talk to? Friends? Financial advisors? Anybody that might have some insight into her relationship with Ratkin."

"Virginia Blount, you know her?"

"The singer?" I'd seen her on *Austin City Limits* a time or two. She was what they call "Alternative Country," meaning she's a wonderful singer and a fine songwriter, but she can't get airplay on country radio for love or money. These days country radio is looking for, well, people like Georgia Burnett: slick, sweet, wholesome, a little vapid.

"The singer, yeah," Linc Breedlove said. "She's a client of mine. Her and Georgia were pretty tight."

"You got her phone number?"

"She might be hard to reach. She's out of town right now. On tour."

"Still. . . ."

"I don't have my book handy, man. I'm driving." Breedlove sounded irritated. "Like I say, she's not in Nashville."

"Neither am I."

"Oh. Where you at?"

"Atlanta."

"Well, hell, why didn't you say so, man? She's doing a show down at the Variety Playhouse tonight."

"No kidding. Where is she staying?"

"Usually I book my people at the Marriott Marquis."

After I got off the phone, I tapped Barrington Cherry on the shoulder. He was busy fooling around with the computer, pecking things out at high speed despite only using two fingers.

"I'm gonna run out for a few minutes," I said.

CHAPTER 19

HALF OF PRIVATE investigating is figuring out ways of starting conversations. In a perfect world, you'd just walk up to people, tell them who you are and what you want, and then they'd be really polite and take all the time in the world to tell you everything you need to know.

Then there's real life. Here's an example of a fairly unproductive way to start a pitch: "Hi, I work for the guy who's been charged with beating your best friend to death, and I was just wondering if I could have a few moments of your time?" It had worked with Linc Breedlove . . . but, truthfully, I had to chalk that up to dumb luck.

And once you've used up your allocation of dumb luck, you're left with two alternatives: fast talking and subterfuge. I'm not much of a fast-talker and I hate lying. So it's kind of toss-up. Given the choice, though, I usually opt for the big fat lie.

The Marriott Marquis was moderately famous for a while because it was the first hotel in the world to have one of those humongous atriums with all the glass elevators and indoor trees. When I was a kid and we were really poor, my mom used to put me in my Sunday dress and take me there, and we'd pretend we were guests, riding up and down the elevators for hours. It still makes me feel good to ride those silly glass elevators.

As I knocked on the door of room 1243 at the Marriott Marquis, I slid a pair of horn-rimmed glasses up on my nose and straightened my tweed jacket. I have twenty-twenty vision, and the only time I wear tweed is when I'm shooting driven grouse in Scotland with my pals in the royal family. Which is to say, infrequently. In other words, they're props. For me, props are the key to getting into character. And getting into character is the prerequisite for selling the Big Fat Lie.

The door opened and a woman of about my age opened the door wide enough that I could see the right half of her face and body. It was Virginia Blount. She looked older and wearier than she had when I saw her on *Austin City Limits*. Her dirty blond hair was pulled back in a ponytail. She wore gray sweats and no shoes.

"Hi, Virginia!" I said enthusiastically, sticking out my hand. "Terri del Amico from *Rolling Stone* magazine! Sorry I'm late!"

Virginia Blount looked at my hand dubiously. "Late?" she said finally. She still hadn't opened the door more than about six inches.

I tapped my watch. "4:15. I know, I know, was supposed to be here at 4:00. Some kind of weather problem up in the Midwest, got every airport in America backed up by two hours."

She just looked at me.

"So where you want to do it?" I said. "In the room? Up in the bar. They've got one of those rotating restaurants, look out over the city, yadda yadda. Whatever floats your boat."

She squinched up her eyes. "I'm sorry, but I don't have the faintest idea what you're talking about." She had one of those east Tennessee hill accents that sounded sort of like she was gulping air when she talked.

I gave her a look of disbelief. "You're telling me you didn't *know*? I just talked to your guy not an hour ago. What's his name? Linc Broadloaf?"

"Breedlove."

"Yeah, yeah, that's him. He said you were on board with this." I put some outrage in my voice. "*Rolling Stone!* The big feature we're doing. Linc said 4:00, give you plenty of time before your show at the Variety. We're supposed to get an hour and a half with you." I pulled out my phone, dialed the number of my gynecologist's office. "Mr. Breedlove please," I snapped to the receptionist. "What do you mean he's not *available*? Jesus Christ, I'm calling from *Rolling Stone*! He's such a big shot these days he can't spare two minutes to talk to *Rolling Stone*?"

Virginia reached out and touched me on the arm. "Hey, hey, no sweat. We can do an interview now if you want."

I snapped the phone shut, smiled brightly. I wondered what my doctor's poor receptionist must have made of the call. "Great, great! Let's get on it, huh?"

Virginia Blount started to open the door and let me in, but then stopped. "You don't mind showing me your ID, do you?" she said. "With all the kooks around, I have to be careful."

I felt a sudden tickle of fear. Now I was screwed.

"Hey, I'm just a freelancer," I said. "What do you think they do, give us a *Rolling Stone* ID bracelet or something?"

She studied my face. "What did you say your name was again?"

"Terri del Amico. I did the cover piece about Smashing Pumpkins last year. Maybe you saw it?"

A trick I use to get through things like this is that I visualize myself as another person, complete with accent, mannerisms, and so on. It seems to help me fool people. In this case, I was visualizing myself as a slightly angrier version of Terri Gross, the host of that public radio show *Fresh Air*.

Somehow I blustered my way past the ID issue and the next thing I knew I was a journalist. Fortunately I'm a country music nut and something of a fan of Virginia's, so I didn't come off like a total idiot. Once I got into my Terri Gross mindset, it wasn't especially hard. "Now I understand your father sang in a gospel quartet back in the '60s. . . ."—that sort of thing. I asked her this and that about her records, her new producer, biah blah blah. It wasn't very hard.

Finally I said, "I understand you were very close to Georgia Burnett. . . ."

Virginia's face suddenly hardened. "Is *that* what this is about?"

"Excuse me?" I said innocently.

"My next album doesn't come out for six months. Why would you guys be talking to me if not for a story about Georgia?"

Good question. I smiled broadly. "Ah. Yes. Well. It's a simple thing actually." So simple I had no idea what it was. I kept smiling until I thought of something. "Lead times," I said triumphantly.

"What's that mean?"

"We got a lot of lead time built into production of the magazine. Most of our articles are written at least six months in advance. Sometimes more."

"Oh."

"Look," I said. "If you're not comfortable talking about Georgia. . . ."

Virginia didn't say anything. She was wiping her hands on her sweat pants. "We were close, yeah," she said finally.

"You knew each other back before she hit it big, right?"

Virginia nodded. "Yeah. We were roommates for a couple years. It was always a kind of big sister/little sister thing."

"You being the big sister, I assume?"

She looked up at me curiously. "Why'd you say that? Whenever I tell people that, most people assume it was the other way around, her being the famous one and everything."

"I knew her in third grade," I said. "Unless she'd changed an awful lot, she wasn't all that much of a take-charge person."

Virginia nodded.

"If I'd had to guess who in our class was going to make it big," I said, "she wouldn't exactly have been at the top of the list."

Virginia smiled a little. "Off the record? If it hadn't been for Jeremy Ratkin, I doubt she would have."

"You don't think she had the talent?" I said.

"One thing I've learned," Virginia Blount said sourly, "is that this business ain't about talent. Nah, she had *enough* talent. What she didn't have was the drive. Or the savvy. Or the ambition."

"Tell me about her and Jeremy," I said. "Everybody's a little curious about that."

Virginia sat up straight suddenly. "Nope. Nope, I'm not talking about her. It's not right."

"Hey, I understand." I reached forward and turned off the tape recorder. I decided a new tack was needed. "Hell, I've probably got enough here anyway."

The new approach I had decided on was the old Good Listener strategy. Lots of times people will start blabbing about things that have been bugging them simply because another person is willing to listen to them sympathetically and nonjudgmentally.

Virginia stood up and looked at me expectantly, like she was ready for me to leave.

I didn't stand up, though. I just shook my head morosely. "God it's so sad though, isn't it?"

Virginia frowned, looked down at me. I put my head in my hands, fastened my eyes on the floor. It was silent in the room for a long, long time. A bead of sweat underneath my blouse had begun running slowly down the back of my arm by the time Virginia Blount finally broke the silence.

"It was my fault," she said finally.

I pricked up my ears at that, you better believe. "Oh?"

The chair across from me let out a groan as Virginia Blount sat back down across from me.

"It was my fault. I introduced them. My first few albums were on ArchRival. They never sold as big as Jeremy hoped, so after number three he dropped me like a rock. He was always pushing me toward doing pop schlock, and that just wasn't me." She paused. "Anyway, I was still with ArchRival at the time. Jeremy threw a party for his artists, and I brought Georgia along. At the time she was still singing demos and playing James Taylor songs in the nightclubs for a living. Didn't even have a band. No focus, no particular style, nothing. Anyway, she came to the party, and I introduced her to Ratkin. Man, I got to give her credit, she just lit up all of a sudden."

I nodded. "I remember that about her when she was a kid. Always wanted to please people."

Virginia laughed softly. "That's why she's so great on stage. I think she's one of those people that's only at home when she's in front of people, and everybody's digging her, applauding, you know? Performers, we're all applause whores. But her? Man!"

"So what happened then?"

"After the party, I didn't see her again for a while. I was touring. But one day I get a break in the tour, fly back to Nashville, she shows up at my house, got her panties all in a wad she's so excited. 'Guess what, Virginia.' " Virginia held up a large, veiny hand. "Man, she's got a rock on her finger the size of a Key lime. I'm like, 'Well, who is it?' I about fell over when she told me it was Jeremy Ratkin."

"Why?"

"Shoot, look at them! She's this twenty-seven-year-

old Southern girl—cute, outgoing, raised in the Pentecostal Holiness church. He's a fifty-year-old Jewish
sphinx from California. You figure it."

"So did they really love each other?" I said. "I mean
you hear all these things about her making a deal with
the devil, marrying him to get famous and stuff. . . ."

Virginia looked off into the distance. "Want a drink?"
she said finally, going over to the honor bar.

"They got Jim Beam in there?"

She pulled out a couple of bottles. "Jack Black,
Johnny Walker, Maker's Mark."

"Hey, Maker's Mark," I said. "Couple pieces of ice,
too, maybe?"

She poured herself a glass of Johnny Walker straight,
then gave me the bourbon on the rocks, and settled back
into her chair. I toasted her silently, took a sip of the
whiskey.

"That's what I don't get about this whole thing," Virginia said finally. "I guess I don't see Ratkin killing her."

"Huh."

"I mean, I don't know if love is the right word. But
they had something. Maybe it was kind of twisted and
fucked up, but it was *something*." She knocked back the
whiskey, then looked into the glass as though wondering
where it had gone. "Funny thing is, I think he wor-
shipped her. You know, the little shiksa princess thing.
Blond, pretty, sweet, all that shit." Her face hardened.
"Of course at the same time he was a totally controlling
guy. Wear this, Georgia. Do that, Georgia. Sing this
way, talk that way, drive this car, the whole bit.
And . . ." She frowned thoughtfully at me. "Did you say
you had known her when you were kids?"

I nodded.

"She probably hadn't changed a bit. No structure in
her life, no . . ." Virginia made a sort of bowl in the air
with her large, strong hands. "She had nothing to contain
all that energy. So she was just all over the place. But
Jeremy, he gave her structure. He told her how to wear

makeup, what angle of her face to show the camera, what hobbies to enjoy, what food to eat. He bought her horses and told her to ride them; he bought her a nice, perky pair of boobs and told her to wear low-cut dresses. For a long time, I think she liked it."

"But it got old after a while?"

She rummaged around in the honor bar, took out the minibottle of Jack Daniels.

"She showed him, though." This time she didn't bother using a glass, just tipped the whiskey straight from the bottle into her mouth. When she was done she had a silly grin on her face.

"Like how?"

The singer leaned toward me, eyes glinting slightly. "She had a little action on the side. I think she was in love—*really* in love—for the first time."

"With who?"

Virginia's face went blank. "She wouldn't tell me. She was pretty tore up about it, though, I can tell you that much. I mean she believed in all that 'till death do us part' crap. In her heart, she was a good little Christian girl."

"So how'd she resolve it?"

Virginia leaned toward me, put her hand on my arm. "Want to know a secret?"

I waited.

Virginia started singing the old Tammy Wynette song, "D-I-V-O-R-C-E."

I raised my eyebrows. "No *shit!*"

"Yessiree, ma'am! She was fixing to divorce his ass."

"Did he know?"

"I have no idea."

"So 'till death do us part' only worked for her up to a point."

Virginia shrugged. "She'd grown up a lot in the past few years. I'm sure she had a place in her heart for Jeremy. But she'd finally started to figure out that she was capable of making decisions, capable of figuring out for herself what she wanted. Buying that farm down here in Georgia, I think that was like her declaration of independence." She smiled an odd, crooked little smile.

"It was those horses that started everything. He buys her a horse, then he's got to buy her a place to put it. Man, she was stone crazy for those horses. I think sometimes she would have been happy living on some crummy little horse farm the rest of her life—riding them, feeding them, currying them, all that physical work. No thinking, no pressure, nobody needing anything from you. You don't have to prove nothing to a horse."

She laughed. "But Jeremy?—man, he hated that place, wouldn't hardly ever come down there unless he had to. Hated the horses, too." The smile faded on her lips, and her eyes went hard. "Well, I guess he finally figured out his days with her were numbered."

"Are you saying what I think you're saying? You think he found out she was going to divorce him, and so he killed her?"

"I don't know what to think." Suddenly tears were dripping down her cheeks.

I didn't say anything, just tried to look sympathetic.

Virginia wiped her face on her sleeve. When she'd finished crying, she added, "I don't know. Jeremy's a son of a bitch, but he doesn't seem like the kind of guy who'd go this far overboard for love."

I said, "You don't suppose it could have been for money, could it?"

The singer curled her lips dismissively, waved one hand as though shooing away a fly. "The guy owns a record company. Why would he need her money?"

I hung around for a while longer, but the conversation drifted away from Georgia Burnett. Virginia had another couple bottles of various kinds of liquor, and then she started in on her romantic problems and how much it sucked living on the road and how all country radio program directors were cretins and jerks. The drawback of the Good Listener approach to interviewing is that if you hang around long enough, your interview subject will eventually bury you underneath a pile of their almost invariably boring problems.

I soon tired of listening to her.

Besides, a certain lack of specificity about the gender of all her romantic entanglements, and a peculiar vibe in the room made me suspect that maybe we were headed toward a lesbian proposition. I decided to scoot before anything embarrassing happened.

As I headed out the door, Virginia called out to me. "Hey, you any relation to that gal on the radio? The *Fresh Air* chick?"

"No," I said. "Why?"

"I don't know, man. You sound just like her."

"Huh. How 'bout that?" I walked away feeling both vaguely pleased and vaguely dirty.

CHAPTER 20

I WENT BACK down home to Fairlie-Poplar, the old warehouse district in downtown Atlanta, and rode the asthmatic freight elevator up to my loft. Barrington Cherry was still hunched in front of the computer.

He swivelled around when I came back in. "Well?" he said.

"She was about to leave Ratkin."

Barrington raised his eyebrows. "Now *that's* interesting."

"What'd you turn up, Barrington?"

"A lot and yet nothing. Ratkin has no criminal convictions on file either on GCIC or NCIC. His personal Dun and Bradstreet looks clean. His Equifax is gilt-edged. He charges between five and fifty grand a month on his cards, generally pays his bills in full every month, runs no balances, fat credit lines, the works.

"I also ran the D and B for ArchRival Records. They don't look as healthy as I had expected. No significant judgments against them, but they're slow-paying their creditors big-time. On the other hand, some businesses do that on principle, so it's hard to know for sure."

"What about BankLine?" I said. BankLine was a company out in Texas that would give you the balance of virtually any bank account in the country. It wasn't precisely legal . . . but it wasn't precisely *not* legal either.

"Lots and lots of money. He's got a joint account with Georgia that's used to pay most of their bills. That one runs a balance of about a hundred grand. Fifty, sixty grand a month runs through it."

"Must be nice, huh?"

Barrington smiled ruefully.

"How much money did he make last year?"

"He reported his income as three hundred and ten grand."

"What about her?"

"Seven hundred and fifty thousand, thereabouts."

"Huh. I read in *People* magazine a couple years ago that she made ten times that."

"I gather the record business is a pretty up and down thing."

"What a bummer. Three quarters of a million in a down year."

Cherry laughed. "Georgia's got some personal accounts, too. There's fifty grand in hers. I assume there's lots more money, but it's probably invested in stock, mutual funds, REITs, limited partnerships, trusts. And without a court order, there's really no way to get our hands on that kind of thing."

I sighed. "Sure would be nice to go into the interview tomorrow knowing to the penny how much money he had."

Cherry looked back at the screen for a minute. "I'll be honest. I'm not seeing a huge money problem here."

"Suppose she left him. Would he have a money problem then?"

"Hm. Honestly, I can't tell. Not with what I've got here. Plus, it would depend on how they split things up. The house in Nashville has a whopping big mortgage. Plus he's got a plane, a bunch of expensive cars, stuff like that." Barrington scribbled a column of numbers on an envelope, drew a slash, added them up. "Assuming he kept the plane and the Nashville place, the Jag, the Range Rover, the boat in Hatteras—yeah, he'd go seriously cash negative. On the other hand, if she kept the plane and the boat, he'd be okay."

"Hm."

"If we wanted to be really, really thorough, we could look at ArchRival, figure out exactly what's going on there. It's basically his company. He founded it, he runs it. Lot of people in that situation tend to comingle their personal and corporate financial situations. They get their company to buy the plane, the boat, all their expensive toys, then they write it off of the company taxes as a business expense. It would be nice to know what percentage of the company's stock he owns, what kind of tax dodges he's running through there. But since ArchRival's not publicly traded, that's basically a private matter."

"Has he been in court recently?" I said. "That's the kind of thing that sometimes gets turned up in discovery for civil cases. If we could find pleadings for a civil trial, we could . . ."

Suddenly I had a hopeless feeling. Barrington must have had the same feeling I did.

"We've got less than three weeks to trial," he said. "Is this the best use of our time?"

"I don't know."

"I mean, we already know Marla's going to testify that there's some kind of conspiracy. Presumably she'll testify that Ratkin's behind it. Even if it's not Gunnar that did the crime, do we really need to spend our time piling on?"

"You got a point. We're probably just duplicating a bunch of evidence that the prosecution will bring out in trial anyway. I guess what we really need to do is work from the other end—figure out who *did* kill Georgia."

"Which brings us back to the crime scene."

"About which we know zip right now."

We sat there in silence for a while.

"You think you could use your high-powered law enforcement contacts to get us a copy of the police files?"

Barrington made a face. "I'll see what I can do. But frankly, given this is all being handled by some hick cop that I've never worked with . . ." He let the rest of the sentence hang there in the air. "You got any beer, Sunny? Wine?"

"Help yourself." I waved at the refrigerator. "I've had enough already tonight."

My loft is all one big room. Bed, kitchen, table, desk, all scattered around in the same cavernous space. I went over and lay down on the bed, stretched out on top of the covers with my shoes still on.

I heard Barrington pop open a beer.

"May I?" he said.

"Sure," I said. He lay down next to me, his cowboy boots hanging off the end of the bed, the beer resting on his chest. This might seem a little weird or presumptuous, but it's not like it sounds. I don't have an easy chair or a couch or anything. If you want to relax, the bed's pretty much the only choice. My standing joke is that I've only lived here for six years, so I haven't gotten around to buying furniture.

Okay, okay, but still I had a funny, awkward feeling with him lying there. It reminded me of high school. Back in those days I was kind of a tomboy, and sometimes I'd end up hanging out with a guy—playing frisbee or soccer or video games, driving around smoking cigarettes, floating down the river and drinking beer stolen from the guy's parents—just kid stuff, nothing boy-girl about it. And then one day there would be this scary moment where our bodies would get close together by some accident. There would be that frightening adolescent sex heat, and some little detail would seize control of my mind: the way his hair curled on his sweating forehead, or the smell of him, or a vein in his neck, or the curve of a muscle in his shoulder. And suddenly everything was new and uncomfortable. It was like we weren't sure if we were going to be boyfriend and girl-friend or not. But once you had that moment, nothing was ever quite the same between you.

"Still and all, Sunny," Barrington said after a while. "I got to say, this beats government work."

I didn't say anything. Barrington made gurgling noises with his beer. I peeped over at him out of the corner of my eye. There was that heat, like high school. But the detail that took my eye this time was on his left hand, the hand that was wrapped around the beer bottle. I'd noticed earlier that he wore a wedding band. It was still there, a simple gold ring, no decorations.

"So, ah—when you planning tell me about this?" I said, touching his ring.

"It's a ring."

I gave it a beat or two, then said, "You know Bar-rington, that's the kind of flip shit that really pisses women off."

The springs in my cheap mattress jangled as Barring-ton Cherry shifted his weight. "I'm sorry, you're right. I was married once, but I'm not anymore."

"You know, speaking as one who has been involved in a certain amount of grief revolving around this par-ticular issue, when I see a single man with a wedding band on his finger, the words 'unresolved issues' start forming in my mind."

There was a long pause.

"My wife died five years ago. I wear it because I loved her. When I find a woman who makes me think it's time to take it off, I'll take it off."

"Mm," I said. I wasn't sure if that was really sweet and loyal or if it was obsessive and creepy.

"You going to ask?" he said after a couple minutes.

"What?"

"How she died."

"Do you want to tell me?"

"I think so."

"Then I want to hear."

There was a long pause. Finally Barrington said, "My last assignment before I got promoted to Deputy SAC here in Atlanta was working fraud cases out of headquarters in Washington. Big white-collar investigations that went on and on forever. Anyway, I found out I was in line to get promoted, and that the promotion was going to be here in Atlanta. We talked it over, and my wife agreed that it was a good move and she was willing to relocate. I mean, she had a good job in D.C. She was a lawyer with the EPA. But she was willing.

"So I went down one weekend to look for a house. I wanted her to come because she had much better taste than me. She really loved beauty, you know? And so I wanted her help. But she had a brief to write and so at the last minute she begged out. I almost cancelled the trip. Came *that* close." Barrington held up his fingers, a fraction of an inch apart. "But I didn't.

"So I came down, checked out some houses, some neighborhoods, talked to some agents about the real estate market, usual routine. It was a pretty busy weekend, and for some reason I didn't call her. I mean I *always* called when I went on business trips, but . . . for some reason this time I just didn't. Didn't get around to it.

"Anyway, trip's over, Sunday night I fly home, drive back to the house, come inside, and there she is lying in the living room surrounded by this huge pool of blood." Barrington's voice was strangely dispassionate, as though he had told the story in these exact words so many times before that they had stopped meaning anything to him, that it was like humming a wordless tune. I imagine it wasn't that way, but that was how it sounded.

"The killer had broken in to burglarize the place, and she must have walked in on him. He overpowered her, stabbed her, then gagged her and secured her to the bannister post at the bottom of the stairs with duct tape. I don't think he meant to kill her. The ME described the stab wound as 'tentative.' That was his exact word.

Problem was, this was a beautiful old house in Capital Hill, built like a rock. There she was, losing blood, and she didn't have the strength or the leverage or whatever to break herself free of the bannister, call 911." He shrugged. "The ME estimated that she'd walked in on the guy on Friday night, and that she'd sat there attached to the bannister for close to forty-eight hours. She was alive until maybe a couple hours before I got home. If I'd called late Saturday night and nobody had answered, who knows, maybe I'd have gotten worried, had somebody look in just to make sure she was okay. The stab wound wasn't even that major, cut some small arteries in her chest, that's all. If she'd gotten to the hospital, she'd have been fine. But it kept bleeding and bleeding and eventually she just bled out. And I never called."

"Jesus," I said.

For the first time since he'd started the story, Barrington looked at me. "So I don't know if you call that an unresolved issue or not. I really loved my wife. I wouldn't want to go through that kind of pain again unless somebody was really worth it."

"You probably wouldn't have to."

Barrington looked at me like a parent might look at a child who'd just said something naive and sweet, something that reminded them of things they'd once believed but now knew better. "There's always pain, Sunny. Cancer, infertility, losing a job, Alzheimer's, getting old, losing a child, your parents dying, *something*. You can't wall yourself off from that. That's part of the bargain when you decide you're going to spend your life with somebody."

"Oh I know," I said. "I just meant . . ." And for a moment I felt hangdog and ashamed, like maybe I was still single at thirty-four because I'd tried to do just what he said, wall myself off from all the pain that went with loving someone deeply.

"I know," he said. "I know."

"Did they ever catch him?" I said.

"The guy who killed my wife?"

I nodded.

He curled his lip slightly, and he shook his head. "Nah."

"That must feel horrible."

"It used to. But you know what, Sunny? People like that, they find their punishment anyway. Whoever it is, I'm sure he ended up face down in a ditch, or doing fifty years in the penitentiary for something else anyway."

"But not knowing . . ."

Barrington held up his hand with the ring on it. "We had sixteen and a half good years. Most of those days were better days than a lot of people find even once in a lifetime. That's what I *do* know."

I sat there for a minute studying his face, thinking: damn, if Barrington Cherry was not in total denial and full of shit, then he was the most mature man I've ever met.

Then again, I supposed, maybe nothing's that simple.

"What's her name?" I said. "You never said her name."

"Her name was Laura."

After a while I heard a clink as he set his beer down on the floor next to the bed.

"Guess I'll run," he said.

"Okey-dokey." I was trying to sound lighthearted or something, trying to defuse the moment. But it just came out sounding kind of queer and embarrassing.

Barrington swung his feet off the bed. His boots went clumping across the floor, then the old freight elevator started wheezing its way up the shaft. I kept staring up at the ceiling, which was crisscrossed by a row of beautiful old heart-pine beams. I had been intending to stain them for about five years now, one of those light, clear stains that brings out the grain. Somehow I had just never gotten around to it.

"See you tomorrow?" I said.

"Actually, there's something I'd like to follow up on."

I couldn't really think of anything for him to do tomorrow anyway. The case was making me feel like I was hip deep in mud. "Be my guest," I said.

CHAPTER 21

I SPENT THE next day spinning my wheels. First I drove up to Floyd County, went into the security office in the staff quarters at Georgia's farm. There I picked up the records of all the loonies who'd sent threatening or otherwise crazy letters to Georgia. Then I drove back down to Atlanta and pored over the letters.

Hoo boy, if there aren't a lot of sick people in the world. One guy sent her about twenty missives from a state crazy house in Mississippi, each note written in neat letters so tiny they could only be read under a magnifying glass. The letters went on for pages and pages describing all the thoughts he'd had about Georgia while masturbating. I'll give him this, he was an imaginative little guy. I called the nut house and found he was still there, under lock and key.

Marla had actually had a couple of the letter writers investigated by a team from the Nashville office of Kroll and Associates—but they didn't turn up anybody that seemed to be a credible threat to her safety. Other than Creepy Guy, she'd never had a bona fide stalker.

It took till well past sundown to wade through the wacko files. And when I was done we were one day closer to trial and no closer to proving Gunnar's innocence.

• • •

Around eight, I buzzed Barrington Cherry up to the loft. He came up the freight elevator carrying a plastic bag that read ANNIE'S THAI CASTLE on the side. Instead of his usual jeans and motorcycle jacket, he was dressed like some high-rolling superpimp or maybe a Pentecostal preacher on the Trinity Broadcast Network: a lemon-yellow four-button suit, pointy red shoes, scarlet necktie, big gold bracelet on his wrist, elaborate gold-framed sunglasses.

"So where you been all day with your bad self?" I said.

Barrington smiled slyly. "Nashville."

"Do tell."

"Bet you didn't know I was a big record producer, did you?"

"No, I did not."

"Yes, indeed. Assistant vice-president at Motown Records." He took out a couple of plates, served up some panang chicken and red curry beef. "In addition to being very phat, very dope, and very down, I'm very interested in buying ArchRival Records."

I raised my eyebrows slightly.

Another secret smile. "You're gonna find this all very interesting." His smile faded. "Only, I don't know if this is a good thing or not."

"So tell me."

Barrington held up one long finger, took a bite of fried rice, chewed, swallowed.

"Here we go . . ." he said. He took another mouthful of the spicy meal, then set down his fork. "Six, eight years ago I was working out of the Nashville field office, and I did some undercover work in a fraud case. My cover was that I was with the publishing division at Motown Records, looking to buy up publishing catalogues. I never ended up testifying in the case, so there are still some folks floating around Nashville thinking that I'm in the music business.

"Anyway, I flew up this morning and tracked down this sleazy little guy that I had had some dealings with back then. Little bald guy named Frankie Bruno. He admitted to me once that he's actually Greek, but he pretends he's Italian, claims people are more scared of Italians." Barrington laughed. "Anyway, this guy supposedly manages singers—but it's all a front for something shady. Loan-sharking or fencing, I never really figured it out. Point is, he drifts in and out of the record business, knows the names and faces, knows a lot of dirt.

"So I went up and told him Berry Gordy at Motown's looking to buy a label, wants to get into country music. Said I'd be willing to pay finders fees to anybody that could help us put together a deal. Told him we'd pay half a percent of the deal price or something. You buy a forty million dollar company, that's a lot of scratch for a few weeks work and some phone calls.

"First, of course, Bruno tries to sell me on some bogus operation he owns. It was just smoke, you know. Just a scam." Barrington smiled a little. "Took me about an hour to shake him off that. Finally he starts naming some outfits in Nashville that are still independent, that might be worth looking at."

Barrington started scooping big spoons full of glistening red curry into his box of rice. He pretended to be very intent on it, getting the proportions right.

"What?" I said finally.

"Oh, yeah," Barrington said. "Sorry. This chicken is *good*!" He licked his lips and jived around in his seat, playing with me.

"Quit that," I said.

"Interesting thing," Barrington said, "is that he didn't mention ArchRival. Which just happens to be the biggest indy label in Nashville."

I frowned.

"He mentions a bunch of little labels I've never heard of, a couple of bigger ones that I had. Then he finally shuts up. So I say, 'What about ArchRival?' He looks at me like I'm nuts. 'Seriously, my brother. I heard ArchRival was in play.'

"Frankie Bruno keeps looking at me like this." Barrington lowered his eyelids, pulled his chin back into his chest, stared at me skeptically. "So I'm saying, 'What, my brother?' He finally says, 'You don't want to waste your time with ArchRival.' 'How come not?' 'Because, amigo, that company isn't worth dick.' "

Barrington raised his eyebrows a little.

"So I say, 'What's wrong with them? They got Georgia Burnett don't they?' Bruno says, 'Yeah. And she's dead.'

"So I said to him, 'Still, the thinking at Motown is that with Ratkin in the middle of this murder trial, we might buy the company at a fire sale price.' He looks at me and says, 'Me, I'm all for fire sales. But not when the place is still in flames.' So I told him I had some inside information that Ratkin was going to get off. He says, 'Doesn't matter. You don't want that company.' "

Barrington picked through his box of food, pulled out a piece of chicken with his fingers. "So I asked him how come not. He said, 'Tell you what, you're really interested, I could round up some financials. That'll give you a flavor what you're looking at.' So I said, 'Fair enough.' Told him to fax it to me at home."

Barrington stood up, wiped his fingers off on a paper napkin, then took a big stack of paper out of his briefcase. He set the faxes in front of me.

I had once committed the youthful error of spending a couple of years on Wall Street. Generally speaking, I'd happily take those two years back and spend them lying on a beach in Tahiti. But every now and then somebody sticks a sheet with columns of numbers on it in front of me—and that's when my two years of stock analyst hell at Donaldson, Lufkin & Jenrette pay off.

The first piece of paper in the stack was the audited financial statement of ArchRival Records.

"Who'd he have to bribe to get hold of these?" I said.

"I don't want to know."

I skimmed over the numbers. Private companies don't usually do terribly detailed statements, and ArchRival was no exception. It was just four sheets of paper: a simple P and L statement, and a balance sheet. No impenetrable footnotes, no long-winded explanations of their inventory control methods.

"I'm no expert on that stuff," Barrington said. "But the bottom line's pretty clear."

I nodded. It was indeed. Literally, the bottom line on the P and L said that ArchRival had lost one point two million dollars last year. The balance sheet showed that the company had virtually no net worth.

I looked up from the paper. "Whoa," I said. "ArchRival was nigh on to bankrupt."

"Makes you wonder, don't it?"

I kept staring at the figures. "The question is, does this help Gunnar?"

Barrington's face sobered. "Short answer is no. Maybe he killed her for the dough. Problem is, our best hope in this case is to demolish the entire murder-for-hire theory. If he has money problems, and she's got money . . ."

". . . then he's got motive."

"Which leaves us with Creepy Guy."

We sat silently for a moment, then the phone rang—the second line.

Out of the little tinny answering-machine speaker I heard Barrington's voice saying the caller had reached the international recruiting office.

After the beep, a woman's voice came on. "Hello. My name is Marla Jeter. I'm responding to the advertisement for the personal security consultant in the *Atlanta Journal*." Then she left her number.

I clapped my hands together. "Ha!" I said. "Better get on the horn."

Barrington was already reaching for the phone.

CHAPTER 22

HE NEXT MORNING bright and early, I was sitting on
the bed in room 1722 at the Sheraton Peachtree downtown, watching a TV monitor as Barrington ushered
Marla Jeter into the adjoining room. As usual, the tall
rangy woman was wearing jeans, a Western shirt, and a
huge fawn-colored cowboy hat. Her red hair hung down
her back in a pigtail.

"Marla," Barrington said unctuously. "Pleasure seeing
you again."

They shook hands, and then Barrington told Marla
about leaving the FBI, saying he was now doing recruitment for an international security firm and wasn't this a
happy coincidence meeting like this. Sorry about the
rush getting her in for an interview, but a real important
assignment had come up at short notice. Then he went
through the song and dance we'd prepared: the job
would be a six-month post protecting an Asian real estate magnate's daughter while she worked on company
business in Atlanta. The backstory was told in an ap-
propriately vague and need-to-know-basis sort of way.

We had secreted two Sony lipstick cameras in the furniture, setting them up so that we could cover the entire
hotel room. The cameras were connected to two moni-

tors in my room, one of which was aimed at Marla's face while the other covered the door and the desk where Barrington was sitting.

Barrington was very, very smooth. He had been modest in telling it, but it was obvious from one of our earlier conversations that he'd been a star undercover agent before being promoted to the mostly administrative post of Deputy Special Agent-in-Charge. It was no wonder he'd done well in the FBI: his whole act was pitch perfect—the vague allusions to the powerful client and the unnamed international personal security outfit, the confidential manner, the pressed chinos and fringed loafers. He'd have been a hell of a con man.

First Barrington led her through a long discussion of her qualifications, let her talk about herself. He was getting her in the confessional habit. Not just the professional qualifications—she'd been in the marine corps, then served on the force in El Paso, eventually struck out on her own as a bodyguard—but he also made sure she talked about her work philosophy, about the broken down ranch her family had worked in West Texas, about her difficulty in finding a job since Georgia's murder. Anything he could think of to keep her talking. When he had pretty much exhausted her personal history, Cherry put his hands together and sat silently for a moment with an awkward look on his face.

"I feel a little funny opening my kimono to you, but you're the most experienced applicant we've got." Cherry cleared his throat. "So, we've got a couple of uncomfortable issues to deal with here, Marla."

Marla had set her Stetson on the table next to her. She picked it up nervously, fiddled with it, set it back down again. She knew what was coming.

"As you know, Marla, I'm former law enforcement so I understand your position. Okay? I know you can't talk about the Georgia Burnett matter. But, ah, first thing there are some scheduling issues to deal with. Thing is, if this trial is going to be some kind of huge distraction. . . ."

He trailed off, let the question hang in the air.

"I really can't talk about it," Marla said finally.

Barrington nodded, frowned earnestly, didn't say a word. The silence hung heavily in the room. Marla fidgeted, finally spoke.

"I guess you've read the papers. Obviously I'll be called to testify." Marla studied the back of one of her long, slim hands. "I probably won't have to testify but for one day. Would that be a problem?"

Cherry smiled, looked relieved. "Oh, that's great. That's no problem then."

Cherry leaned over a boilerplate applicant evaluation form that was sitting in front of him, made some notations, then started writing a long paragraph, which he continued on the flip side of the paper. It seemed to take forever. I studied Marla's face on the monitor as she nervously studied the top of Barrington's head. He was using the time and the silence, breaking her down. Her nervousness continued to grow. She picked up her Stetson, put it down, picked it up again. Cherry kept writing.

Finally he looked up.

"Last thing. Marla, frankly, I don't know if this issue can be resolved right now given your, ah, legal predicament."

Marla waited expectantly.

"Personal security is a trust business, Marla. Now my understanding is that you've been indicted on an obstruction of justice charge, and that you've gotten some kind of immunity deal. That's what they say in the papers. You've got to understand, I like you for this position. But I'm new at this job. I don't want to look like a jackass. If I recommend you, I have to know that you're not going to get up on the stand and say that you did something terrible."

"I know, Mr. Cherry, but—"

Barrington cut her off with a wave of his hand. "The

client for this assignment, as I said earlier, is an Asian. Personal loyalty is a big thing in this gentleman's culture. Maybe more important than whether you have or haven't had some kind of minor brush with the law. I mean, if you did something, oh I don't know, out of loyalty to your employer. . . . See what I'm saying? That would go a long way toward allaying their fears."

Marla sighed. "Look, is this something that we can keep between you and me?"

Cherry tapped his pen on the bogus form he'd been filling out. "Naturally I'd have to document it. But our personnel files are 100 percent ironclad confidential, believe me."

Marla nodded eagerly. "It's exactly like you said, I was just serving my client. And I did something stupid."

"Uh-huh."

"See, maybe it sounds silly and old-fashioned, but I literally put my life out there for my client. If my client gives me an order, I just do it. No questions asked."

Barrington Cherry smiled warmly. "I wish there were more like you. It would sure make my job easier."

Marla smiled back at him, reassured. "See, what happened is that my client asked me to do something for them. And I did it. I did it without asking any questions."

"Your client, meaning Georgia Burnett?"

"No. I—" Marla looked frustrated. You could see she wanted to come right out and blab everything she knew. But still she hesitated. No doubt the Floyd County DA had put the fear of God into her about not talking to anyone about her immunity deal. She sighed loudly. "No, it was Mr. Ratkin. After Georgia was killed, he asked me to do something for him, and I just did it. It was just a little thing. Or it seemed that way at the time. So it wasn't until later that I realized that this little thing I did had actually gotten me involved in covering up a murder." She sighed loudly. "But once it was done, it was done."

Cherry watched her carefully. I noticed I was holding my breath. We were *so* close.

"Man, that's tough," Cherry said. "So the GBI or the cops, they held it over your head, this thing you did. And they said you have to testify or they'd send you to jail for obstruction."

Marla nodded.

I took a slow breath. *Now,* Barrington. *Do it now.*

"Again, Marla. I don't mean to push. But this is all a little vague."

Marla swallowed, looked away, fretted with the fawn-colored Stetson in her lap.

Barrington smiled encouragingly. In a voice that was light as a feather, he said, "I mean, we're not talking about running a dead body through a meat grinder, right? Maybe you heard something? Saw something?"

She nodded eagerly. "There was a . . ."

My heart was beating in my throat. Come on. Come on.

"There was a videotape." Marla blew out her breath sharply. "Okay, okay, the hell with it. What happened was, there was a video surveillance camera. When Mr. Ratkin got there, he asked me for the tape."

Cherry clicked his tongue in sympathy. "How come the man didn't do it himself?" he asked in an injured tone.

"He didn't know how to run the video system. It wasn't like your garden-variety home VCR. You know, there were a bunch of different machines, various codes you had to know, stuff like that. So he had me do it."

"Wow! And he asked you to throw out the tape?"

"No, I gave it to him."

Barrington nodded. "So this tape. . . . Are you saying it actually *showed the murder* or something?"

Marla's eyebrows went up. "No! Of course not. It was just a camera at the front gate. It showed who went in and who went out."

"So you had Gunnar Brushwood on tape driving onto the property."

"Right before the murder."

"And what was Ratkin's justification for ditching this tape?"

Marla shrugged. "He made it seem like it was some stupid little housecleaning thing. I mean, I knew it was crap at the time but I was so . . . I mean my primary had just been murdered. I considered Georgia a friend. I was . . ." Marla held the Stetson up in front of her face for a moment, hiding like a little girl. "Oh God, I couldn't even think straight."

"So let me be clear, Marla. You just went in, you got the tape, you handed it to him. And that's what this whole obstruction of justice thing is all about."

Marla nodded.

Cherry looked thoughtfully up in the air, frowned. "Huh. They must have more on him than *that*. I mean, getting rid of a tape, that seems a little thin for a conspiracy-to-commit case." The way he said it, it wasn't like he was asking her a question—it was more like it was something interesting that had struck his fancy.

"I overheard some things," Marla said, her voice suddenly cautious.

"What like?"

Marla cleared her throat. "I really can't talk about that."

Cherry paused, thought about it for a while. "Well, okay, good, good," his voice was suddenly full of enthusiasm. "I don't see that this is going to be a problem."

"So do I have the job?"

Cherry stood up, held out his hand. "I'll have to talk to a couple more people. Company policy, all that good stuff." He smiled confidentially as they shook hands. "But let's say you're in strong contention. *Very* strong."

Marla put on her big Stetson and got ready to leave. As she opened the door, Cherry did something unexpected. Looking up from the desk with a big smile on his face, he said, "The baseball bat. You put it in Gunnar's trunk, didn't you?"

She turned slowly, her hand on the door lever. Even over the grainy video monitor, I could see the brief moment of confusion, and then the blood draining out of her face as she realized this whole thing had been a put-on.

The tall woman pointed a long finger at Cherry's face and said bitterly, "I would *never* lay a hand on her. Never!"

I glanced at the second monitor, the one showing Cherry's face. He raised his eyebrows. "Shucks, who said you did?"

After Marla left, I called for room service. Barrington and I sat in the hotel room discussing the conversation he'd had with Marla. " 'I never laid a hand on her,' " he said. "I ask her if she'd hid the bat, and she says she never laid a hand on Georgia. Isn't that an odd thing to say?"

"Maybe she denied it because she did it. Maybe she made up the whole thing about Ratkin and the tape."

Barrington nodded. "Makes you wonder, doesn't it?"

CHAPTER 23

LOCATED OFF HIGHWAY 53 just north of the city of Rome, the new Floyd County jail is constructed of a reddish-tan brick—like the skin of a Sicilian with sunburn—its slitty windows covered by startling blue bars. As you approach from Rome, the most noticeable feature of the jail is a large blue-steel armature over the stairwell of one of the cell blocks; from a distance, it looks like the crosshairs of a huge rifle.

Jeremy Ratkin's lawyer, Mike Friend, was waiting for us in the interview room, but Ratkin himself had not yet arrived.

Mike Friend stood up and shook my hand, gave me a condescending little smile. He was a short, stubby man with an explosive little tuft of hair beneath his lower lip, like some jazz sax player from the '50s. He wore an ochre-colored Italian suit with four buttons up the front, an ornately embroidered gold paisley vest, and two-tone brown-on-brown wingtips. He was an ugly little man, and the extravagance of his clothes did nothing but point up his physical inadequacies.

"I'm consenting to this, okay, Sunny?" Friend said. "But before they bring in my client, we need to set some ground rules."

"You talked to Quentin about this?"

The nasty little smile went away. "I don't kowtow to anybody when my client's rights are at stake. Not Quentin, not anybody."

"That's noble of you, Mike."

"First thing, I've got written instructions from Quentin for you to be here, so any notes you take are going to be attorney-client work product. You try admitting any documents into evidence that arise from this meeting, you'll open the door to having every lick of paper you or Quentin have generated produced in open court."

"Fair enough."

"Second, if I instruct my client to shut up, you cease asking him questions or I'll pull him right out of the interview. This is a courtesy to you. Abuse our goodwill, it's over."

I smiled girlishly and tried to pretend I was my mother. Mom is much more accomplished at being nice to people she despises than I am. For now, there was no percentage in pissing him off.

"I understand your position."

Friend straightened his chocolate-colored necktie, banged on the door behind me with his fist.

Ratkin settled into his chair. As usual he was expressionless, cool, just a little gloomy in appearance.

After some awkward preliminaries, I began by asking, "How much do you know about the crime?"

"Too much and not enough."

I waited. Ratkin gave me nothing else, so I turned to Mike Friend and said. "Goddamn it, this is not a negotiation here. We're supposed to be sharing information. Would you instruct your client not to be a dickhead." So much for being nice.

Friend whispered something in Ratkin's ear. Ratkin nodded impassively. "I'm preternaturally tight-lipped," he said to me. "That doesn't mean I'm trying to jerk you around."

Yeah, right. I smiled again, despite my real feelings.

"I'm sorry," I said. "I shouldn't have called you a dick-head. Anyway, when did you get to the crime scene? What did you see?"

His mask wobbled briefly, a flash of emotion running beneath the surface, then disappearing. "I got there too late to find out much of anything. She was killed in the bedroom. They had it roped off. You know, with yellow tape, just like in the movies. They had already removed the body."

That was disappointing. Georgia law requires all forensic evidence be turned over to the defense at least ten days before trial. That meant that eventually we would have the ME's report and some photos of the scene. But the sooner we knew what we were up against, the better. Knowing the Floyd County DA's office, we would get the material exactly ten days before trial and not a minute sooner. Without sufficient time to get our act together, we would be playing catch-up throughout the trial.

"The approximate time of the murder, so far as we know, was around noon. Where were you at that point?"

"I was in Nashville getting ready to fly down to Atlanta."

"Commercial flight?"

"No. I own a Gulfstream IV, which I fly myself."

"Any passengers?"

"Just me."

He then filled in the details, the exact time of take off, and the landing time at Charlie Brown Airport, a small general aviation field in Atlanta. He added that he picked up his Range Rover, which he keeps parked at the airport, and began driving to the house at about 2:00 P.M.

"Had you heard about the murder by then?"

"Yes. Marla called me on the cell phone right after I landed."

"When you reached the house, who was there? GBI people? County cops?"

"Just the Floyd County police guys. GBI got there later. I gather the Floyd County cops called in the GBI crime scene technicians to help with the investigation."

"And how did they seem to view you? Did you sense that they viewed you as a suspect in a murder-for-hire scheme?"

"Frankly I've never felt excessively comfortable around heavily armed Southern Baptists." I suppose he was joking, but you couldn't tell it from the masklike face. "I don't know how they felt about me."

"But they weren't openly hostile?"

"No."

"So you don't think you were a suspect at that point."

"No."

"When did you perceive yourself as becoming a suspect?"

"The next day. I came back to Atlanta, stayed at the Ritz Carlton. I couldn't stand to stay out there. Not after what had just happened. The next morning the GBI showed up to interview me. It was quite grueling. And somewhat hostile."

"Did they charge you that day?"

"The next."

"What precipitated the arrest?"

Ratkin eyed me for a moment. "Marla. She made up some kind of story, this murder-for-hire nonsense."

"Why? Why on earth would she make up a story like that?"

"I guess she didn't like me much."

"Why would you say that?"

"I wanted to fire her after the kidnapping. Georgia nixed the idea, but I'd already made it clear to Marla that I wasn't overly impressed with her work."

"Did they ask you about the videotape?"

The record executive glanced furtively at his lawyer.

"Okay, goddammit, where did you hear about the tape?" Friend said to me.

"We've talked to Marla."

He looked unbelievingly at me. "How?"

"Let's just say my operative didn't walk up and blithely identify himself as an employee of Gunnar Brushwood."

Friend looked at me for a moment, then fingered his silly little jazzman beard. "Okay, I think the appropriate response to your question about the video tape is, 'No comment.'"

"Get real, Mike," I said. "The tape is gonna come up in trial. That's going to be a key point in Marla's testimony."

Friend was about to speak, but Ratkin put a manacled hand on his lawyer's arm. "She's right, Mike. It'll come out. The explanation is innocent enough." He turned to me. "The videotape is a special surveillance type. Like you see on TV sometimes when they show robberies at 7-11's? They're not continuous motion, they just capture eight or ten frames a minute. Point is, these tapes run twenty-four hours before they get filled up. This is kind of stupid, but . . ." Ratkin made a face of annoyance. "I wasn't thinking straight. Georgia had been seeing . . . this is so stupid . . . she'd been seeing some quack, some psychic. He had come the night before the murder and so his face was on that tape. I just didn't want this whole psychic business ending up as part of the media feeding frenzy that I knew was about to happen. It was stupid, but that's why I did it."

"And you destroyed the tape?"

"Sure. Threw it in the trash at the Ritz Carlton."

I took some notes, then looked up from my legal pad. "Is there any other reason why Marla would think that you had hired Gunnar to kill Georgia?"

"Other than the fact that he happened to show up more or less at the time of the murder? No."

"Absolutely nothing at all? No paper trail, no unexplained phone calls, no nothing?"

There was a momentary hesitation, then Friend gave me his little counterfeit smile. "Look, my client has made me aware that you left Gunnar's employ because you believe that Mr. Ratkin engineered the kidnapping of his wife."

"I know damn good and well that's what happened."

"Okay, fine, that's your opinion. Now my client is not under any circumstances going to admit to having engineered a bogus kidnapping."

Ratkin then said, "Without admitting to anything with regard to the kidnapping, let's just say that after Gunnar heroically rescued my wife, I rewarded him unusually generously."

"Careful . . ." Friend said.

"In other words, you paid him off to keep his mouth shut," I said.

Ratkin shrugged slightly.

"How much did you pay him?" I said.

"Fifty thousand dollars."

"That ain't gonna look good," I said.

"I'm well aware of this," Ratkin said.

"My client's position," Mike Friend said, "is that the generosity was a reward for Mr. Brushwood's heroism."

"When exactly did you pay him?"

Ratkin made a face. "That's the problem. I didn't pay him right off the bat. We had a little cash flow problem, and I didn't get around to paying him until the end of November."

"You sent him a check for fifty grand a week before your wife got murdered."

Ratkin cleared his throat. "Actually, about three days before."

"Oh, sweet Jesus, no!" I said. "I assume you're not prepared to testify that the payment was made because he knew you'd staged the kidnapping?"

Friend laughed loudly.

"I take that to mean no."

"We're going to beat this case on its merits," Friend said. "If we drag in—and I'm talking hypothetically—if we drag in some kind of crazy story about a kidnapping staged as a publicity stunt, what does that do to my client's credibility? Or yours for that matter? The jury members would be fighting one another for the opportunity to pull the switch on both of them."

"Okay," I said. "I'm personally certain that Gunnar didn't commit this murder. But—just looking at all the angles here—that doesn't mean you might not have hired somebody *else* to kill your wife."

Ratkin looked at me with cold black eyes. "I could never do that. I loved her."

"Maybe a little too much? Hm?"

"What's that supposed to mean?" Ratkin said sharply.

"I understand she was going to leave you. Maybe you weren't willing to let that happen."

For the first time Ratkin seemed uneasy, almost melancholy. "Not true. We had our problems. We had started going to a counselor. But that was all."

"Have you ever had domestic disputes?"

"You mean like raising our voices?" Ratkin said sarcastically. "Expressing annoyance? Pointing our fingers at each other?"

"I mean like cops showing up, bruises, trips to emergency rooms."

"Absolutely never."

"Okay, fair enough. Now while we're on touchy subjects, there's something else I have to ask. Was Georgia having an affair?"

Ratkin looked at me steadily, his black eyes as unreadable as ever. After a moment he said, "Nope."

"Virginia Blount says she was."

"Virginia Blount is a terrific singer, she's got a lot of musical integrity, blah blah blah. But, guys, *Please*—the woman's a bitter, boozed up, unhappy dyke who had a love jones for my wife. She dislikes me intensely because I dropped her from my label. As a result, she made a major project out of trying to split us apart. My supposition is that when she finally conceded the fact that playing munch-the-rug with Georgia wasn't in the stars for her, she invented some big hairy man as her proxy. Anything but me and Georgia being in love and working out our problems."

"No boyfriend?"

Ratkin's eyes grazed the floor for a moment. "If there was, I wasn't aware of it. Whatever you want to say about our relationship, we were honest with each other. And she never told me about another man."

I had another line I wanted to pursue, but wasn't sure quite how to angle into it.

"Georgia had a lot of money," I said. "The case is liable to be made that you were after her dough."

Friend held up his hand. "Absolutely off limits. My client is a very wealthy man, and that line of argument is totally without merit. Okay? So I'm not going to have you blundering around in his financial affairs trying to make a case for the prosecution."

"Yeah, but—"

Friend shut his briefcase with a snap, gave me a sarcastic smile. "You want us to walk out right now? Is that it?"

"Okay, okay," I said. I badly wanted to pursue this line of questioning, but I could see that Mike Friend was dead serious. I took a moment to scribble down some notes, then finally said, "Look, if it wasn't you and it wasn't Gunnar, and there was no murder-for-hire, who did this thing? Marla? The milkman? You got a theory?"

"I have more than a theory. I know. It was that lunatic."

"What lunatic?"

"This guy, Creepy Guy, whatever you want to call him, that peeping Tom freak who was living up on the hill and spying on us." For the first time Ratkin seemed genuinely outraged.

I frowned. "I thought he was part of the kidnapping scheme."

"Who?" Ratkin said.

"The *guy*! Creepy Guy! I thought you staged that whole thing so you could use him as the villain in your kidnapping stunt."

Ratkin looked at me for a moment, then said, "Give me a moment with Mike, Sunny."

I got up, banged on the door. The guard let me out. We had a brief conversation about the possibility of snow in the forecast, then Friend gestured through the Plexiglas window for me to come back in.

I sat down and Ratkin began to talk.

"When I graduated from Berkeley back in 1964, I went out to Hollywood and took a stab at the movie business. I even wrote, produced, and directed my own picture. Typical low-grade piece of shit horror picture. Lost my ass on it. Anyway, that's not important. Point is, I think of the world in terms of stories. Even as a record producer. I mean that's all country music is, right? Stories. Boy meets girl; boy loses girl; boy gets pick-up truck; whatever. So even when I develop an artist, I'm always thinking, *How do I sell this guy's story*? Small-town boy, mother dies at ten, raised by his alcoholic father, saved from a bleak life by music, yadda yadda. That's how I sell a singer: I tell a story. Good singer? Who gives a damn. Every broke, desperate, redneck asshole in Nashville can sing. You want to be rich and famous in this day and age, my friend, you better have a story."

Ratkin paused and watched me for a minute, letting me absorb what he was saying. I had a hunch where he was going.

"So let's say, hypothetically speaking," he continued, "that I'm thinking about Georgia's career. Songs, chord changes, musicians, multitrack recording? Fuck that. I'm thinking about it like a screenwriter does. I've got access to the same talent pool as every other record company executive in Nashville. The same thirty songwriters, the same twenty-five studio musicians, the same fourteen recording engineers, and the same nine producers in Nashville. Singers like Georgia are a dime a dozen. So you have to have something extra."

"A story," I said.

"A story. So let's think like screenwriters instead of record company executives for a minute. What's in the screenwriter's toolbox? You know, all the usual cliches: the perfect crime, the locked room mystery, the flamboyant sleuth, the beautiful sidekick, the big fight scene, the same old crap."

Mike Friend put his hand on Ratkin's arm. "Now Jeremy . . ."

Ratkin didn't smile, but his black eyes seemed to gleam a little. He ignored his lawyer. "Again, hypothetically, one can imagine a scenario in which one actually . . . well . . . *devises* a story. But at a certain point, you want your story to fit into reality. For instance maybe one develops a script in which there's a kidnapping. According to the first draft of that script, your villains are a team of former KGB or Stasi operatives. High-tech gadgets, Central European accents . . . you know, the whole *Mission Impossible* vibe. You following me?"

"Maybe," I said.

"This lunatic sitting up on the hill with his telescope—maybe he's not in the first draft. He's not part of the story at all. I mean he's *real*. Do you understand me, Sunny?"

"You're saying he wasn't part of the original plan."

"I'm saying that, hypothetically speaking of course, once one found a guy like that, maybe one might decide to scrap the first draft of the story. Because this kidnapping, it's unfolding in real time and so on—well, maybe one would say, hey, look! Here's a *real* villain. Here's a guy who might *really* do a thing like this. Not just some bogus Hollywood scenario. Maybe we got ourselves a living, breathing, bad-smelling, true-life shithead."

"A fall guy."

"Hypothetically speaking? Yeah. Because if he got caught, he'd take away any potential heat that might fall on *us*. See?"

"So you're saying you changed the plan in midstream. You set it up so that this Creepy Guy dude would look like the kidnapper." I thought about it. "Wait. What about the black Toyota, the Land Cruiser?"

Ratkin smiled ironically. "If a bigshot wheeler-dealer such as myself can't find a guy to buy him a black truck, he's in deep trouble."

"So the whole deal with the guy driving around talking on the cell phone and then abandoning the Land Cruiser and escaping onto the subway—that was all staged to make a false connection between this creep and your bogus kidnapping."

"Hypothetically," Friend interjected.

"Hypothetically," Ratkin said. "Yes, if I were orchestrating a scam like this, that's the way I would have written the second draft." Ratkin's lips twitched in a ghost of a smile. "But of course I would never have been involved in such a flagrantly illegal and unethical thing."

"You need to find that guy, Sunny," Friend said. "The guy with the telescope, he's our boy."

"That kidnapping was just a stunt. It was harmless. Nobody got hurt," Ratkin said, his eyes furious. "My wife getting beat to death? That was no Hollywood script, Sunny. It was real, and it was him."

"The guy in the woods."

Ratkin's voice suddenly grew urgent and he leaned toward me. "That son of a bitch. That *monster*. He got tired of watching, Sunny. He got tired of fantasizing up in those woods, and so he came down and broke into my home. And when his sick little fantasy didn't play out like he'd hoped, he flipped. He killed my beautiful wife."

"Where'd he get the bat?"

Ratkin sighed a long, wracking sigh and stared for a

moment out through the little Plexiglas window. "It's my bat, Sunny. I kept it in the bedroom. I've always kept a bat in my room, since I was a kid. I know it's silly, but it makes me feel safe."

"And how'd it get in Gunnar's trunk?"

"That's easy," Ratkin said. "Gunnar shows up right after this bastard kills my wife. The guy's still in the house. Gunnar probably rings the doorbell, and when nobody answers he wanders around back to see if anybody's out at the stables. This son of a bitch sees his opportunity, throws the bat in Gunnar's trunk, heads off into the woods."

"How'd he open the trunk?"

"Every car in the world has a remote trunk latch now. Probably just opened the front door, hit the latch button, dropped the bat in the trunk, and walked away."

Suddenly I was excited. I had never even considered the idea of a stalker. But to make it work as a defense strategy, we had to find out who this nut was. What was his real name? Had he served time? Had he been in the loony bin? Restraining orders, police complaints, reports of weird behavior—anything I could turn up would help.

"One last thing," I said. "If you could make a list of everybody who might have been on your property that day. Or on a regular basis, for that matter. Cable guy, bodyguards, cleaning lady, pool boy, whatever. Anybody with access."

Friend opened his svelte rhino-skin briefcase, took out a typed list with names, addresses, and phone numbers. "Already done. Feel free to contact any of them. We've already instructed them to answer any questions you might have."

"Which one's the psychic?" I said.

Ratkin's eyebrow twitched. "I left him off. I don't want him involved in this."

"Dammit—"

"Look, we know he wasn't involved, okay?" Friend said. "I already had a PI in Nashville check him out. He lives in Nashville, and he flew back the night before the murder. He was having lunch in broad daylight with three people when the murder happened. Forget him. Scratch him off your list."

What could I do? If Ratkin wouldn't tell me, he wouldn't tell me.

"I'd like to go by the house," I said. "It's a long shot, but with an obsessive freak like this guy, who knows, he might still be hanging around somewhere."

"Good. And while you're there," Ratkin said, "The security office in the staff house has the records of the investigation they did when he was following Georgia around on the tour last year. It didn't get very far, but there might be something useful there."

CHAPTER 24

I PULLED MY old Cadillac up to the gate of Georgia Burnett's farm and studied the layout. Fronting the two-lane rural road was an eight-foot stone fence with a bare electric wire running along the top. Behind the electrified fence was a stand of trees that sheltered the house from the view of the road.

The wrought iron gate was arched, twelve feet high or so, and swung inward on two arcs of metal track. A wooden guard shack stood to the left of the gate. Just in front of the guardhouse, a stainless steel post stuck up four feet out of the grass. Mounted at the top of the post was an intercom and an access keypad for opening the gate. Weeds had grown up along the road since the last time I had visited, and a custom-painted For Sale sign touting the property had appeared.

I noted that a video camera was mounted on the fence to the left of the gate so that anyone punching in a code on the security keypad or stopping to talk to the guard could be easily videotaped. That must have been the source of the video that Marla had given to Ratkin.

I punched in the code, and the gate swung smoothly inward. The Cadillac crunched slowly up the stone drive through a stand of maples, oaks, poplars, and sweet gum trees, then broke out into the open pasture in front of the house.

After parking in the semicircular drive of crushed rock that lay in front of the house, I got out of the car. Although weeds had sprung up everywhere around the house, a hay baler had recently been run through the pastures. Big round bales were lined up at the far edges of each pasture.

I walked around behind the building, scanned the woods. I assumed that if the Creepy Guy had in fact been hanging around prior to the murder, he wouldn't have come back to the same little hummock he'd been on before. Unless Marla was an idiot—and she wasn't— she would have made sure that her team patrolled down there periodically.

I wandered through the stables. The horses were all gone, and the rich stink of animals and manure and feed—though still lingering—had lost its pungency. It was very cold, and I realized I hadn't dressed as warmly as I should have, so I didn't hang around long.

I started walking down the path toward the woods, the same one I'd ridden on with the big security guard, Ben Pryor. It seemed a hell of a lot further on foot in cold weather than it had on horseback on that beautiful Indian-summer day back in October. After a while I started jogging just to keep warm.

As I was jogging, I tried to think like a stalker. If I'd already been caught in the act once, then obviously I'd have to be more careful this time around. I would want to avoid the place where I'd been caught before. I'd also want to avoid the horse trails where I'd be easy to spot. But at the same time, I'd still want to be in a position where my telescope would have a clear view of the house.

Unfortunately this strategy didn't lead me to any evidence of Creepy Guy's presence. The lower edge of the pasture butted right up against a hardwood bottom, with only a wire fence dividing the two areas. When I got to

the edge of the pasture, I worked my way along the

forest side of the fence. It was slow going; brushy and
choked with briars. It was a good enough place to hide,
but the lay of the land wasn't right: the curvature of the
terrain rising up across the pasturage blocked off any
view of the house. That was why the hillock where
Creepy Guy was camping had jumped out at me the first
time I'd come here: It was the only spot on the back
side of the property with a clear view of the house.

I spent a good two hours working my way through creek
bottoms, woods, and even skirting the edge of an over-
grown jungle of recently replanted clearcut to the north
of the property, but I found nothing for my trouble. No
suspicious trails, no apparent hideouts, no cast-off food
containers, no tents.

I was freezing and frustrated and bleeding from a
dozen briar scratches by the time I headed back up the
hill, my fingers numb and my feet full of pins and nee-
dles. At the top of the hill I fumbled with the keys to
the staff house, finally opened the door, went inside.
Unlike the huge "cottage" next door, this house had a
distinctly middle American feel. Cheap wooden panel-
ing, decorative touches in the icky greens of the early
'70s, hollow core doors, worn shag carpet. It had obviously been the original farmhouse back before Georgia
had built her big house—back when this had been a
working farm. Though the house was not as frigid as
the outdoors, I could still see my breath blossoming in
the still air each time I exhaled. I cranked up the thermostat and was gratified to hear the sound of the gas
furnace going *whooomph* in the basement.

I wandered through the house. Ben Pryor and Marla
Jeter had bunked here, but there was no particular sign
of recent habitation. All the rooms were bare and empty
except for the one that had been Marla's office.

The office—a wood-paneled room that had probably
once been a den—contained the same cheap desk, the
same computer, the same cheap copier, the same bank
of television monitors and VCRs, and the same gray

filing cabinet as it had when I had come here during the kidnapping investigation in October. The only thing new was a light coating of dust on every surface.

I dug around in the filing cabinet until I found the file on the Creepy Guy. The first item in the file was a brief, single-spaced report signed by an investigator for the Nashville branch of Wackenhut, an international private investigation outfit. The upshot of the report was that they had been unable to turn up the guy's identity. As Marla had told me some months earlier, Creepy Guy had been using the name of Robert Smith, but that had turned out to be a bogus identity.

They had been successful in obtaining his fingerprints off a glass, but had not gotten a hit when they ran them through AFIS or the Tennessee Bureau of Investigation's fingerprint system. I flipped through the file to look at the supporting documentation. Whatever you want to say about corporate outfits like Wackenhut or Pinkerton, they do good paperwork. Surveillance reports indicated they had tailed "Robert Smith" for about a month. He had stayed in moderate-priced hotels, driving from city to city of the tour in a black Toyota Land Cruiser. The surveillance reports revealed nothing especially remarkable—other than the fact that the guy managed to support himself without working. That suggested somebody with an independent income. "Robert Smith" had either saved up a lot of money, or he had a trust fund.

At the back of the documentation was a sheet that read "Fingerprint Search Itinerary" at the top. There was a long list of fingerprint databases with little boxes next to them. The only ones that had been checked were the AFIS and the TBI state system. Among the databases they hadn't used were some private systems, military databases, foreign databases, the RCMP's computer, Interpol, and some with cryptic acronyms that I'd never even heard of. It was a pretty normal thing to limit your search to those two databases. But still, it made me wonder: what if we ran some more databases? It was worth a shot.

I turned on the little desktop copier, copied everything, and put the report back in the file.

Just for yucks, I turned on the video equipment. The
monitor blinked to life, giving me a view of the front
gate. I checked the VCR that was used to record the
images, but there was no tape in the machine. I checked
the room to see if there were any old tapes lying around,
but there weren't. Most likely the Floyd County investigators had taken them away.

I sat in the room for a while, thinking. Had "Robert
Smith" been scared off for good when we found his
hideout two months ago? My sense was that obsessive
freaks like Smith didn't get scared off that easily. But I
hadn't found any hidey-holes out in the woods.

Well, it was irrelevant. The guy was probably long
gone by now. I couldn't think of anything else to investigate, but I kept sitting there anyway. The truth was,
the house had gotten nice and warm, and I didn't feel
like going back out in the cold.

Down in the basement the gas furnace came on again,
making its deep *whooomph* sound. Suddenly a thought
struck me. The crawl space.

I turned off the thermostat, locked the staff quarters,
and walked briskly over to the big house, making my
way around the perimeter of the building until I found
what I was looking for: a small plywood door set in the
base of the house. The access to the crawl space. A small
padlock dangled from the latch—but when I touched it,
the lock snapped open. Someone had set it to make it
appear to be locked—when, in fact, it was not. I had a
sneaking suspicion I knew who would have done a thing
like that.

I felt enough of a nervous prickling on the back of
my neck to make me draw my pistol before opening the
door and ducking into the crawlspace. The space was
dark and cold, dirt-floored, with pink insulation jammed
up in the spaces between the joists. I pulled the string
on a bare bulb mounted on the wall. The light revealed

a swarm of ugly hunch-backed cave crickets along the brick.

I forged into the darkness, my eyes adjusting enough to see a trail of scuff marks in the red clay. Someone had worn through the dusting of pale mildew that covered the dirt. I followed the trail slowly—first bent over, then eventually on my knees as the floor sloped gently up toward the joists. I still had the Smith & Wesson clutched in my right hand.

I have never liked the dark. I have never liked enclosed spaces. I have never liked cave crickets. Crazed stalkers were never high on my list either, for that matter. But I kept going anyway, deeper and deeper into the darkness until finally I was going by feel alone. The only sound I could hear was the shuffling scrape of my knees on the clay and the rushing of my blood in my ears.

It had grown so dark that I could see nothing at all.

I was finally about to give up when suddenly the ground fell out from under me and I pitched forward. As I hit the ground I heard the bang of a gun and light from a muzzle flash exploded, briefly illuminating the dirt floor around me.

Then I was blind.

CHAPTER 25

I HOUGH IT PROBABLY only took me the span of a few
seconds to figure out what had happened, those few
seconds seemed an endless stretch of terror. As I had
fallen forward, my finger had tightened reflexively on
the trigger of the Smith. It had been my own gun that
had gone off. As my panic subsided and my heart
slowed from its jackhammer pace, I realized I was lucky
as hell not to have shot myself.

I lay there for a while, my eyes slowly adjusting again
to the dark. Above me, I could see something hanging
from the joists: another pull string for a light. I felt
something soft under me, smelled the stink of sweat and
mildew.

I reached up and grabbed the string, pulled it sharply.
Suddenly the area where I lay was flooded with light.
Again I got that prickly feeling on my neck.

My God, I thought, looking around. It was all here.

Robert Smith—or whatever his real name was—had
been living under Georgia's house. He had hollowed out
a coffin-sized hole, put a sleeping bag at the bottom. It
was into that hole that I'd fallen. Mounted on one of the
joists above me was a blue, plastic electrical junction box
full of neat splices. Spidering out from the blue box in all

directions was a maze of electrical cords. Apparently our boy had tapped into the electrical system. One cord ran down to a space heater, another to a two-burner hotplate, still another to a square metal box sitting on the clay floor. After examining it carefully, I realized the metal box was some sort of filter with a powerful fan inside. You had to give the guy credit: he was filtering his cooking fumes so that no one upstairs would smell him.

There was another wire dangling down, but it didn't seem to be connected to anything. I examined it and realized it wasn't a power cord, but a coaxial cable, the kind used for cable TV lines. All the comforts of home—the son of a bitch was even picking up free cable!

A sick feeling ran through me: we'd chased this creep off the hillside two months earlier, only to drive him closer to the source of his obsession.

I ran my finger across the surface of one of the stove burners. It was thick with dust. "Robert Smith" obviously hadn't been here for a long time. I felt a mild sense of relief. Even with the gun, I didn't relish running into the guy down here.

I decided I'd better not touch anything else. It was time to get the cops involved. Maybe this would convince them that this wasn't a murder-for-hire conspiracy after all.

I drove to the Floyd County Police office, which is located in a brand-spanking-new building just off Broad Street in Rome, told a nice lady sitting behind a bulletproof glass window that I was looking for the investigator in charge of the Georgia Burnett murder. Several convict trustees in white jumpsuits were milling around in the lobby staring at me while keeping up the vaguest pretense that they were emptying a wastebasket.

After a while a civilian aide led me upstairs and down a long hallway to an office that said Chief of Police Ray

Robard on the door. "I wanted to talk to the lead investigator," I said. "Not the chief of police."

The aide was a good-natured woman with a plump face that was half covered by a bright-red birth mark. "He *is* the lead investigator," she said.

"Oh." Great. So some small-town Barney Fife was leading the charge here. The guy probably couldn't fill out a traffic ticket and here he was leading a complex murder investigation. No surprise they had jumped so quickly to the conclusion that a rich, long-haired Jew from Nashville had hired somebody to whack his own wife.

"Hi there, hon," the police chief said pleasantly, getting up and shaking my hand, then ushering me to a chair with a hand on my arm.

"You know who I am, I assume?"

"Sure, sure," the police chief of Floyd County said, smiling. He was lean and hard looking, about forty years old, with the look of a man who exercised a lot. He wasn't quite the Barney Fife I'd expected. On the credenza behind him was a varnished two-by-four with a gold painted sixteen-penny nail sticking out of it. Carved into the side were the words NAIL THE BASTARD. Next to it was a trophy for practical pistol shooting. I revised my diagnosis: even worse, he was a small-town cop who wanted to be a gunfighter. "Well, what can I do you for, Miss Childs?"

I told the chief all about the information I had on Creepy Guy, explained to him about what I'd found in the basement of Georgia's house.

He made a little tent of his fingers and looked thoughtful. "Interesting," he said after a moment.

Then about a minute and a half of silence.

"Uh," I said. "Does that mean you're going to take a look?"

He narrowed his eyes slightly. He seemed vaguely amused by me. "See, I know what y'all think about us down there in the big city. You think country cops are a bunch of dopes who know zero about real law enforcement. May be true of some redneck sheriffs and county mounties in the state of Georgia, but not this one. I was a homicide investigator up in Charlotte, North Carolina, until five years ago. I'm not some dipshit who jumps to conclusions based on zero evidence, or some hick fool who thinks it would be dandy to throw a long-haired Jew in prison just because the voters find such things amusing, or some jerk who fabricates or ignores evidence. The reason I'm leading this investigation personally is because I happen to know more about homicide investigation than anybody in this part of the state."

I felt a little sheepish. He'd just kicked over every suspicion I'd been developing about him since the case began. "So you'll check it out?"

"Of *course* I'll check it out." He looked moderately insulted. "Anything else, Miss Childs?"

I shook my head.

The chief stood up. "We *will* check this out, hon. I'm embarrassed we didn't find it ourselves. We should have, and it's my screwup. I'll send the GBI crime scene people in there and if there's blood or anything else to change a reasonable man's mind about who killed Georgia Burnett, than I'll do the right thing."

"That's all I ask." I stopped, turned toward Robard.

Robard smiled, then steered me gently by the elbow all the way to the front door of the building, just as he had steered me to my seat earlier. It wasn't as obnoxious or condescending as it sounds: it was just a gesture, the kind of thing a well-bred man does in Floyd County.

I had gotten to my car when I heard the chief call out to me. "This ain't gonna change a thing, Ms. Childs. We got Gunnar Brushwood nailed. When I nail a man, he stays nailed."

I drove home with an ominous feeling in my gut. For the first time I wondered. This chief seemed like a straight shooter. If he said he had Gunnar nailed, he meant it. What evidence did they have that we hadn't found yet?

A question kept worming around in my head: *could* Gunnar have done a thing like this? Sometimes I used to sit around in the trophy room of his house, all those dead animals looking down at me, wondering what moves a man to killing on that kind of scale. And to this day I had never come up with a satisfactory answer.

No. But it couldn't be. I *knew* Gunnar. Didn't I?

CHAPTER 26

"**Y**EEEE-HAH," BARRINGTON CHERRY said dryly.

I had wanted to knock some ideas around, so I'd called up and asked him to meet me back at my loft. Now he was sitting on the floor, drinking a bottle of Sam Adams and wincing. I'd put on a Buck Owen CD, the *Live at Carnegie Hall* album, and it didn't seem to agree with him.

"Hey, this is one of the great country records of all time!" I said.

"That's precisely the trouble," he said.

I laughed, then got serious, updating him on what I'd learned today. "Something's troubling me about all of this," I concluded. "I'd like to believe Ratkin's theory, that it was this wacko who did the deed, this Creepy Guy. But people like this just don't come out of the woodwork. Wackenhut ran this guy's latents through AFIS and nothing came up. It seems hard to believe such a sick bastard could make it this far without any sort of police record."

"Which leads us back to the theory that he was part of the kidnapping setup."

"And if he was part of the kidnapping, then Ratkin's a lying scumbag."

"Which means that Gunnar—"

"No!" I cut Barrington off. "No. That's not on the table here."

Barrington took a pull on his beer, his face betraying nothing. I could see he wasn't convinced, though, that he never had been.

"So, let's assume that this guy under the house is the real deal," I said. "What's a logical explanation for why he isn't in the computer?"

"Got me."

"Take a look at this," I said, pulling the Wackenhut report out of my briefcase and setting it on the floor next to Barrington's leg. He picked it up and leafed slowly through it.

"Seems pretty thorough," he said finally, closing the file. "I mean they could have run the prints through some additional databases. There are some private databases, foreign databases, stuff like that. But that's a long shot. AFIS is the best database available, and they ran it through there."

I looked at him for a moment, a thought running through my mind. "Something just struck me. When I talked to Marla Jeter back in October, she said something that seemed odd. She said that this guy, Creepy Guy, he never spoke. He'd come backstage after the concerts and sometimes he'd give Georgia a note saying that he'd enjoyed the show or something. But never a word."

"So?" Barrington said.

"AFIS is an American database, right? So most of the criminals in the database will be American. Stands to reason."

Barrington raised his eyebrows slightly. "So what if he was a foreigner? If he'd talked, they'd have heard the accent. But he never talked."

I nodded.

"Well," Barrington said. "It's a thought."

"It *is* a thought," I said. After a moment I took out

the card that Chief Robard had given me, went over to my phone and dialed his direct line.

"Chief," I said. "It's Sunny Childs."

"Oh, hey." He sounded distinctly unthrilled to hear from me.

"You have your guys take a look under the house?"

"Uh-huh."

"Find any fingerprints."

"I can't tell you that!" the Chief said.

"Reason I'm curious, I've already got a pretty clean set of latents that an investigator picked up from a guy who was stalking Georgia last year. I believe it to be the same guy as the one under the house."

"So?"

"The investigator ran them through AFIS about six months ago, and nothing came up. What I'd like to do is fax them over to you. If you get any prints out from under that house, you could compare them and see if they're the same."

There was a long pause. "I appreciate your taking time out of your busy schedule to assist our investigation." The Chief's voice was cool. "But that doesn't mean I'm going to help *you* out."

"Sure. But here's the thing. I don't think this guy is an American. I have reason to believe that he has a record in another country."

"You have reason to believe. Like, *what* reason?"

"I can't really reveal that to you." I hoped Chief Robard didn't have his blarney meter tuned too high.

"What country?"

"I don't have that information."

Suddenly Barrington pulled my sleeve. "Interpol!" he whispered urgently. "Interpol has a new multi-jurisdiction system."

"All I'm saying," I said, "is if you could run it through the Interpol computer, it would help."

"*Interpol!*" The Chief laughed. "Hon, you think maybe this boy's already killed him a string of country and western singers over in Belgium? Maybe South Korea? Mozambique?"

"Look," I said. "If you run it through Interpol and the guy comes up clean, that's just one more nail in my client's coffin."

After a long pause, Chief Robard said, "I'll think about it."

CHAPTER 27

FOR NEARLY A week Barrington and I spent fourteen hours a day driving to every hotel, motel, bed-and-breakfast, and rooming house in upstate Georgia fruitlessly pushing blurry surveillance photos of "Robert Smith" in front of people who had never seen him. Or claimed not to have. Or didn't care one way or the other. I went by to see Gunnar a couple of times at the Floyd County Jail. The second time I went, he had a black eye because another inmate had tried to steal his shoes. After that I couldn't face him anymore.

But then one evening as I came out of yet another crummy motel office down on the Stewart Avenue porn strip in Atlanta, my cell phone rang.

"Chief Robard here," the voice said.

"Working late, huh?" I said. Out the window of my Cadillac I watched a Jeep pull up next to a bony white woman in a miniskirt. A transaction was arranged under the dim streetlight, then the woman got in the Jeep and they drove off into the darkness. "To what do I owe the pleasure?"

"Tomorrow morning makes ten days to trial," the chief said.

"And?"

"As I'm sure you know, state law requires us to turn over all forensic evidence to the defense within ten days of trial."

It took me a moment. "You got a hit on the fingerprint," I said.

"Uh-huh."

"How long have you been sitting on this?"

"Honey, no offense, but this is a courtesy call. I could have buried this information in the back of the chem lab attachments to the ME's report and you wouldn't have found it for another three days."

"You're right. I'm sorry. It's been a crappy week. So what did you find?"

"First, we didn't find any prints under the house. Everything was wiped clean. But because I'm a thorough guy, I ran the prints you sent me through the Interpol computer. They came up with a match. An Australian national by the name of Ian Bollard. Looks like he was a bad boy Down Under."

"What did he do?"

"Can't tell exactly. Spent three years in prison in Queensland. I don't know if that's the name of a prison or what. I'll fax you the report."

Suddenly I felt a spurt of hope. "Chief," I said. "You're a good man."

"I know that," he said.

When I got back to my loft, the Interpol report was lying in the bin of my fax machine. Like most crime computer reports, it was a bit cryptic—but clearly Ian Bollard had been convicted of something fairly serious.

I looked at my alarm clock. 8:15. I wondered what time it was in Australia. Somewhere around nine or ten in the morning maybe? I pulled out my National Geographic atlas of the world and peered at it for a while.

Then I made an international call, got hold of an information operator in Australia, and had them connect me to the police department in Brisbane, the biggest city in the province of Queensland.

It took me about fifteen minutes, paying god knows what kind of extortionate telephone rates, but I finally reached a Detective Inspector Archie Loomis in the Queensland Police Service who claimed to have heard of Ian Bollard. Loomis had a nasal Australian twang, and the scratchy throat of a three-pack-a-day man.

"Made a bit of a splish, actually," he said.

"What for?"

"He's one of those celeb stalkers."

"Hallelujah," I said. "You are officially my hero for today."

"You heard of Tori Nilssen, the actress?"

"No."

"She's a big film star down here. She was in *Missing Edgar*. Did you catch that one?"

"I'm afraid I missed it."

"Damn funny picture, that." Detective Inspector Archie Loomis began going into a long and involved description of the movie's plot.

Finally I interrupted. "Not that I'm not interested. . . ."

"Oh, sorry, dear, sorry. I've a tendency to run on a bit. Anyway, like I said, Tori Nilssen is this film star. This arsehole Bollard started following her around, you know, showing up wherever she was going and that. Next thing you know, they find he's been living under her bloody house. She gets him arrested for trespassing, but he's got a good lawyer, and he ends up walking away, promises to check into a madhouse, go to a psychiatrist and that. Well, as soon as they let him out of psychiatric hospital, he shows up at her door with flowers and candy—you know, like he was about to go on a bleddy date. She starts screaming, he barges in, starts going at her with a knife.

"Lucky for her, she was dating some chap who was a karate expert or some'ink. He beats the bleddy snot out of this Bollard. This time they throw the book at him. Turns out he'd done some similar things in Adelaide a couple of years earlier. Not with a film star, you know, but the same general pattern. Stalking some poor bird, slowly escalates, he ends up thumping her about a bit."

"Thumping her about?"

"You know, assaulting her. Bit nasty actually. Believe he used a cricket bat."

"A cricket bat," I said. "That's like a baseball bat, isn't it?"

"Bit like that, yeah. Long, flat piece of wood. The bowler throws the ball at the wicket, the batsman tries to hit the ball with it."

"I assume you have access to the records on all that stuff?"

"Sure."

"Can you fax them to me?"

There was a brief pause. "You said you're in law enforcement?"

"I'm a private detective."

Maybe it was just satellite delay, but it seemed like he hesitated for a beat or two. "Oh. That makes it a bit more difficult. The international angle and that. Bit fussy about paperwork round here."

"This guy has killed somebody here in the States. A famous country singer."

There was a long pause. "Georgia Burnett, is it? I saw some' ink about that on the telly. I fancy country and western music a bit, myself." He started singing *Your Cheating Heart*, fantastically out of key, and with a wretched voice. He had forged deep into the second verse before I cut in.

"Sorry!" Detective Inspector Archie Loomis said pleasantly. "Running on again, eh? Anyway . . . hold on! I thought her husband got nicked for that already."

"He did. But this evidence about Bollard has just popped up. It's looking like the police made a mistake."

"Wait a minute, wait a minute!" Loomis sounded angry. "Are you telling me you're representing a *defendant* in this case?"

Cops, they were the same the world over. Didn't want to give defendants the time of day.

"It's the same MO!" I said. "Sleeping under the house. Spying on her through a telescope. Killed with a baseball bat. It's *him*, sir. It's got to be Bollard."

I could hear a match firing, the lighting of a cigarette. "All the crazy bastards in the States, you had to find an Australian to blame it on?"

"He was *there*. He was in her house."

"How do you know that?"

I stretched the truth more than a little. "Where do you think we got the fingerprints from?"

The Australian sighed. "Tell you what, let me check with my boss, see what he says. Maybe we can get you the information."

"I'll need the investigation files on both those two cases, plus any other criminal convictions he's had, plus any history of psychiatric evaluations, commitments or whatever."

"I'll see what I can do."

"We're less than two weeks from trial. If that information doesn't get here in time, two innocent men are going to the electric chair!"

"Yeah, yeah, yeah," Loomis said distantly.

As soon as I got off the phone, I called Quentin. "Habeas corpus," he said when I finished gushing about my big breakthrough.

"Huh?" I said.

"That's Latin for 'Bring out the body.'"

"I know what it means," I said.

"My point, this is fine work, hon, don't get me wrong—but we got to have the man. We got to have him in the actual flesh. We got to put this sumbitch Bollard on the stand."

"But if we've got the records—"

"Records, hell, even if we get every police file in the entire country of Australia, that don't mean dook at trial. For any records involving criminal activity by Bollard to be admissible in court, they got to have foundation. To get foundation, we got to fly a detective up from Australia to testify as to the authenticity of the documents. Meantime, we got no subpoena power outside the confines of the United States, no way to compel some Australian cop to fly up here, and a budget that, frankly, is not bottomless."

"Jesus. I hadn't thought of that."

"Bollard's who we need, Sunny. Ian Bollard, in the flesh."

"Okay."

"Find him or we got nothing."

"I understand. But we've been beating the bushes and—"

"Just goddamn *find* him!"

I set down the phone feeling considerably more subdued than I had when I'd picked it up.

CHAPTER 28

THE NEXT MORNING I went out for a doughnut at the Krispy Kreme down on Ponce. When I came back I found a terse message from Quentin on my machine. "Ten o'clock, Sunny, meet me at the Floyd County Jail."

The interview room at the jail. Same old hateful smells and sounds. I was starting to dread the place the way you start to hate the smell of a hospital when you've been sick.

I got there before Quentin, so I had the guards go ahead and bring Gunnar in. I told him about Bollard and for the first time since he'd been inside he started to look hopeful. His black eye was even beginning to fade.

Then Quentin showed up.

The lawyer sat down hard in his chair, and I sensed something different about him. He'd been working without a break for weeks now, but it was more than just that. He looked somehow betrayed.

"What?" Gunnar said finally.

Quentin opened his briefcase. "The DA sent over the forensic material today. ME's report, Crime Lab results, so on." He pulled out a piece of paper, tossed it in front of Gunnar.

"Could you put my reading glasses on, darling?" Gunnar said. With his hands shackled, he couldn't get at the glasses in the pocket of his prison jumpsuit. I took them out, slid them on his nose. He looked down at the piece of paper Quentin had put in front of him. His eyes narrowed slightly, then his face went white, and he literally fell backward so hard he nearly slid out of his chair. It was as though someone had momentarily disconnected his brain from his muscles.

"What is it?" I said.

"You want to goddamn *explain* that, Gunnar?" Quentin said.

I pulled the piece of paper over to me. It was a report on GBI Crime Laboratory stationery, a fingerprint comparison signed by the lab's fingerprint expert.

The report summarized the results of a comparison of two fingerprints: print number one was a standard rolled booking card impression inked when Gunnar was arrested; print number two was a latent left in the blood found on the bat that had been taken from Gunnar's trunk. The crime lab's fingerprint man had found seventeen matches between the two prints.

The room was silent for a long time as Quentin stared accusingly at Gunnar's ashen face.

Finally Gunnar looked up. "I never touched that bat, Quentin. Never."

"Then how'd your bloody fingerprint get on there?"

Gunnar looked at the lawyer for a long time, then looked at me. "Tell him, Sunny," he said in a soft, pleading voice. "You *know* me. You *know* I didn't do this thing."

What could I say? I just sat there. After a minute the tears started coming down my face.

Gunnar stood up then, shuffled backward to the door, and started kicking it with the heel of his shoe. His leg chains jangled musically. "Guard! Guard! Get me back to my cell you rotten sons of bitches!"

ON TRIAL

CHAPTER 29

T **HE PHONE CALL** to Australia had been our high-water mark. I was dead sure that I'd found the real killer and that I had my fingers only inches away from the evidence needed to prove it. But then day by day, everything had gone to hell.

The Brisbane police were dragging their feet on sending us Ian Bollard's files. They claimed it was all about their internal procedures, but I suspected it had more to do with the fact that they were cops and we were defendants, and so they were going to kick and scream and jerk us around as much as they possibly could.

Quentin had been feverishly working government channels, had hired a barrister in Brisbane who was filing motions on Gunnar and Ratkin's behalf and was on the phone to Australia for hours every day. But it was no good. Other than the Interpol fingerprint report, we had not received a single scrap of paper detailing Ian Bollard's criminal record.

Getting a witness from Australia? Sh'yeah, right. Even the prospect of a free vacation to the States was not enough to entice Detective Inspector Archie Loomis or any of his compeers from down under to come up here and testify.

And still, there was the fingerprint on the bat. No wonder Chief Robard had been so cocksure.

Our last, distant hope—Ian Bollard. And he was nowhere to be found.

There's a strange and almost dreamlike quality about a murder trial. Every sensation is heightened, every breath signifies, every emotion becomes mysteriously concentrated.

And when it's a trial like this one, complete with crowds of reporters, TV trucks pulled up on every sidewalk, mobs of fans and thrill seekers and wackos milling around—you can't escape it. Every bad feeling, every setback, every twinge of self-doubt and mistrust reverberates through your mind till you feel like you've got your head jammed up inside some huge clanging cathedral bell. I couldn't even turn on the TV without being assaulted by the trial. Every day teenage girls and sad looking old women carrying crude, hand-lettered signs on flimsy posterboard—WE'LL ALWAYS REMEMBER! and GEORGIA LIVES! and FRY THE BASTARDS!—would mob the jail, screaming abuse at the unmarked cars that transported Gunnar and Ratkin from the jail to the courthouse. Everyone connected to the trial received hate mail and threatening phone calls.

People approached me in restaurants—sometimes to insult me, sometimes to ask for an autograph. As the trial approached, I had to change my phone number twice in one week. The bell-clang of trial was everywhere, and I couldn't get my mind straight.

Barrington Cherry and I had continued canvassing every hotel, motel, flophouse, bed-and-breakfast, and rooming house in upstate Georgia in the increasingly desperate attempt to locate Ian Bollard. We'd printed up hundreds of copies of his picture from the surveillance photos taken earlier in the year, we'd passed out fliers, we'd done everything we could think of. We'd even hired somebody to make us a goddamn web site. And

Ian Bollard was nowhere to be found. So amid all the frenzy and activity there was one constant, a sickening sense that time was running out.

As the district attorney of Floyd County stood up, buttoned the jacket of his best blue suit, and walked to the podium in Courtroom A of the Floyd County Courthouse, we were no closer to clearing Gunnar than we had been a month earlier.

The district attorney of Floyd County was a young man named Gorin Maples, reeking of ambition, who had the look of a deacon at the First Baptist Church. Which I imagine he was. His short blond hair was already thinning at the age of thirty-two; his blue suit had a Rotary Club pin on the lapel; his small, pale, wretched, vain mustache served only to highlight—rather than cover—the scar left by an operation for a cleft palate. But he had the confidence that comes with knowing he was riding a winner. And that trumps a good mustache any day of the week.

Maples walked gravely to the podium, looked at the jury and made his speech. He used no notes and didn't stutter, pause, hesitate, or lose his way. And when, on a couple of occasions, he got worked up, he strutted around the room like a Pentecostal preacher calling down judgment on the wicked, striding manfully and waving his arms at the ceiling. In short, he put on a good show.

When he was done with the facts of the case, he paused for a moment and just looked at the jury. "Now we're all aware of the spotlight that is shining upon this room. Only a liar or a fool would claim that that light is not seductive or distracting. I've already had calls from movie producers and agents from New York. And once this thing is over, y'all may get some of those calls, too. But when the bright lights fade, and the TV cameras are turned off, and the reporters have wandered away to gaze upon the next appalling tragedy, you and I will be left with the stillness of our own hearts.

"All I ask is that you listen to the testimony and the evidence with care, and then consult with your heart. If you do that, this case will be appallingly, horrifically simple."

Gorin Maples sat down, and Quentin stood up. Ratkin's lawyer, Mike Friend, had wisely opted to let him make the main opening remarks.

The past month had been nothing but one sixteen-hour day after another for Quentin Senior, Jr. But today he looked like the very archetype of all masculinity, all staunchness, all self-assurance, all male beauty. He wore a charcoal gray suit tailored to flatter all that remained of the body that had made him an All-American tight end—broad in the shoulder, lean in the hip, tall in the saddle.

Quentin was famous for shmoozing juries, for seducing them, for kissing up to them. But that didn't seem to be his strategy today. Today he was brooding and angry—sort of like the figure of Moses, righteously pissed.

"What kind of *fools* does the district attorney take us for?" he said finally. His face wore a small, scornful smile. "Listen to your *hearts*? Let me tell you something, folks, if you listen to your hearts, you will be nauseated, because what this case has been about from the get-go is publicity. It's been about a famous woman dying tragically. It's been about rounding up one of the leading record executives in America and one of the most distinguished private investigators and slapping them in jail without the least semblance of due process in order to glorify and magnify the career of one Gorin B. Maples, attorney at law. Moreover—"

At this point the DA popped up and said, "Your honor! He's making an argument!"

The judge—a thin dyspeptic old guy named Roynell Deaks—pushed a pair of ugly black-framed glasses up on his nose, then lifted his gavel and pointed it at Quentin Senior, Jr. "Mr. Senior," he said in a grating little voice, "I better not have to instruct you on how to do your job. Talk about the evidence or don't talk at all. You want to make an argument, you better wait till the end of trial."

Quentin smiled at the jury then, like: *See? Didn't I tell you how this would go?*

For all intents and purposes Quentin had declared war—not just on Maples, but on Deaks. Because, as he had explained to us earlier, Judge Deaks was the man in charge out here. Maples was just Deaks's front man. It was a dangerous strategy. But what else could we do?

"I'm sorry, folks." Suddenly the look of anger and passion slid off Quentin's face. "I've forgotten myself. My job right now is to talk about evidence. The judge is right. I'm angry and I let my anger carry me away." Anybody who knew anything about Quentin Senior, Jr. knew that he was full of it, that everything he did was planned down to the least detail.

Quentin smiled easily. "The judge wants me to talk about evidence? Let's talk about evidence," he said. "I listened to that whole speech Mr. Maples made, and you know what I never heard? I never heard about the stalker."

Quentin's eyes widened and he stood there letting the words sink in. "The stalker! I never heard Mr. Maples mention the fellow who followed Ms. Burnett from city to city for six months, showing up in restaurants and bars and theaters and coliseums and hotel lobbies, silently watching her with a frightening and predatory gleam in his eye. I never heard Mr. Maples mention how the stalker terrorized Ms. Burnett. I never heard Mr. Maples mention how she filed a restraining order against the stalker in the state of Tennessee. I never heard him mention how the stalker camped out on a hill on Ms. Burnett's beautiful piece of property over there on Little Texas Valley Road and watched the most intimate details of her life through a thirty-power telescope.

"I never heard him mention how Ms. Burnett was kid-

napped and held for ransom by person or persons unknown not two months ago. I never heard Mr. Maples
mention how the stalker had slithered up under Ms. Burnett's house, hollowed him out a dirty little hole to sleep
in, wired himself up a little rat's nest not ten feet from
where she ate breakfast and not thirty feet from where
she was beaten to death. I never heard Mr. Maples mention how this sick little man sat down under that house
cooking his meals in secret, sleeping in secret, dreaming
his foul and secret dreams.

"That stalker is not fiction, folks. That stalker exists.
He's the one who killed Georgia Burnett. And before
this trial is over, we're gonna put a name and a face on
him. We're gonna convince you that he not only had the
opportunity and the means—but unlike these other two
gentlemen, he had the motive."

"Now as y'all know, folks, the state gets the opportunity to make its case first. And you're going to hear a
lot of *circumstantial* evidence about Mr. Brushwood and
Mr. Ratkin. I guarantee you they'll pile it high. Indirect.
Circumstantial. Over-the-hill-and-around-the-bend. But
high, brother. Oh, yes, very high!" Quentin's voice had
taken on the tone of church orator. Maples hadn't done
a bad job in that department, but he looked pretty pale
in comparison to the old master.

"See, folks, what they won't be able to do is show
you evidence demonstrating that these are the kind of
men who'd do a thing as horrible and sickening as beating a young and beautiful and innocent and talented
woman to death. Only a monster could do a thing like
this. As we will demonstrate, the defendants are men of
spotless character, men of stature, men who don't have
so much as a ticket for jaywalking on their records. So
keep asking yourself as they pile up all these little co-
incidences and little innocent mistakes and little bitty
technical-sounding pieces of forensic whoopty-do—
keep asking yourself this: Has the state yet shown me a
man with the mind of a monster?

"Because, folks, the time will come when the defense *will* have the opportunity to show you the mind of a predatory monster." Quentin's eyes widened. "The time will come! And when it does, we'll show you who *really* did this horrible crime.

"So stay tuned, folks. Listen hard, listen skeptically, and stay tuned."

After the speech, we broke for lunch and headed across the street to a little café called the Partridge Restaurant.

"Well, Quentin," I said. "That was certainly . . . tantalizing."

Quentin smiled tightly. "You mean because I never mentioned Ian Bollard by name."

I nodded.

We took a moment to order. At the Partridge, the waitress doesn't write down your order; instead you have to circle the items in pencil on a barely legible photocopied menu. I went with the chicken livers on rice, plus turnip greens and pickled beets.

"Truth is, Sunny," Quentin said after the waitress had carried off our orders, "we don't have any admissible evidence yet to prove that Ian Bollard was under that house, or staring through that telescope, or doing much of anything else besides going to a few concerts. If you don't turn up something we can use in the next five, six days, and if we can't pry something out of the goddamn Australian police, then all we got is some dingbat—we don't even know his name—cooking scrambled eggs under Georgia's house."

"You barely mentioned the kidnapping either," I said.

Quentin laughed silently, his eyes squinching up at the corners. "That's the thousand-pound gorilla in this case."

"How do you mean?"

"My whole case, right now, is going to be based on character. I'm laying the groundwork for the worst-case scenario, which is that we don't find Bollard and we don't get anything out of the Australians. In that case, we put up some anonymous creep, this stalker whose name we're barely going to be able to mention. It ain't much, but at this exact moment it's all we got."

Quentin took a sip of his iced tea, flirted with the doughy young waitress, then turned back to me.

"Far as the kidnapping goes, Sunny, I had to at least mention it. Depending on how things go, we may have to use it as a Hail Mary. If we get enough stuff on Bollard, we don't want to touch it with a ten-foot pole, though. Because there's at least the possibility that the state could, ah, shall we say, make a compelling case that it was faked."

"Which would destroy Ratkin and Gunnar's credibility."

"Right. And there goes the character defense, which is the ace in the hole of our the-crazy-man-done-it strategy."

The waitress brought our food and Quentin paused to take a bite of his drumstick.

"Tricky situation," he said after he'd cleaned every scrap of meat off the fried chicken leg. "If I didn't mention the kidnapping at all, Gorin Maples is gonna say, 'Why is he so scared of bringing up the kidnapping? There must be something hinky there.' Then we're in *big* trouble."

"I see," I said.

After lunch I called Barrington on his cell phone. He was still trudging around the state trying to find Ian Bollard. "Any luck?"

"We need a new strategy," he said irritably. "I went to twenty motels this morning. Nothing. Even with a lot more manpower, this whole approach is a loser."

"What choice do we have? I'm open to any suggestions, but right now I don't know anything else we can do."

CHAPTER 30

"**S**TATE CALLS **CHIEF** Ray Robard."

The chief walked up to the front of the courtroom, where he was sworn in. He wore a full-dress uniform, every crease knife sharp, and carried a broad-brimmed hat military style under his arm. When he sat down, he placed the hat carefully on the witness stand next to him. It even had a silver star on the crown like in a cowboy movie. He looked calm, cool, firm, fair, and handsome. From Gorin Maple's perspective, central casting couldn't have handed him a better witness.

For us, it only got worse.

The district attorney went through the preliminaries, and then said, "Chief, when you found out that Georgia Burnett had been murdered, you appointed yourself lead investigator on the case, did you not?"

"Yessir."

"How come you didn't leave it to one of your investigators?"

"Well, sir, I actually had a good deal of homicide experience prior to being named chief of police here."

"Oh?"

On came the litany of experience: seventeen years on the Charlotte, NC, police department. Five years as a homicide detective. Investigated over fifty homicides in his career. Commendations for bravery as a patrolman in Charlotte. Youngest man in the city ever promoted to detective. Highest case-closing stats of any homicide detective in Charlotte. Lead investigator in the successful investigation and prosecution of two of the most complicated murders in Charlotte history. In short, a poster boy for law enforcement.

Robard concluded by saying, "While I have several fine detectives on my staff, the low crime rate we're fortunate enough to have around here means they have limited experience with complicated homicide investigations. Frankly, I have more homicide investigation experience than all my investigators combined. So I figured that in a case which was likely to be as complicated as this, the demand for experience on this thing overrode my natural inclination to delegate."

"Shee-it," Quentin muttered softly.

"I'd like to turn to the day of December 9 of this year. Could you tell us what happened on that day?"

Most law enforcement people tend to jargon you to death with law-enforcement-speak when they get on the stand. It's all "This officer responded to a ten-twenty-one whereby I apprehended a male white who had on or about his person a distinct odor of beverage alcohol" ... and so on. Not Chief Robard. He understood that a jury wanted a story, a story told in human terms with normal words.

"It started with a 911 call," he said. "My office is in the back of the police department. The 911 operator is up front. My door was open that day, as it usually is, and I heard somebody holler up front. Almost like a scream. I thought somebody'd been attacked or something. So I ran up front. When I got there, the gal who handles the 911 line looked up at me and said, 'Georgia Burnett's been killed.'" Chief Robard shrugged. "I can remember the sinking sensation I had."

"So what did you do next?"

Without batting an eye, Robard said, "I put my hat on."

Everyone in the room laughed. Quentin just shook his head. I looked over at the jury and saw that every one of their eyes had eventually come to rest on that hat, that pristine Stetson with the star on it. Hokey? Yes. But it was still a potent symbol of something, some John Wayne notion of righteous authority that everybody in America wants to believe in. Suddenly the laughing stopped and everyone looked a little sheepish.

"My God," Quentin whispered. "Where'd they find this beautiful son of a bitch?"

The DA smiled slightly. "Fair enough. Then what?"

"I contacted the Georgia Bureau of Investigation, authorized them to send up a team of forensic experts. We frankly don't have the depth of technical expertise here in the Floyd County Police Department that a case like this demands. I wanted things done right.

"Then I grabbed every detective in my department, told them what the score was and asked them to accompany me up to Ms. Burnett's farm.

"When we got to the farm, two deputies were already on scene. I've got my boys pretty well trained, so once they had determined that Ms. Burnett was beyond medical help, they had started securing the scene to avoid contamination. I made a cursory examination of the scene."

The district attorney nodded. "What did that examination turn up?"

"Well, what I found was a young woman who appeared to have been beaten to death in her own bedroom. Of course like everybody else, I've seen Ms. Burnett on TV, so I recognized her. But only just barely. She had been beat so bad you could hardly make out who it was.

"There was a good deal of blood in the room. I expect you'll have some additional testimony on that score later, but suffice it to say that there were streaks of blood across the walls and ceiling, indicating that she had been struck repeatedly with a weapon which then slung her blood around the room each time the killer lifted the weapon to hit her again."

Gorin Maples nodded. "So you came to the conclusion this was murder?"

The chief smiled sadly. "Put it this way, sir, she didn't just fall down in the shower."

After that, the chief brought out some charts and showed where the body fell. Then came a photograph, blown up for the jury to see. The DA put it on an easel that was aimed discreetly so that only the jury could see it. But Maples made sure to flash the media a brief glimpse as he was setting it on the easel. It showed a bloody figure, half-naked and streaked with blood, lying in a ragged heap. I'd seen the picture after the defense produced it, but still it shocked me. In some respects it looked less like a woman than like a pile of body parts.

The chief then talked some more about the crime scene. But most of that testimony was obviously being left for the forensic science witnesses.

"Did you question any witnesses?" Gorin Maples asked eventually.

The chief explained that he had questioned the bodyguards, Marla Jeter and Ben Pryor. "At that point, Mr. Ratkin arrived. I believe he had been flying down from Nashville at the estimated time of the murder, so naturally we questioned him."

"How would you describe that interview?"

"He seemed a little cool, frankly. A little less cut up than I would have expected. But at the time I put that down to his character. He seemed like a reserved man. Maybe even somewhat . . . calculating."

Ratkin's lawyer, Mike Friend, popped out of his chair. "We object to this gratuitous character assassination."

Judge Deaks smiled thinly. "I expect you do. Chief, try to avoid characterizations of the defendants and stick to what actually happened."

"Yes y'honor."

"What did you learn from Mr. Ratkin?"

"Not much. I asked if he knew who might have done this, and he told us about the kidnapping that had happened several months earlier. He also mentioned that some fellow had been camping out in the woods back there a while back, and that they'd had to run him off at some point."

"Did either of these seem like credible suspects?"

The chief shrugged. "In a murder investigation, everything's credible at first."

"Was there anybody you looked at early on, but were able to rule out?"

"Well, the people in closest proximity to the crime were Marla Jeter and Ben Pryor. So naturally we had to look at them. But they were together the entire morning."

"They alibied each other, you're saying?"

"That's right. Very firm, very credible alibis. They were playing cards together all morning."

"Anybody else?"

"A Domino's pizza delivery man named Mance Verdun delivered a pizza around noon to Ms. Jeter and Mr. Pryor. We questioned him briefly, and his story checked out. He had no motive, no priors, and he was back at his job in a period of time consistent with dropping off a pizza and then driving straight back to work."

"Okay. Please tell us how the investigation proceeded from there."

"We processed the forensic evidence with the help of the GBI crime scene technicians and the medical examiner, Dr. Preston. That day we continued to interview people close to Ms. Burnett. On the following day we received some information that led us to want to question Ms. Marla Jeter again.

"At that point we brought her down to the police department. In the course of the interview she admitted—"

The DA jumped in, "We'll get to that in Ms. Jeter's

testimony. I'd just like to know kind of the flow of things here."

"We questioned her for about five hours, during which point she made some admissions as to knowledge about elements of the murder. At which point she suddenly requested a lawyer. Her lawyer insisted upon involving your office, the office of the district attorney, I mean. So I believe you came over, Mr. Maples, at which point Ms. Jeter requested an immunity deal. An agreement was struck, and that's when Ms. Jeter told us—"

"Again, Chief," the DA said, "to avoid hearsay, let's reserve the details of Ms. Jeter's agreement until she can testify about it herself."

"Gladly. Anyway, the upshot is that after working out this immunity deal, Ms. Jeter admitted certain peripheral involvement in the murder—after the fact, I must add— and then she proceeded to implicate the defendants, Mr. Brushwood and Mr. Ratkin. We then arrested Mr. Ratkin at the Ritz Carlton Hotel in Atlanta.

"At that time, we were not prepared to arrest Mr. Brushwood. We did, however, serve a search warrant on Mr. Brushwood that allowed us to take a peek around his property. In the course of doing so, we found evidence strongly indicating that he was involved in the murder."

"What was that evidence?"

"We found a baseball bat in the trunk of his car. A bat with what appeared to be blood, as well as several blond hairs adhering to it."

"Was Ms. Burnett a blond?"

"Natural blond, no. She dyed it blond, though."

"So what did you do then?"

"We put the cuffs on Mr. Brushwood and hauled him off to jail."

"Thank you, Chief."

The DA sat down.

Judge Deaks looked over at our table. "Mr. Senior? Mr. Friend?"

Quentin stood up.

"Could you tell us a little more about this conversation you had with Ms. Jeter? What did she tell you that led you to believe these two men, Mr. Brushwood and Mr. Ratkin, should be considered suspects?"

"Basically she said she'd overheard a conversation in which they'd discussed a murder-for-hire scheme. Mr. Ratkin hiring Mr. Brushwood, in other words."

"I see. And did it occur to you that maybe she was lying to protect someone? Herself, for instance?"

"Sure. But after we'd gone over what she told us, it became clear she couldn't have done it."

"Oh? How was that?"

"I'm not sure how far I can go without getting into hearsay. . . ." The chief looked up questionly at the judge.

"This goes to his further course of action," Quentin said.

"You can answer it."

"She said that she and Ben Pryor, the other security guard, were playing cards together during the period when forensic evidence indicates that the murder took place. We asked Pryor about it, and he confirmed her story."

"Thank you, Chief."

CHAPTER 31

THE NEXT WITNESS was the medical examiner, a woman of about thirty-five named Dr. Regina Preston. Her plain, round face wore no makeup, and her dull-brown hair was cut in a short, practical, styleless bob. At first glance, my guess was that she was painfully shy and read a lot of science fiction.

"How's the leg, Doctor?" the DA began with an unctuous smile.

Dr. Preston smiled back, but it didn't look convincing. "Getting better, thanks."

"Skiing accident?"

"Karate, actually." She had the loud, uninflected slightly aggressive voice of somebody with a large collection of strong opinions.

"Remind me not to mess with *her*!" Maples winked at the jury, then looked sorry he'd been flippant. He quickly dove into a discussion of Dr. Preston's qualifications, then brought out the Georgia Burnett autopsy report to be marked as an exhibit.

"Could you outline for us your findings, Doctor?"

The medical examiner said, "It was my finding that Georgia Burnett was beaten with a blunt instrument. The beating resulted in several distinct fractures to the cranium and facial bone structure. I observed lacerations of the cerebrum and cerebellum as well as a massive sub-dural hematoma. Any one of these injuries would likely have been fatal. Her spinal cord was partially severed at the third cervical vertebra. Also a potentially fatal injury. I observed broken bones in the right ulna, the right collar bone, the third cervical vertebra, and the posterior aspect of the right fourth and right fifth ribs. There was also bruising on her back, her chest, and on her left forearm."

Gorin Maples had an anatomical chart brought out by an assistant, then the doctor stood up and marked all the breaks and bruises with a red magic marker. When she was done, the chart was covered with slashes and blobs of red, and I was feeling queasy.

"So how many times was she hit? Once? Twice? Four or five times?"

Dr. Preston gave the DA a wincing smile. "I can't conclusively say how many times she was struck. But I'd estimate she was hit about twenty times."

"Could this have been an accident?"

"Certainly not."

"Suicide?"

"No."

"So in laymen's terms, what caused Georgia Burnett to die?"

"Somebody beat her to death."

"Based on your analysis, are you able to make any sort of reconstruction of the sequence of the crime?"

"This isn't an exact science."

The DA hesitated a moment, as though expecting her to continue. Finally he said, "But I trust you were able to make some sort of analysis?"

"Yes, I was." She stood and pointed to the chart. "The fracture to the ulna, that's this bone in the right forearm, and the bruise on the left arm are what we call defensive wounds. Ms. Burnett was right-handed. It's typical for a person, when realizing they are about to be struck, to try to ward off the blow." The doctor assumed a flinching posture, both arms in the air in front of her face. "On right-handed people, the right hand tends to be in front. That would explain why the right arm was fractured, whereas the left was only bruised."

"Anything else?"

"She's hit. It breaks her arm. After that I suspect she tries to escape by rolling backward and to her right. She's still got her arm lifted, but now her elbow's forward because she's trying to favor the now-broken forearm. Plus she's probably trying to cover her head. The next blow glances off the back of her upper arm here, striking her ribs, causing this bruise." Using a pointer, she indicated a red blob on the anatomical chart. "Ms. Burnett continues to roll until she is curled up in a ball, thus receiving two or maybe three blows on her back, which cause the fracturing and bruising on her right rear ribs, just below the shoulder blade. Again, this is more art than science, but my analysis is that the next blow fell on Ms. Burnett's neck, crushing the third cervical vertebra, here."

At this, Dr. Preston whacked the chart with her pointer. A pale woman in the front row of the jury box flinched visibly.

"This blow very likely caused unconsciousness or paralysis or both. At that point her body relaxes and the protective ball she has assumed collapses. Maybe the assailant rolled her over, or maybe she just naturally presented frontal targets at this point—but, whatever the case, the assailant then began to strike her in the head and chest. The assailant then hit her about ten or fifteen more times, crushing her face and skull as well as causing major wounds to the torso."

I felt a rising sense of nausea as she described the event in her cold, loud, flat voice.

"What, if anything, happened then?"

"That was it. She was left, if I may put it in these terms, in a heap."

"Can you estimate the time of death?"

"When I arrived at the house at 3:05 P.M., her core temperature was eighty-nine degrees. Based on the ambient temperature of the room, which was seventy-one degrees, I estimate she had been dead anywhere from two to four hours."

"So she was killed somewhere between eleven and one o'clock?"

"Roughly, yes. Certainly no earlier than eleven."

"Any other significant findings, Doctor?"

"Not particularly. She was a normal, healthy woman. Toxicological tests indicated there were neither illicit drugs nor poisons present in her blood."

"Anything else of interest? Anything at all?" Gorin Maples's face was very sober, very serious. But I sensed he was holding back some sort of expression of glee.

"Well," the medical examiner said. "She was two and a half months pregnant."

The pale woman in the front row of the jury box gasped loudly and put her hands over her mouth. The whole room rumbled. Judge Deaks glared around the court. The noise subsided.

"Nothing further, your Honor."

CHAPTER 32

"P REGNANT! MY GOD, it just keeps getting better,"
Gunnar said. We were sitting around in an end-of-
the-day strategy session in a broom closet–sized
space to the courtroom.

"We knew it was coming," Quentin said. "It was in
the ME's report."

"It was?" Gunnar sighed, put his head down on the
table. "How could I have forgotten a thing like that?"
He was wearing a suit for trial, but they still cuffed him
every time he left the courtroom. As long as he was in
view of the jury he was keeping up a good front, but
each time he was out of sight of them, he seemed to
deflate more and more. For the first time in my life I
was noticing how old he looked. A sudden premonition
ran through me that some kind of medical malady was
going to overtake him, a heart attack or a stroke.

"Why'd they end the ME's testimony with that *particular* fact, though?" I said.

Quentin shrugged. "Standard trial strategy. Build sympathy for the victim, you also build hatred for the alleged
perpetrator."

"Still . . ."

"Pregnant," Gunnar muttered again. "I can't believe she was pregnant."

"Look, let's not get bogged down in that," Quentin said, just as Barrington Cherry walked into the room. Quentin turned to him. "Any progress finding Bollard?"

Barrington shook his head. "No. But I got an idea."

CHAPTER 33

BARRINGTON CHERRY'S IDEA was named Lucretia Kolwicki. When he called me early the next morning before we went to her office, Cherry said, "I have one word for you. Layers."

"Huh?"

"Underneath your winter clothes? Dress very, very lightly."

"I don't follow you."

"She's a little strange, that's all."

"Strange like how?" I said.

Cherry laughed mysteriously.

Lucretia Kolwicki, Ph.D., had been a civilian profiler with the famous Behavioral Sciences Unit at the FBI for a couple of years. According to Cherry she had been very good, but she'd been hired from outside the Bureau and never fit in very well with their buttoned-down culture. If anything, he suggested, the few years she spent there had exaggerated certain oddities of character that she had already had. Now she was teaching psychology at Georgia State.

We knocked on a door that read DR. EVELYN HO. "Dr. Ho?" Barrington called.

No one answered.

"I thought her name was Kolwicki," I said.

Barrington put his finger over his lip, winked at me, then knocked a second time.

This time a voice answered from inside the office.

"Yes? Who is it?"

"Barrington Cherry. Here for the appointment."

"Are you with anyone?"

"Like I said on the phone, I brought an associate. Her name's Sunny Childs."

I heard the sound of three or four locks opening, then the door opened. "Quickly!" a woman said in an urgent voice. The room was so dark I couldn't see anything as we entered. The door closed and various locks and bolts were rapidly shot home.

As my eyes began to adjust to the darkness of the room, the woman walked around to the other side of a desk and sat down. The windows behind her were completely covered with black velvet curtains. It was insufferably, chokingly hot.

"The heater broken?" I said.

She shook her head sharply. "Can't be too careful," she said. "I heat the room to precisely ninety-eight degrees. That way they can't pick you up on infra-red."

"They?" I said.

"Whoever," she said, waving her hand. Now that I could finally see, I saw that she was a lumpy woman of about forty, with a square face and very short hair. She wore nothing but a jogbra, a pair of bicycling pants and a .357 magnum revolver hung on a web belt dripping with speedloaders. Small rolls of fat squeezed out at the edges of the bra and the bicycling shorts. Dr. Kolwicki sat and got right down to business. Her only jewelry—if that's the right word—was a key that hung around her neck on a cheap metal chain, like the kind used as a pull cord on a light.

"Don't like beating around the bush," she said. "I believe we agreed my consultation fee would be fifteen hundred dollars. If I testify, it'll run you two hundred bucks an hour."

"Yes, ma'am," I said.

"Cashier's check or cash only."

"Yes, ma'am." Barrington had warned me about this. I took the cashier's check out of my purse and handed it over to her. She turned on a small ultraviolet lamp on her desk, squinted at the check under the light through a magnifying glass, looking at both sides several times before finally putting the check into a drawer in her desk, and locking it with the key that hung around her neck.

She smiled brightly. "Good. I feel much better now."

"So, Lucretia," I said. "Did you have a chance to review the material we messengered to you last night?" I had sent over a file containing every document we had received, as well as a summary of what I had learned from the Australian police about Ian Bollard.

"Of course," Lucretia snapped. "And please call me Dr. Kolwicki, Ms. Childs. I detest bogus informality."

"Yes, ma'am," I said.

"Now. I reviewed the files. Let me first say this. Ian Bollard didn't kill this woman."

My heart sank. Fifteen hundred dollars, right down the toilet.

"Well, ah, if I may . . ." Barrington said.

"No, you may not." Dr. Kolwicki placed one plump hand majestically on a stack of documents that were arranged perfectly square in the center of her pristine desk. "I shall now review the substance of my findings."

I realized I was dripping sweat. Fortunately, I had done as Barrington suggested. Underneath my black pants and black blouse, I wore nothing but a thin T-shirt and a pair of cotton running shorts. While Dr. Kolwicki began her lecture, Barrington stripped down to almost nothing. Somewhat apprehensively, I followed suit. I noticed Barrington didn't stop until he was wearing only a Speedo. Not much was left to the imagination.

His copper skin was beaded with sweat. For a forty-five–year-old guy, he had held up exceptionally well. He was muscular, but not in a pumped-up weight-liftery way, and there wasn't an ounce of fat on him. Kolwicki didn't seem to find him quite as distracting as I did.

"Let us begin with the circumstances of the crime. The victim was killed in her own bedroom. She was found naked. Furthermore, there were no bloody clothes found in the vicinity of the scene. Furthermore, there was no smearing of blood to indicate that any clothes were removed. Therefore, she was almost certainly in an unclothed state when the attack began."

Dr. Kolwicki flipped to the next page of what apparently was her report.

"Let us move to the crime itself. Except in cases of self-defense where one uses whatever weapon comes to hand, bludgeoning is an act of punishment, frequently of rage. We may safely rule out self-defense in this case. In cases of self-defense we may expect a few blows beyond the disabling blow . . . but not many. And those blows are typically not to the head or face. In this case, the majority of the blows took place *after* the victim had long since been rendered helpless.

"This, too, indicates that the victim was being punished. In all likelihood, that punishment was not for, say, welshing on a debt. Generally beatings related to financial matters are administered to the limbs, indicating the attacker's power over the victim's—"

I decided it was time to cut to the chase. "Dr. Kolwicki, we are in the middle of a trial where two men's lives are at stake. Quite literally, our time is infinitely precious. We can read your report at leisure, but right now I really don't give a hoot in hell what you *didn't* find out. I don't care who *didn't* commit the crime. I need you to tell me who you think actually did this."

Lucretia Kolwicki looked at me levelly for a moment. She seemed to be considering my outburst. Finally she said, "Yes. You're exactly right. My apologies. Every once in a great while I give in to self-indulgence."

She stroked the stack of documents again, lovingly, as though trying to scoop some essential meat out of them.

"Now, one final issue. The position of the victim. The victim's body was found in a contorted heap, one arm flung out, one over the torso, legs twisted. She died as she fell, and the killer did not move her. This is highly inconsistent with the act of someone like a stalker. Stalkers consider themselves to be in love with their victims. As soon as stalkers kill the object of their obsession—and the killing itself may be quite brutal—they tend to feel remorse. If the killing takes place in a protected area such as this, a stalker, an Ian Bollard type, will almost invariably attempt to tidy up the scene. They may straighten out the corpse, perhaps drape a shirt or sheet over them, perhaps move them to a more 'dignified' location such as a bed."

Kolwicki flipped to the next page of her report, studied it for a moment.

"Here, then, are my findings, Ms. Childs," she said finally. "First, the victim's state of undress indicates one of two things: either she was surprised by someone who launched immediately into the attack, or she had an intimate relationship to the killer.

"Second, according to the information you gave me, the baseball bat used to kill her was Mr. Ratkin's. That means it was not brought to the scene by the killer, but that it was close at hand. The logical conclusion is that the killer knew of its existence prior to entering that room. All of which argues against the conclusion that Bollard was the killer.

"That said, it's possible that a person with the pathology of an Ian Bollard could have snuck into the victim's room, found her naked, had an altercation when she resisted his advances, and then killed her with the weapon at hand. But, as I said earlier, it's highly unlikely that such a person would have left her in a heap like that."

Out in the hallway, a door slammed. At the sound, Kolwicki burst out of her chair and fell to the floor behind her desk. I looked questioningly at Barrington. He raised one hand a few inches off his bare thigh, indicating to me not to move. We sat in silence for at least two minutes.

"I think it was just a door slamming, Dr. Kolwicki," he finally said softly.

She peeped up over the top of the desk apprehensively. Apparently seeing no immediate threat, she got back in her chair, her face resuming its imperious mask. I noticed, though, that her .357 was not in the holster anymore. I assumed she was holding it in the hand that lay in her lap behind the desk.

"So that's it, really," she said brightly.

"I'm sorry," I said. "Am I missing something?"

"I wouldn't know," Kolwicki said grandly.

"I mean, you just ruled out a bunch of people. But who do you think actually *did* do it."

"Isn't it obvious?" she said.

I shrugged. "Not to me."

"Well, it can't be her husband because he was in his airplane. He has the airport logs to prove it. It can't be Ben Pryor and Marla Jeter because they alibied each other. It can't be the pizza delivery man, both because she wouldn't have let a stranger into her room while she was naked and because he wouldn't have known about the bat. It can't be Bollard because the crime scene is inconsistent with his pathology.

"Therefore, clearly the killing was staged, planned in advance. The intent was to make it appear to be an attack by—if not by Ian Bollard—then by someone like him. Only they didn't realize that the killer was leaving a crime scene that was completely inconsistent with a murder committed by a romantic obsessive. Only a hired killer is likely to leave their victim in a heap like that, to objectify them, to treat them contemptuously so as to gain psychological distance from the victim's pain."

Kolwicki stopped, put all her papers back in a single stack, straightened them, then smiled pleasantly.

"I'm sorry," I said. "But I'm not sure I understand what you're suggesting."

"I'm saying that given the facts in evidence, the only logical conclusion here is that Mr. Ratkin hired Mr. Brushwood to kill his wife."

When we got outside, the air felt bitterly cold on my sweaty skin.

We had walked several blocks before Barrington spoke. "Well, Sunny?"

"What the hell were you thinking, Barrington?" I said finally. I was so mad I could barely get the words out.

"Now look, Sunny, I know she's a little wacky. But she did good work for the bureau."

"A little *wacky*? Wacky? Jesus, the woman's afraid even to put her own name on the door. She's clinically paranoid."

"Maybe, but her analysis—"

"Her analysis was crap and you know it!"

Barrington stood on the corner, the chill wind tugging at his coat. "Oh?" he said finally. "What *exactly* was wrong with her analysis?"

"It all relies on the notion that some psycho like Bollard is so predictable that we know for sure what they'd do in a situation like this. Oh yeah, first he'd smash her face in and then the next minute, you know, he'd practically be giving her corpse a makeover. That doesn't make a lick of sense, Barrington! And even if it did? Maybe Bollard got interrupted. Maybe he heard the pizza guy's car driving up. Maybe he heard Gunnar knocking on the front door. Maybe he just freaked out. Whatever. So then he goes booking out the back door."

"He freaked out." Barrington looked at me coolly. "He got interrupted, and he freaked out. Only he still had the presence of mind to plant the bat in Gunnar's car."

"The hell with you!" I said.

"Why are you getting mad at me?" Barrington said. "I'm just trying to put a cold, clear eye on the evidence."

"Maybe that's your problem. You're too cool, you got no faith in anybody."

"You don't know me well enough to say a thing like that." Barrington's hazel eyes looked cool then, sure enough. "Anyway, look, if that's how you feel, maybe you don't need me." He turned and started walking to his car.

"Where's the motive?" I shouted.

Barrington put his key in the lock, opened the door. "I quit," he said. "You don't want my help, fine. Go it alone."

"Where's the *motive*?"

CHAPTER 34

NEXT MORNING THE first witness was Georgia's business lawyer, a woman named Celeste Williams. I don't know why, but I had a bad feeling about her as soon as she got on the stand.

Maybe it was because as soon as she got up there, Gorin Maples started stroking his pathetic little mustache—a habit he seemed to indulge in when anticipating a particularly damning piece of testimony.

"Ms. Williams," he said. "Did you have occasion to meet with Ms. Burnett in the weeks prior to her death?"

"Yes, I met with her on several occasions in early November. That would have been a month or so before her death." Williams was the quintessence of a certain kind of Southern woman: just barely on the wrong side of gorgeous, her makeup laid on with infinite care, long hair dyed blond and elaborately coiffed, red nails painted just so. Her emerald green suit had a small, flaring peplum—an item of fashion that, in my opinion, should be reserved for women who are built like runway models. Which Celeste Williams was not.

"And could you tell us what the occasion of your meeting was?"

"Ms. Burnett wanted to make certain alterations in her financial situation. . . ."

"Go on, Ms. Williams."

"Well, I kind of need to back up and tell you about something I'd done for her some months earlier."

"That's fine."

"Back during the summer she had come to me and explained that . . . well, basically she told me that she had been having an affair with someone."

A wave of muttering ran through the room.

"She told me that she loved this person, but the whole thing was really torturing her and so she hadn't made up her mind about what she wanted to do. At any rate, she wanted to figure out what the financial implications would be if she left her husband."

Williams touched her dyed hair with a long red fingernail, then went on. "Georgia had also said to me that her husband had been experiencing some financial problems. She said that she had helped him out recently, but that his situation was still not stable. It was my concern that under such circumstances, her assets might be vulnerable if she divorced him. He could potentially sue her for a share of her assets, under the claim that all of her earnings had derived from his efforts as her producer, advisor, manager, mentor, and so on, and that he therefore had a right to a share of them.

"While I thought the claim would ultimately be found meritless, it was nevertheless a serious concern. With that in mind, I advised her to take steps to keep her assets out of his hands."

"What steps?"

"My recommendation had been that she establish a trust. By transferring her assets into that trust, she could obviate any claims Ratkin might make in a divorce proceeding."

"Whoo, that sounds complicated," Maples said with a

folksy grin. "You think you could break that down for me a little?"

"Basically a trust is a legal entity that controls a potful of assets. And that trust has a purpose spelled out as to how the money is to be used. You could establish a trust for charitable purposes, for instance, so that your money will continue to be used, oh, to fund cancer research after you died or something like that. In Georgia's case, though, the point of the trust was to preserve her capital and to ensure her a steady income over the course of her life."

"Was any provision made for her death?"

"Sure. If she died, the trust was to be liquidated and distributed to her heirs."

"But she didn't have any heirs, did she?"

I started to get a sinking feeling about where this was going.

"Well, no, that's not accurate. By virtue of the fact that they were married at the time that I established the trust for her—again, that's about six months ago—Mr. Ratkin was her sole heir."

Gorin Maples raised his eyebrows theatrically. "Oh, he *was*?"

"Sure. Like I say, she had not made a decision at that time about whether or not to stay married."

"Okay, so does that bring us up to these meetings you had in November?"

"Yes. See, when she came to me in November, she wanted an amendment to the articles of trust. She wanted it spelled out in the articles of trust that if she gave birth to a child—even if she did remain married—the trust was to be maintained for the benefit of the child."

"Okay, again, I'm a little hazy on this technical stuff," Gorin Maples interrupted. "Let's say she has a baby and then she dies. What happens to the money?"

"Objection, your honor!" Mike Friend said. "This is hypothetical."

Judge Deaks adjusted his black-framed glasses. "It's probative, counselor. Overruled."

"Again, Ms. Williams," the district attorney said. "A baby's born and Ms. Burnett passes away. What happens to the money?"

"My firm would administer the trust until the child reached majority. That's basically their twenty-first birthday."

"And Mr. Ratkin? Could he put his hands on that cash?"

"Couldn't touch a single penny."

The DA got his fingers up in his little mustache and started rubbing away. When he finally got tired of feeling his mustache, he said, "Once Ms. Burnett gets pregnant, are there any circumstances under which Mr. Ratkin could get control of that money?"

Mike Friend and Quentin both hopped up, livid. "Objection!"

Deaks blinked a couple of times. "Fellows, I don't like hypotheticals in my courtroom as a rule. But, again, I think this has probative value."

"Exception!" Friend shouted.

"Duly noted, counselor. Now sit down." Judge Deaks turned to the lawyer. "You can answer the question, Ms. Williams."

Gorin Maples repeated himself. "Once Ms. Burnett gets pregnant, are there *any* circumstances under which Mr. Ratkin could ever, ever, ever get control of that money?"

Celeste Williams glanced nervously at the defense table. "Well, I guess Georgia would have to get killed. And she'd have to do it before that baby was born."

I looked over at Quentin. His face was red with anger.

As soon as Ratkin was led into the conference room next to the courtroom, Quentin said, "Did you know that your wife was pregnant?"

Ratkin clasped his hands together for a moment. Then, in his usual expressionless voice, he said, "Yes."

"And did you know about this goddamn trust?"

Neither Friend nor Ratkin spoke.

Quentin shook his head slowly. "I can't believe you sons of bitches. Did you actually think these people wouldn't find this out?"

Ratkin didn't speak.

"When did you find out the details of this trust?"

"She told me as soon as it was done. Mid-November."

"And the pregnancy?" Quentin's voice had risen to a roar.

"She called me that morning," Ratkin said softly. "That's why I flew down."

"Look," Mike Friend said, "I'm not going to be apologetic about this. You know as well as I do that our interests in this case are not completely coextensive. We had no obligation to share this information with you."

Quentin ignored the lawyer, turned to look at Ratkin. "If you were gonna kill her, boy, December 9 was sure the right time."

Ratkin looked at him for a moment. His face seemed completely calm—at least it did until the moment he suddenly rose up out of the chair and hurled himself at Quentin. Mike Friend grabbed him just as his manacled body slammed into Gunnar's lawyer. The whole gang of them went down in a pile.

"Hey! Hey!" I yelled as Friend pulled Ratkin off of Quentin. "This is not helping."

"I *loved* her!" Ratkin screamed. "Why can't anybody understand that? I loved her more than my own life." Suddenly he was sobbing, a horrible deep groaning coming out of him. Sitting there looking at him I couldn't help thinking that, even if he'd hired somebody to kill his wife, this was one of the saddest things I'd ever seen.

Mike Friend reached over and hugged his client, and the record producer leaned against him, his hands straining against the manacles and clutching at the lawyer's suit.

It took a long time for the crying to subside.

"Alright, alright," Quentin said, straightening his jacket. "So now we know. We'll deal with it." He turned to me. "Sunny, where the hell is Ian Bollard?"

I shrugged. I knew I needed to tell him that Barrington Cherry had quit. But I couldn't bring myself to do it. I figured it would be better to try and salvage things myself, let Quentin worry about the trial. That's how I rationalized it anyway.

"We'll find him," I said. "I promise."

CHAPTER 35

AFTER THE DISASTROUS day, I decided I'd better do something about mending fences with Barrington Cherry. It was that or hire a new operative—and I just didn't have enough time to do that. Not and get them up to speed while the trial was still going. So I called Barrington and asked him to meet me at Manuel's, a bar over in Decatur.

"You look like somebody just died," he said after we ordered our beer. His eyes were cool and distant.

I told him about the trust that Ratkin hadn't bothered to reveal to us and how Georgia's pregnancy provided Ratkin with a possible reason for wanting to get rid of his wife.

"That's why they've been so cocksure," I said. "Aside from all the forensics, they've had motive all the time."

Cherry blinked and then leaned back in his chair with an unreadable look on his face. After a second, he crossed his arms tightly over his chest. He didn't say anything.

"Look, Barrington, I'm sorry about unloading on you this morning," I said finally. "I'm just really stressed out. I want you to come back and finish the case with me."

Barrington pursed his lips, then said, "Hang on for a second. I want to show you something."

He stood up, walked out the door of the bar. When he came back, he was carrying a small flat leather case just a little larger than a clutch purse, its cover flap fastened with a corroded brass snap. The leather was worn but still supple as he opened the case. Inside, nested in faded purple velvet, lay a row of gleaming steel tools: several pairs of scissors in different sizes and shapes, a couple of crimping tools, a curling iron, a steel comb, some other implements I didn't recognize. Each tool's handle was inlaid with mother of pearl.

"This is my prize possession," he said. He pulled out a straight razor, opened it, slid his thumb across the blade. Then he handed it to me. "Feel that."

I felt it with my finger. The blade made a soft ringing noise as the ridges of my finger scraped across the keenly honed metal. "Sharp," I said. "But what's that got to do with Gunnar Brushwood?"

"You know," he said. "I was a disappointment to my father. He wanted me to be a doctor."

"Oh?" I said. I realized that he was working through something and that he'd get around to talking about the case in his own good time. "Was he in medicine?"

Barrington Cherry laughed. "My father came to the States from Trinidad right after World War II, worked for five years as a common laborer so he could save up enough money to start a business. He was a barber. The slogan of his shop was, "At Mr. Cherry's, every man is a king!" By the mid-'50s, he had seven chairs in his shop. It was probably the most famous black barbershop in Chicago."

Barrington closed his eyes for a moment. "You should have seen that place. Everything gleamed. All his barbers were light-skinned men from Trinidad. They dressed like diplomats. I mean, *sharp!*" He smiled fondly, thinking back, eyes still closed. "No one was allowed to curse or even use first names on the premises.

It was Mr. This, Mr. That. 'Mr. Johnson, may I have a word with you in the process room?' He used to advertise on the black radio station in Chicago back in the '50s that he had the most exclusive process in the free world."

"Process?"

"You know, conks? Hair straightening? His process was a secret formula. Had him a special room in the back for doing the process and nobody was allowed to watch. It was like the confessional seal. You went in as a fallen creature and then you came out reborn, clean, risen. All kind of rigmarole involved in it, special towels and special tools, beaucoup fussing around. It was all hokum, I suppose. But it was good-spirited hokum. Black people appreciate theater in daily life in a way that y'all chilly northern Europeans don't."

"You obviously haven't met my mother," I said.

Cherry laughed. "All the famous blues musicians used to come to Dad's shop. Muddy Waters, Little Walter, Sonny Boy Williamson, all those guys. Getting conks, DBs, fingerwaves—you name it. The big gangsters, too."

"Oh yeah?"

"Even back then I wanted to be an FBI agent. I'd walk around wearing this little plastic G-man badge I got from a cereal box, and we'd play arrest. These guys, these hoods and thugs, they'd point at one another and say, 'Get him, G-man! Mr. Worthy over there, he the biggest pimp on the South Side.' Of course, they'd have to say it quietly so my father wouldn't hear them. Or 'Mr. Slidell, there, he got him the dirtiest dice game West of Halsted.' So I'd go over and this pimp or this gambler would put out his arms and let me pretend to handcuff him. Then they'd give me a nickel.

"But my father? Oh, he was strict! Every morning he made his men line up for inspection. If there was a piece of lint on your suit or if your shoes weren't shined or if your razor wasn't the absolute apotheosis of sharpness, he'd dock you a dollar. And, sister, a dollar was a lot of money for those men.

"One day I remember I was playing arrest and one of these gangsters had about had it with me. This dude was in the numbers business, and I mean he was stone psycho. A known killer. Of course *I* didn't know what these people were capable of. I tried to play arrest with him, and he turns to my father and says, 'You want to shut this little motherfucker up, man?'

"My father turns to this numbers man—this is a guy with a gun in his coat, a switchblade in his shoe, brass knuckles in his pocket—my father turns to him and says, 'Mr. Reynard, I don't countenance that kind of language in my establishment. I would be pleased if you would leave and not return.' And you know what he did, this stone killer? He just stands up and walks out. Because he saw what he was up against. My father was what we used to call a 'do-right' man. That gangster, he didn't want to go up against that. Not because he thought he couldn't do whatever he wanted to my father, but because he could see this was a man with standards. Even bad men can recognize that, admire that. That man left my father's shop because he was ashamed."

I handed the razor back to Barrington, and he set it on top of the leather case.

"Every year on my father's birthday, I sharpen up this razor, strop it, shave with it."

"To remind you of him?"

"To remind me of his *standards*."

I nodded.

"Standards," he said. "To me this little package of tools represents everything my father was about. Standards, craftsmanship, seriousness. Living by what you believe. Sharp as a razor."

"Okay? And. . . ."

"Do I have to say it?" Barrington picked up the razor and started ticking things off on his fingers with it. "We know about the bat in the trunk. We know about the

bloody fingerprint on the bat. We know about Dr. Kolwicki's analysis. We know about the fifty grand that
Ratkin paid to Gunnar. We know Marla's going to testify that Ratkin destroyed evidence. And now you tell
me about this trust, about her being pregnant? You asked
me about motive this morning—there's your motive."

"So?"

Barrington was looking a little frustrated by now. "So
I don't see how any rational person can conclude that
Gunnar didn't do this thing."

"Maybe I am irrational," I said. "Still, I know Gunnar.
I know this man could not do a thing like this."

Barrington kept looking at me, his eyes hooded and
unsympathetic.

"He *couldn't,* Barrington!"

Barrington Cherry hesitated a moment, leaned a fraction of an inch closer to me, and then said, "Can I tell
you my impression of Gunnar Brushwood? I mean, he
seems like a good guy..." Barrington seemed to be
searching for a way of phrasing what he wanted to say
without making me mad. "But he's always putting on a
show. You know? You watch the Gunnar Brushwood
Show for a while and eventually you start to wonder:
hey, what's for show and what's for real? What's going
on underneath all the fish stories and the big laughs and
the jokes and the handlebar mustache? I for one don't
have a clue."

He had put his finger on the same thing that kept
running through my head. It was horrible to doubt—
even in the smallest way—someone who'd meant so
much in your life as Gunnar had in mine. It made you
doubt your own capacity to judge anyone, to trust anyone close to you.

But all I could say to Barrington was, "There has to
be an explanation. There *has* to be."

"When I quit the FBI, I did it because I was tired of
committees and political decisions and clock-punchers
and people bitching about not getting vacation when

they wanted it. All those little compromises you make when you work in a bureaucracy. I wanted my life to be like this, you know?" He held up the razor, its blade and its gold fittings catching the gleam of the dim lights in the bar. Highlights shimmered in the iridescent mother of pearl handle. "Sharp, clean, full of purpose. Feels like I lost that somewhere along the way at the Bureau."

He snapped the razor shut, slid it back in the leather loop, then folded the case back up.

"I want to be a razor again, Sunny."

"Hey," I said. "Don't we all."

"Sunny, dammit, this Ian Bollard thing, it's a mirage. He didn't kill that poor woman. We're slogging through quicksand, trying to catch up to something that's not even there. I can't do this anymore, can't work for something that I know isn't right."

"I have faith that I'm doing the right thing."

"Yeah, but I don't."

"Okay, okay. Forget about the case for a minute." I don't know what came over me, but suddenly I felt something turn inside me, change direction. "Look at me, Barrington. What I'm asking is, do you think you could have faith in *me*?"

Barrington fiddled with the razor. From the look of sadness and pain in his eyes, I knew as sure as the world that he was thinking about his wife. "That's a hell of a thing to ask."

"I have faith in the case. All you have to do is have faith in me. Be *my* instrument."

Barrington looked at me, and he seemed as naked as any man I've ever known. "Alright then," he said quietly.

I raised my beer, and I smiled at him. But in my heart I wasn't sure anymore. How well *did* I know Gunnar? How well do you know anyone? I downed my beer and then I excused myself and went into the bathroom to throw up.

When I got back to the table, I said, "Man, I think I'm losing it."

He looked at me curiously.

"Would you come home with me tonight, Barrington?" My hands were shaking.

His eyes widened half a notch and his head tilted downward slightly. "You mean like *come home* come home?"

I nodded.

"Hey, Sunny, hey." His voice was gentle. "One thing at a time."

CHAPTER 36

THE NEXT DAY brought a parade of minor—but damning—witnesses. Keisha Reece, the administrative assistant at Peachtree Investigation came on first and testified that she had received a phone call between 9:00 and 9:30 on the morning of the murder from someone claiming to be Georgia Burnett's secretary. The caller had requested that Gunnar visit the farm in Floyd County that afternoon to meet with Georgia.

Next a banker from Tennessee Federal in Nashville testified that ArchRival Records' four million dollar loan had been placed on the "nonperforming" list at his bank due to ArchRival's poor financial situation and their resulting erratic loan repayment record.

An investment banker from Montgomery Securities in New York then testified that Jeremy Ratkin and his investors had retained the bank to attempt to sell ArchRival, but had been unable to find any buyers due to the financial weakness of the company. He further testified that with an appropriate infusion of capital ("say, in the neighborhood of five million") and a few hit records, the company could rapidly get on its feet again.

The last witness before the lunch break was Ben Pryor. His testimony took no more than five minutes. The big ex-football player came up to the stand and sat down heavily. He looked awkward, nervous, out of place—a big, straight-shooting country boy who was at his best only when out of doors.

"Mr. Pryor, tell me about your routine as a body-guard," Gorin Maples said after Pryor's preliminaries were out of the way.

"Basically, when Ms. Burnett was home, I was on an eight-hour evening patrol shift. When you hear body-guard, you think of somebody following a person around every step they take. That's kind of the way it worked when she was on tour. But when she was home, I was just a glorified security guard. I'd patrol the property, work the front gate, check on noises, things of that nature."

"Did you ever go into Ms. Burnett's house?"

"Sure. She had been kidnapped about three months before her death, so she was kind of spooked. Some-times she'd hear something and call me over." He smiled a little. "You know, I'd take my flashlight, poke around in a closet or something. That was about it."

"Ever go into her bedroom?"

"Yes, sir. Like I say, she'd called me over a couple times to check on things. Plus, when she was up in Nashville we patrolled the house as a routine matter, checked the doors and windows of all the rooms."

"Let's turn to December 9 of last year. What were you doing that day?"

"I got up late since I work the four-to-midnight shift. I had a cup of coffee then went for a ride on my horse. Well, it was Georgia's horse, really, but she let me ride it. At about 10:00 A.M. Ms. Jeter, my boss, who lived in the staff house same as I did, she asked if I wanted to play cards."

"And how long did you play?"

"About four hours. We started at ten, ended around two."

"Have lunch in there somewhere?"

"Yes, sir."

"So I guess one of you got up and went in the kitchen for a while?"

"No sir. We ordered it to be delivered. There's a Domino's over in Rome."

"Nobody went out for a smoke break?"

"Nope."

"So you were with Ms. Jeter from eleven to two. With her the whole time."

"Pretty much every minute, yes sir."

"You and Miss Jeter, what game were you playing?"

"Go Fish," Ben Pryor said. "Gin rummy. Couple other games."

"Thank you, Mr. Pryor," Gorin Maples said. "That'll be all."

Quentin approached the podium and the big witness eyed him nervously.

"You said you had a cup of coffee that morning. Did you ever step into the little boys' room to relieve yourself?"

"I might have."

"So when you say Marla didn't leave your sight for those four hours, you didn't mean that literally."

"Well, look, I don't have prostate problems or nothing. We're talking about maybe thirty seconds or a minute that I might have went in the toilet."

"Ah! So she *was* out of your sight for some period of time, though." Quentin didn't wait for a response. "Now when you were patrolling Georgia's house, did you ever check the lock on the door to the crawl space, make sure it was secured?"

Pryor suddenly got a defensive look in his eyes. "Yes, sir, I did. It was always locked."

"Oh really?" Quentin let the question hang in the air

for a while. "Sir, are you aware that the Floyd County Police have since found evidence indicating that someone was living underneath Georgia's house?"

Pryor hesitated, then finally said, "Yes, sir."

"Some nut is camping out under the house not a hundred feet from your bedroom, you never saw this fellow?"

"No, sir."

"Never caught him sneaking around in the bushes?"

"Nope."

"You must have been doing a fine job over there."

Pryor had been looking queasy the whole time, but now he got angry. "I would have done *anything* to protect her," he shouted. "Anything!"

Quentin ignored the outburst. "Mr. Pryor, have you ever heard of a man named Ian Bollard?"

"No, sir."

"Thank you," Quentin said airily. "I have no more use for this man."

CHAPTER 37

DURING LUNCH I called Barrington on his cell phone. "Any luck?"

"Maybe," he said. "I'm up in Jasper." That was a small town about an hour north of Atlanta. "Talked to a lady who runs a campground up here. She said she thinks she recognized Bollard from his picture. She wasn't real sure, but she said he had an English accent."

"Yes!" I said. English, Australian—most Americans couldn't tell the difference. It had to be him. "Did she keep records of his vehicle or his plates in her registration book?"

"Yeah, he signed in but the entry was illegible. He obviously didn't want to be tracked."

The afternoon's testimony promised to wrap up the prosecution's case. Gorin Maples had saved his star witness for last.

"Ms. Jeter, before we get started, I want to get something straight." Gorin Maples was in his best Young Republican ensemble—white shirt, blue suit, black wingtip shoes, and a red tie with a splattery design that put me in mind of bird droppings. "You're testifying in this matter under grant of immunity, isn't that correct?"

"Yes it is." I almost didn't recognize Marla Jeter. The DA must have hired an image consultant to give her a makeover, because there was no way she'd come up with this look on her lonesome. Her coppery hair was wrapped around her head in a simple chignon instead of dangling behind her back in its usual long braid. Her face was tastefully made up in warm browns and reds that—without making her look like some kind of fake girlie-girl type—softened the hard angles of her face. In a pair of tan cords, low-heeled brown boots, and a lovely raw silk blouse, she looked downright statuesque.

Still, there was something in the eyes that gave her away, something of the farmer's daughter: like Ben Pryor, she was not at home in places like this courtroom.

Maples continued. "Grant of immunity. That means you did something wrong, didn't you? You did something wrong, and because we needed your help in this matter, we were willing to offer to overlook what you did in order to get you to testify. Isn't that right?"

"Yes it is." She was doing everything right: looking him in the eye, leaning forward, back straight, jaw firm. Nothing defensive about her.

"We'll get into what you did in a moment, but I think it's only fair to let the jury understand where you're coming from before you speak. Sound fair?"

"Yes, sir. I made a mistake, and I want to be aboveboard about that."

It was an obvious strategy. Maples wanted to defang Quentin, who would inevitably come out on cross-examination and imply that Marla was a scoundrel and a liar and a criminal who was willing to fabricate anything the DA told her to in order to escape prosecution for her own part in the murder.

"Good. That's admirable of you." The district attorney smiled earnestly. "But let me ask you something. Did we ask you to lie?"

"No, sir."

"Shade the truth a little to make our case sound stronger?"

"No, sir."

"We didn't put any pressure on you? You sure of that?"

"Yes, sir. I told you I'd done something wrong, and that if you'd offer me immunity I would tell you everything I knew. Just like the oath says, the whole truth and nothing but the truth."

Maples's little blond mustache twitched. "Alright then. Let's turn to the day of November 1 of this year. You remember that day?"

"Yes, I do."

"Did anything significant happen to you on that day?"

"Yes, sir. About a month before that, my boss, Georgia Burnett, had been kidnapped. Mr. Ratkin had hired Gunnar Brushwood to help out with the ransom. In the course of the ransom exchange there was a shoot-out and Mr. Brushwood saved Georgia's life.

"Anyway, about a month after that, Mr. Ratkin decided to throw a party to thank Mr. Brushwood for what he'd done. It was sort of a media event really—TV crews and everything. So the date you mentioned, that was the date of the party. As head of security, my job was to sort of mingle with the crowd—you know, be unobtrusive but keep an eye on things.

"While I'm doing my thing, I go out onto the deck and I see Mr. Ratkin and Mr. Brushwood having a conversation. It looks like Mr. Brushwood's mad at Mr. Ratkin about something. He's got a cigar and he's kind of like jabbing it at Mr. Ratkin's face.

"Now I don't want to bother them—but at the same time it's my job to make sure there's no trouble at the party. So I circle around and come up on the back side of the deck. There's stairs going down both sides, see, so I was able to circle around and then kind of skooch up to where I could hear them.

"So I'm about ten feet away, hiding behind one of

these little trees in a pot. A ficus? A rubber tree? Something like that? They're still arguing and Mr. Brushwood's voice is getting louder and louder. I hear Mr. Brushwood say, 'You know this is wrong, Jeremy!'

"Mr. Ratkin says, 'It's just business.'

"Mr. Brushwood says, 'Well, I'm not comfortable with it.'

"Mr. Ratkin goes, 'Fifty thousand bucks, Gunnar. You and I both know why I'm giving it to you. And it's damn sure not because you're a hero.'

"Mr. Brushwood stands there for a minute like he's thinking, then finally he says, 'Alright, alright,' or something like that.

"Then Mr. Ratkin pokes him in the chest with his finger and says, 'Okay. It's done. Fifty thousand. Now you do *your* part.' "

The district attorney nodded. "Okay, now let's turn to December 9. Tell me everything you can recall about that day."

Marla's eyes dropped, and she put her hands over her mouth sort of like she was praying.

"Miss Jeter? Are you alright?"

Marla took a deep breath, nodded. "On the day that . . . on the day that Georgia was killed, I was playing cards with one of my guards, Ben Pryor. We were rooming together in the staff quarters. Neither of us was on duty, so we started playing at around ten, then at around noon, we ordered a pizza. The delivery boy came around 12:15. At that point, me and Ben are still playing cards.

"Then maybe fifteen minutes later I get beeped by the intercom from the front gate. We had a guard who's usually there, but he had taken a patrol around the property so he wasn't manning the gate. Anyway, the person at the gate identifies himself as Gunnar Brushwood, says he's come out at Georgia's request. He said he'd called over to the house and she didn't answer. So I said go ahead and . . ."

Marla suddenly began sobbing. "It's all my fault," she kept murmuring. "It's all my fault."

"What do you mean it's all your fault?" Gorin Maples said after Marla finally got control of herself.

Marla blinked, daubed at her eyes. "I let Mr. Brushwood in. If I hadn't let him in . . ." She took a deep, wracking breath.

The DA nodded. "Well, now let's not put the cart before the horse. What happened next?"

"Nothing, really. I looked out the window, saw Mr. Brushwood get out of his car, go up to the front door. I didn't really look any longer than that. A few minutes later I heard the car drive away."

"Then what happened, Miss Jeter?"

"Well, me and Ben got tired of playing cards. I didn't have anything better to do, so I figured I'd take a quick patrol around the property. I walked around by the front of the house and noticed the front door was open, so I kind of yelled through the door. There was no answer, so I called again. Then I went inside. I figured she was in the shower. But since the kidnapping, obviously I couldn't let something like this ride, so I just went through the house." She took a deep breath. "That's when I . . . I went to her room and found her body. She was . . . oh God, there was blood everywhere and the . . . oh God, God . . ."

This time when she started crying, she couldn't stop.

The judge called for a fifteen-minute break.

After the jury filed out, Quentin and Gunnar and I had a quick, whispered conversation.

"It's crap," Gunnar said. "You see that, don't you? That conversation I had with Ratkin was about the kidnapping. You listen to how *vague* that whole thing was? I was giving Jeremy grief about how he'd faked the kidnapping, and how I didn't appreciate being put in that position. The whole thing had been bugging the hell out of me and frankly I was thinking about going to the news media about it."

"So basically Ratkin offered to buy you off?" I said.

Gunnar sighed. "Aw, you know, it wasn't exactly like she told it. We'd talked about the fifty grand before. You know, he'd said that I deserved it as a bonus for all my good work, saving his wife, that sort of thing."

"It was a bribe," I said sharply.

Gunnar looked at the floor. "You don't have to tell me I'm a goddamn fool. That's plain enough by now."

A few minutes later, Marla Jeter's testimony continued: "Chief Robard got to the house around 2:25. Mr. Ratkin arrived from the airport a few minutes later. He talked to the cops and then he kind of took me aside and demanded for me to give him the security tape."

"Ah, let's back up," Gorin Maples interrupted. "Tell us what you mean by 'security tape.'"

"We had installed a video camera at the front gate. It was a commercial type system made specifically for video surveillance. It records sixty frames a minute as opposed to a normal videotape recorder that records about fifteen hundred frames per minute. That way, instead of having to mess with changing tapes every two hours, you only have to change it once a day."

"When did you ordinarily change the tapes?"

"At the end of day shift. Four o'clock."

"So the tapes in the recorder had been recording since four P.M. the previous day?"

"Right."

"Okay. Now that we've clarified that, go on and tell me about your conversation with Mr. Ratkin."

"Well, he kind of pulled me aside and said he wanted me to give him the tape. I asked him why. He wouldn't say. He just told me to give him the tape."

"How'd you feel about that?" the district attorney said.

She looked blankly out into the courtroom. "Numb. I was just numb. I went back in the room and I got the tape and I gave it to him. Then he said not to say nothing to the police about it."

• • •

After the next break it was time for cross-examination.

"So you and Mr. Pryor played cards for almost four hours. Did you ever go to the bathroom?"

"I may have."

"You *may* have?"

"Well, yeah, probably I went to the bathroom."

"And did Mr. Pryor come into the bathroom with you?"

"Of course not."

"So, in fact, both you and Mr. Pryor were alone for some period of time."

Marla shrugged. "Maybe for a couple minutes, yeah."

"I hate to be indelicate about this but, ah, did you go number one or number two?"

Marla's eyes widened a fraction. "Excuse me?"

"When you went to the bathroom, was it number one or number two."

"How should I remember?" Marla's cheeks flushed slightly.

"So if it was number two, it might have been more than a couple minutes."

"Objection!" I was surprised the DA had taken this long to pop out of his chair.

Quentin was ready for him, though, with a speech that was clearly aimed at the jury and not the judge. "Your honor, a man's life is at stake here!" Quentin said in a loud, grave, and theatrically aggrieved voice. "The issue of who could have done what to whom could be decided by a matter of minutes. Of *seconds*, even! Ms. Jeter and Mr. Pryor have both *claimed* that they could not have committed this heinous crime because they were together for every single, solitary instant of the period during which the murder occurred. And now all of a sudden this witness is getting extremely vague about a period of time that could have lasted, who knows . . . ten minutes! Ten minutes is a long, long time. Long enough to commit murder."

Judge Deaks looked at Quentin sourly. "Alright," he said finally. "The witness can answer the question. But no more prying into anybody else's potty habits, Mr. Senior."

"Yes, your honor." Quentin turned back to Marla. "So how long were you in the bathroom, Ms. Jeter?"

"I don't remember."

"Could it have been ten minutes?"

"I don't *remember*."

"A lot of murdering can get done in ten minutes." Quentin smiled. "Can't it, honey?"

Gorin Maples jumped up howling objections, but he was too late. Quentin had already hit his mark.

"I'll withdraw that. But one last issue we need to grapple with," Quentin said. "It's been established that you're testifying under immunity here today."

"Yes, sir."

"Now you destroyed some evidence that may have been material to this case, correct?"

"Like I said to Mr. Maples, I just gave it to Mr. Ratkin."

"But you knew this was evidence pertaining to a murder."

"I guess so."

"How'd the police find out about that?"

"I believe Ben Pryor saw our conversation and reported it to the chief of police, who was the head investigator there."

"So they sat you down later that afternoon and grilled you about it?"

"Yes."

"And at first you denied that you'd helped destroy evidence."

"I was scared. Confused."

"I bet you were." Quentin smiled thinly. "Let me show you Exhibit forty-six, which I believe you have already identified to Mr. Maples as your immunity agreement made with the district attorney." Quentin studied the document with exaggerated care, then set it on the edge of the witness box. "This is a very impressive piece of legal work here. So I guess you must have a lot of legal training, drawing up a nice agreement like this."

Marla looked momentarily confused. "No, sir. It was drawn up by my lawyer."

"And his name is . . ."

"Lee Brett."

"Oh, Lee Brett, sure. Mr. Brett's quite a well-regarded criminal attorney around Atlanta. So I guess you have a top-notch big city lawyer on retainer waiting around to do criminal defense work for you?"

"No, sir."

Quentin mugged for the jury. "Well, my gosh, how'd you find him then?"

Marla sat there for a moment, then said, "Mr. Ratkin recommended him."

"Ah! Let me draw your attention to the third paragraph of this document. Could you read that to me?"

Marla read the paragraph. "The District Attorney of Floyd Country shall hold Marla Jeter harmless for all acts, known or unknown, committed by the witness with regard to the aforementioned criminal act, to wit, the murder of Georgia Burnett."

"Thank you. Did the DA's office write this language up?"

"Uh, I guess so . . ."

"You guess so."

"Wait. No, my lawyer did."

"Did the DA's office ever write up an immunity agreement and offer it to you?"

Marla looked confused. "They may have."

"Did they or didn't they?"

"Well, yeah, okay. They wrote something up, I guess."

"But you didn't sign it?"

"No, sir."

"Mr. Maples went to all that trouble to write up a nice paper for you, and you didn't sign it? How come?"

"My attorney, he told me not to. He said he would write something up that would be better."

"Ah! So this agreement was more favorable to you than the one that Mr. Maples offered you."

"I guess."

"What was the difference?"

"Well, my lawyer . . ." Marla again looked a little confused. "I guess this one was just better."

"Just better. Better how?"

"I'm not sure."

"What, did it smell better? Look prettier? Did they print it up on nicer paper?"

Marla just sat there looking at him.

"Are you familiar with the term 'limited immunity'?"

"I guess."

"Could you define if for me?"

Suddenly Marla was looking very nervous. "Uh . . . limited immunity would be like when you sign an immunity deal where you're immune from prosecution for a specific thing."

"In this case, for instance, if you had been granted immunity from a charge of obstruction of justice, but *not* from a charge of, say, criminal conspiracy—that would be limited immunity?"

"Yes, sir."

"What about transactional immunity? That term mean anything to you?"

"Uh . . . I'm not sure I could define it for you."

"If I said that transactional immunity allowed you to avoid prosecution for *anything* you did connected to a particular crime, would that definition sound about right to you?"

"I guess so."

"So might it have been, Ms. Jeter, that the first agreement, the one you refused to sign, that it was a limited immunity deal? Might it have been that it didn't hold you harmless for—I'm quoting here from the immunity deal drawn up by *your* lawyer—'for any and all acts, known or unknown, committed in connection to the murder of Georgia Burnett'?"

"I don't understand."

"Were you holding out for transactional immunity?"

"I was doing what my lawyer advised."

"Okay, fine, but if I read this correctly, you are now free to admit to any role in this crime without fear of prosecution."

Marla looked beseechingly over at the DA, who started rising out of his chair. But he didn't make it in time.

"Isn't it true, Ms. Jeter," Quentin pursued in a stentorian voice, "that according to this agreement, you can now admit to killing Georgia Burnett . . . and then walk away free as a bird?"

CHAPTER 38

THAT NIGHT WE had a big blowup. Marla Jeter was the last prosecution witness and now it was time to decide what kind of defense to put on.

Everyone was agreed that the finger of blame had to be pointed at someone in particular, that making vague allusions to a bunch of potential suspects wouldn't likely get Gunnar and Ratkin off the hook. But beyond that, Quentin and Mike Friend were at loggerheads.

"Who've we got?" Quentin said. "We got the pizza delivery guy. That's a loser. Agreed? No motive, no time, no criminal record, no nothing."

Friend nodded.

"So that leaves Marla Jeter, Ben Pryor, or Ian Bollard. Marla admits she was in the crapper, or at least that she might have been. So that gives us a window for both Ben and Marla. With Marla we've got credibility issues . . . but frankly I don't think the jury's going to buy the notion that just because she knuckled under to her boss and lied about it for a few minutes that she could therefore be a murderer. Where's the motive? I say we go with Pryor."

"What's *his* motive?"

"I'd argue he was shagging the missus," Mike Friend

said. "No offense, Jeremy. Pryor finds out she's pregnant, she tells him, 'Hey, big guy, because of this child I'm going to stick with my marriage, go take a hike.' He can't deal, so he whacks her."

"Aw for chrissake, hoss!" Gunnar said. "You got zero evidence of that."

"We bring up Georgia's friend Virginia Blount, she'll testify Georgia was having an affair. Right? Then I'll put Pryor on redirect," Friend retorted, "Give me a morning with that moron, I'll have him confessing to the Kennedy assassination."

Gunnar made a face of annoyance. "You're underestimating that boy, son. Five bucks says he ain't as dumb as he looks."

"It's got to be Bollard," Quentin insisted.

"We don't have jack on this Bollard guy!" Mike Friend shouted. "One six-month-old fingerprint off a water glass from Boise, Idaho, and a cryptic-looking one-page crime report from some foreign country. We can't unambiguously place the son of a bitch inside the state of Georgia! That's not going to hack it, guys."

"Barrington just found a campground where he stayed," I said. "He's out there."

Mike smiled patronizingly at me. "So what? Our case isn't going to take but three or four days. So if you haven't found him by then, we're dead."

I nodded glumly. Fact was, he was right.

Friend was the kind of guy who couldn't resist twisting the knife. "And Sunny, *you're* the one who said you were going to get that material from Australia. Where is it, Miss Ace Investigator?" It was the unstated fact of my every waking minute: this whole case was on my shoulders. And I was losing it. Which didn't improve my mood much. "I've been calling down there and bugging those jerks every day. Quentin's got a lawyer down there. But there's a limit. They're stonewalling."

Quentin added, "If the Australian police don't feel like sending that stuff, we can't compel them."

"Hey, I'll send somebody down to Australia myself." Friend said. "Let's try a *competent* investigator for a change. I guarantee you I'll have those records in our hands—along with an Australian policeman to put on the stand—in five days."

"Kiss my white ass!" I said. "If you're such an investigative genius, then—"

"Five days?" Quentin interrupted my budding tirade. "We don't have five days worth of witnesses!"

"I'll *find* five days worth of witnesses. Get me one DNA expert, I'll stall for two full days, easy. Give me a fingerprint expert, I'll give you another day and a half . . ."

"We're not putting a goddamn fingerprint expert on the stand!" Quentin's voice neared a shout. "They'll just confirm that my client's fingerprint is on that bat and that'll be the final nail in his coffin."

The voices rose and rose and Quentin started jabbing his finger in Mike Friend's chest. Just as it looked like someone was about to be punched in the nose, Jeremy Ratkin said in his quiet, firm voice. "Please. Guys. Shut the hell up."

Everyone looked at him. He had a report in his hand and was reading it through his Hollywood glasses. He paused for a moment, then looked up. Finally Ratkin looked up, waved the document in his hand. "I was reading this report from your paranoid friend, Dr. Kolwicki . . ."

"And?" I said.

"She says Bollard didn't do it. But look, she's got a long paragraph here about this guy's psychological profile. Let me read this: 'The celebrity stalker, like the serial killer, draws sexual gratification from his power to affect the life of the victim. Stalkers generally consider themselves to have a sort of cosmic link to their victim. Celebrity stalkers, in particular, typically compensate for feelings of inferiority by drawing on the power, glamour, influence, and media attention that surround celebrities. Blah blah blah. The obsession draws them to all things related to their victim. Blah blah. Celebrity stalkers are well know for their obsessive attendance at events related to their victim: concerts, plays, movie premieres, etc."

Ratkin looked at us expectantly.

"What?" I said.

Ratkin, as usual, looked disappointed that our trifling intellects couldn't keep up with his. "If Mohammed can't come to the mountain. . . ."

"Wait a minute, wait a minute!" I said. Suddenly I felt like dawn was breaking. It was so obvious. Why hadn't I seen it before? "I just thought of something . . ."

CHAPTER 39

JEREMY RATKIN'S PR man, Gill Merrit, had outdone himself. Starting at six o'clock the previous evening, he had mobilized every public relations asset available to ArchRival Records. A web site had been set up; e-mails sent to a proprietary database of country music fanatics; announcements made on country radio stations throughout Georgia, South Carolina, and Tennessee; fliers had even been posted on telephone poles throughout the city of Rome.

And all of them with one message: the promotion of a "spontaneous" prayer vigil organized by "a groundswell of die-hard Georgia Burnett fans." The event was to be held in the Rome High School gymnasium, a location that Gill had secured through a combination of subterfuge and substantial donations to the school's athletic booster club.

The day's testimony was spent, as Mike Friend had suggested, by farting around with an unsufferably dull DNA expert from Emory University—solely for the purpose of buying time to see if we could turn up Ian Bollard.

• • •

It was half an hour before the vigil was supposed to start. Barrington Cherry and I were preparing for the event.

"Limited access," I said. "That's the key. Every single person will come through one door at the corner of the gym. We'll have a video camera set up there. A 'volunteer' will be handing out candles that will be lit during the vigil. That'll make everybody stop to look toward the camera so we can get a look at them before they go in. Then, just inside the door we've set up a big sheet of paper where people can write messages in memory of Georgia. Again, the purpose is to get people to stop and look in one direction for a period of time."

I pointed at a long piece of poster paper along the wall of the gym. It read WAVING GOOD-BYE TO GEORGIA at the top. "We've also put a bunch of colored paint out there, and we've seeded it with some hand prints. Dip your hand in the paint, then leave your print on the wall. 'Waving good-bye,' get it? So maybe even if we don't recognize him because he's wearing a disguise, we'll get his fingerprints. Then we can work backward from the fingerprint to the disguise. Soon as we're done here, we've got two private fingerprint guys who'll go over the whole thing, comparing print by print with the one they pulled off Bollard back in the spring."

"Think anybody's gonna show up?" Cherry said.

"Let's go see," I said.

We walked over to the door of the gym, opened it, and looked outside. Then we stared for a long time. Finally I spoke.

"Oh. My. God."

The crowd was enormous—probably a thousand people already. There were also camera crews, news trucks, bright lights, and parked cars playing country music at deafening volumes.

A pretty face that I recognized as belonging to a "reporter" from *Entertainment Tonight* elbowed her way toward us. "Hey!" she said. "Can we get in early, get some shots as people come in?"

I slammed the door in her face.

Gill Merrit came up behind us and said, "Ready?"

"Let's do it."

Barrington Cherry and I sat next to each other in the girls' locker room, watching the two video monitors intently. We had four blowups of Ian Bollard's face pasted next to each screen: there was a straight photo, plus several computer modifications: one showing him wearing his blond hair much longer, another with a mustache, and still another with a beard and sunglasses.

"So what do we do if we spot him?" Barrington said as the first fan, a chubby high school girl with red-rimmed eyes, came through the door.

"Oh," I said. "I forgot to tell you. Each candle has a drip card around the bottom with a number on it. Gill's going to have a drawing at which some items associated with Georgia will be given away. A pair of her cowboy boots, some signed photos, stuff like that. If and when we spot the guy, we use the walkie talkie to notify the girl at the door who's giving out the candles. She tells us what number is on Bollard's card."

"What if she messes up?"

"We'll have somebody sidle up to him and read the card. In any case, when the drawing takes place, Gill calls out Bollard's number. He'll go up front, and Gill will tell him to go over to the men's locker room to claim his prize. At which point, we'll take him down."

"*We?*"

"We've got a material witness subpoena on him. If he flees, we can request that the county police hold him until he testifies."

Cherry shook his head slowly. "We're gonna look like maximum idiots if that boy doesn't show up."

I kept my eyes glued to the monitor. The mob stretched out to the far edges of the screen. "You got *that* right," I said.

•   •   •

By seven-thirty, the gym was getting dangerously crowded, and neither Barrington nor I had spotted Bollard. We kept admitting people for another ten minutes.

Suddenly I saw the form of Chief Robard swim up on the monitor. He was followed by a man in a black cap and a white uniform. He had a short, sharp conversation with the girl who was giving away candles. I watched the candle girl, one of Gill's assistants from the record company, lift her walkie talkie to her mouth. "Uh, Sunny? Some police guy wants to talk to you."

"Send him back," I said.

A minute or so later, Robard walked into the girls' locker room. "What in the samhill is going on here, Sunny?" he said.

I considered bullshitting him—but I suspected he wouldn't buy it. So I went ahead and explained what we were doing.

The man in the black cap interrupted. "I can't have this," he snapped.

"And you are . . ." I said.

"Trent Tidwell, I'm fire chief of the city of Rome." He was a beefy, chinless man with a peevish look in his brown eyes. "And y'all are in violation of the city ordinances here."

"How's that?"

"Look!" he said, pointing out the door of the locker room. The gym was standing room only by now. "This dadgum place is rated for three hunnert fifty souls, young lady, and you got close to a thousand in there already."

"What are you going to do?" I said. "All these well-meaning folks who want to share their pain about this tragedy—you want to just tell them to all go home?"

"That's exactly right."

I was trying to keep my eye on the monitor, but it was hard to do while I was talking.

I got on the walkie-talkie to the candle girl at the door. "How many more people have we got?"

In the monitor I saw her shrug. "A few hundred. And we're running out of candles."

"Damn it!" I said.

"Right now, young lady," the fire chief said loudly.

"Five minutes," I said. "We'll just let a few more in then open up the doors, make an announcement that the crowd's too big, and then we'll move the whole thing into the parking lot."

"Chief Robard," the fire chief said. "If this young lady don't clear this place right now, I want her arrested."

"Okay, okay, okay," I said. "But I'm not the one doing crowd control."

"Who is?" the fire chief said belligerently.

"A guy named Gill Merrit. You'll see him up front. Tell him I said to make the announcement. We'll clear out, go into the parking lot, and do the vigil out there."

Barrington sighed as Robard and the fire chief left the locker room.

I called Merrit on the walkie-talkie, filled him in on what was going on. "Slow them down!" I said. "Stall them, tell them the PA isn't operational, something."

"I'll do what I can." Merrit's voice crackled from the little speaker.

"He should have been here by now," Barrington said. "If he was going to be here. . . ."

"Maybe he's being careful," I said. "Maybe he *suspects* a trap, and he's being cautious."

"May be," Barrington said dubiously.

A man in a Braves baseball cap, dark glasses, and a T-shirt that read GEORGIA LIVES FOREVER appeared in the monitor. He wore black hair and a close-cropped black beard—but there was one feature that was unmistakable.

"Barrington?" I said.

Barrington turned to my monitor, studied the man. "Son of a gun," he said finally. "He can't hide that nose, can he?"

It was him! It was definitely Bollard.

I radioed the candle girl. "What number?" I said frantically.

She was handing a candle to the man. She stopped, hesitated, looked at the candle. "Four twenty-one," she said into her microphone.

In the monitor I saw Bollard look at her, then look at the candle. Then his eyes narrowed suddenly as he mouthed something. He started backing away from the door. The girl with the candle said something to him, trying to put him at ease, waved the candle at him a second time.

Bollard studied her from a distance of about ten feet, then turned and walked rapidly out of the camera's view. "Get Chief Robard!" I yelled to Barrington Cherry. "I'm going after them."

I tore out of the locker room and fought my way through the crowd. The fire chief was right. We had let *way* too many people into the gymnasium. I elbowed and fought, but everyone was so jammed together I could barely move.

Then suddenly I broke free and was out the door. "Which way?" I yelled to the candle girl.

She pointed wordlessly. In the middle of the parking lot outside the gym I saw a figure running away at top speed. I realized then how stupid I'd been. *I* should have gotten Chief Robard while Barrington ran out this way. I'm in pretty good shape, but there was no way I could out-sprint a healthy, vigorous man. And as he disappeared over a grass berm at the other end of the parking lot, Ian Bollard was showing no signs of a limp or a heart problem.

As I started running toward the spot where I'd last seen Bollard, I noticed Chief Robard's car parked at the edge of the lot. The door was open and the keys were in the lock.

What the hell, right? In for a penny, in for a pound. I jumped in, fired up the police car, and started driving.

By the time I hit the edge of the parking lot, I was

doing at least sixty. I skidded into a turn, pulled out in front of a pickup truck full of Mexican laborers, stomped on the accelerator. Bollard was running down the street. There were cars parked all along the sides of the road, and I assumed he was heading back to his vehicle.

I tore down the road, pulled in front of him, and slammed on the brakes. He looked up with an expression of panic, then dove off the road into the woods.

I threw the cruiser in park, jumped out and started running after Bollard again. He plunged into the strip of woods bordering the high school grounds. My heart was pounding and my breath was coming hard. I drew my Smith & Wesson, but it seemed pointless. Once again I was in a losing footrace. Bollard was *fast*. Nevertheless, I kept after him, watching as he dodged through the pines.

I was about to lose him when suddenly he tripped on something and fell in a heap. I ran around a patch of brush and there he was, clutching his leg.

"Chroist, my leg!" he said in a strong Australian drawl. "I just broke my bleddy damned leg."

I pointed my pistol at him and screamed, "Don't move!"

He rolled slowly around, looked at me angrily. I reached into the pocket of my jacket, pulled out a piece of paper and threw it on his chest.

"Ian Bollard," I said. "You are hereby served to testify in Floyd County Court, the State of Georgia vs. Gunnar Brushwood and Jeremy Ratkin."

Bollard sat up slowly, clutching his shin, and looked defiantly into my eyes. "I want a lawyer," he said. "I'm not saying a *bleddy* word."

CHAPTER 40

IAN BOLLARD DIDN'T lie. He got a lawyer, and he shut his mouth and he didn't say a word. Not until he got on the stand. And even once Quentin put him in the witness box first thing the next morning, he didn't make it easy. He admitted his name was Ian Bollard, but after that it was like pulling teeth.

"Mr. Bollard, what is your nationality?"

Bollard was still wearing his dyed black beard and his dyed black hair. He ran a finger meditatively through the beard. "Like to think of myself as a citizen of the world," he said finally.

Quentin turned to the judge. "Permission to treat the witness as hostile."

"Go ahead, counselor," Deaks said. "But before you get started, let me warn you this court ain't going allow you to go up hill and down dale with this witness just to confuse people. Keep this dog on a leash."

"Yes, your honor." Quentin turned back to the Australian. "Are you an Australian citizen?"

Bollard shrugged. "What if I am?"

"You ever been in trouble in Australia?"

"Yeah. Big trouble. Sometimes when I was a lad, I

was negligent in my studies, and my mum got quite irate about it."

Quentin sneered at his witness. "I was speaking about trouble with the law."

"Oh that. Now I believe on that subject I'm going to have to invoke my fifth amendment right to protection from self-incrimination."

We had learned a good deal more about Bollard's history on the phone with the Australian police. The problem was that we still had no documentation. "Did you ever know a young woman named Edna Peel?"

Bollard sniffed, wrinkled his long nose. "Don't believe so, no."

This was the point where a trial lawyer typically said *Let me refresh your memory* and then slapped a police record in front of the witness. Only Quentin had no files to work with. "You don't recall sending her threatening notes?"

"I believe I'd best invoke that wonderful fifth amendment of yours," Bollard said cheerfully. He seemed to think the whole proceeding was a joke.

"Do you recall being charged with attacking her?"

"That charge was dropped. It was a boyfriend-girlfriend misunderstanding, that's all."

"I see. How about Tabitha Ferrell? Was she your girlfriend, too?"

Bollard shrugged. "Not really."

"But you knew her?"

"A bit."

"And were you charged with harassment of Tabitha Ferrell under the Australian stalkers law?"

"That charge was dropped, too."

Quentin tapped his Bic pen thoughtfully on the podium for a moment, then said, "Do you know what a cricket bat is, Mr. Bollard?"

"Sure."

"Would you tell us?"

"It's an implement." He smirked again.

"What sort of implement?"

"An athletic implement. It's used in a game called cricket."

Quentin was obviously frustrated, but he kept cool. The danger, he understood, was that Gorin Maples would start objecting and Judge Deaks would shut down the whole line of questioning.

"Is it like a baseball bat?"

"A bit, yeah."

"Weren't you, in fact, charged under the Australian stalker law because you threatened to beat her with a cricket bat?"

"How would I know what's in the cops' heads? This one detective had it in for me. Once again, they dropped the charges. You might note that I filed suit against him for unwarranted police action."

"Is it true you've been diagnosed with obsessive-compulsive disorder?"

"I'm taking the fifth."

"And that you've been hospitalized several times in Australia?"

"I was suffering exhaustion, that's all, mate."

"So you *have* been hospitalized?"

Bollard leaned forward, ran his finger down the side of his long blade of a nose. With a thin smile, he said in slow words, as though speaking to a child, "Fifth amendment."

Quentin gave the jury a significant look. "Does the name Tori Nilssen ring a bell with you?"

Bollard lost his smirky look. His expression became guarded. "Sure."

"Who is she?"

"She's quite a famous actress—in Australia anyway."

"She was in a movie called *Missing Edgar,* right?"

Bollard nodded. "Yeah."

"Did you ever threaten her?"

"No."

"You ever break into her house and live in her basement?"

"No."

"You ever attack her with a cricket bat?"

"*No!*"

"I'd remind you that you're under oath. You are subject to being charged with perjury if you lie."

Bollard leaned forward toward the microphone. "So what, mate? I'm telling the truth."

"Oh really?" Quentin smiled, took the single piece of documentary evidence that we actually had in our possession and handed it to the clerk. "I'm going to mark this document as Defense Exhibit 12, your honor."

Gorin Maples finally stood up and said, "Your honor, I've been patient here, but I have to object. We've been listening to a bunch of unsubstantiated accusations about one thing or another and now Mr. Senior is dragging out some kind of piece of paper that I've never seen before, that's never been produced, and, ah, I'm just going to have to object to this whole line of questioning as being irrelevant."

"Could we have a brief sidebar?" Quentin said.

Deaks twitched one finger at the lawyers, and they all trooped up front. There was a lot of whispering and gesturing, but I couldn't hear anything. It was obvious, though, that Quentin was arguing that the defense had a right to present an alternate theory of the crime and that he was attempting to admit evidence of prior similar acts by Bollard. When the sidebar was over, Quentin didn't look happy.

"Just a couple more questions, Mr. Bollard," Quentin said. "Have you served time in prison in Australia?"

"I'm taking the fifth," Bollard said defiantly.

Quentin studied his face for a moment, then said, "Could you look at the document we've marked as Defense Exhibit 12. Are you familiar with Interpol, Mr. Bollard?"

Bollard shrugged. "Some type of international police agency, I believe."

"And Mr. Bollard, would you read the top line of this document?"

Gorin Maples said, "I object! Your honor, there's no foundation for this document. He's trying to badger this witness into admitting something using a document that we have no reason to believe is or is not real."

Deaks smiled broadly. "He's right, Mr. Senior. You messed up here. Until you lay some foundation, that document stays on the clerk's table."

It was a crushing blow. Quentin had taken a strategic gamble and lost. In hopes of ambushing the defense with Bollard's testimony, he had failed to put somebody from law enforcement on the stand to lay foundation for the Interpol document. He could have called Chief Robard up and laid the foundation for the document that way. But that would have tipped Maples off, and the district attorney might have moved even quicker to shut down this line of questioning.

Quentin's face was slightly pale as he set the paper quietly on the clerk's table. He took a moment to compose himself. "Is it not true, Mr. Bollard," he said, "that you followed Georgia Burnett around to all her concerts earlier this year?"

"I'm a bit of a fan, yeah."

"And that you showed up in restaurants where she ate?"

Bollard smiled a little. "That may have happened occasionally. We shared similar tastes, that's all."

"And did you also obtain backstage passes to many of her shows?"

"A few. What's wrong with that? I liked her music."

"Is it also true that after the tour was over, you trespassed on Georgia's land, that you set up a tent there, that for several months you lived on her land while spying on her with a telescope?"

Bollard's face tightened. "I believe I'll invoke the fifth again, mate."

Quentin raised his eyebrows slightly. Finally he'd scored a hit. Taking the fifth wasn't a perfect bull's-eye, but it was better than nothing. "And is it not true that after you were discovered there squatting on Ms. Burnett's property, you decided to change your hidey-hole? Isn't it true that you broke into the crawlspace under Georgia's house?"

Gorin Maples stood up again. "I'd like to renew my continuing objection to this whole fishing expedition!"

"Consider it renewed." Deaks was looking at the witness narrowly as though he were considering something. "Now go ahead and answer the question, Mr. Bollard."

"I'm taking the fifth again," Bollard said.

I turned to Barrington Cherry and whispered, "Why's he doing this? Why not just lie and deny everything?"

Barrington shook his head. "Maybe his lawyer instructed him to do that under the assumption that we've got more on him than we do."

Quentin finally took the plunge, thundering, "Is it not true that you had an obsession with Georgia Burnett, that you finally broke into her house, that she rebuffed your advances, and that when she did so, you killed her?"

"Objection!" Gorin Maples yelled.

Bollard stood up in the witness box and screamed. "Not true! Not true! I never hurt her! I would never do a thing to harm Georgia!"

Judge Deaks hammered his gavel until everybody shut up. "Alright, alright," he said in his creaky little voice. "I believe I've seen enough. Mr. Senior, you're done with this witness."

"But—"

"Sit *down,* counselor."

I had been watching this whole scene with a sinking feeling in my stomach. Quentin was a good lawyer, it was true, but he'd let his legal instincts get in the way of his human instincts. He'd structured his entire presentation with the intention of getting as many questions asked in front of the jury as possible. Knowing his problems with documentation, he didn't expect to get answers. And he certainly didn't expect to get any sort of admission of guilt out of Bollard. All he had been aiming to do was expose the jury to the notion that Bollard was an obsessive crank who may have exhibited a pattern of behavior that would lead the jury toward reasonable doubt.

He'd tried, and from where I was sitting, he'd failed. Now that it had happened I knew what we should have done. Twenty-twenty hindsight.

Without thinking, I stood up and shouted, "Wait!"

Deaks put on his glasses and looked at me malevolently. "Who are you?" he demanded, knowing full well the answer.

"My name is Sunny Childs, I'm a private investigator for Mr. Brushwood."

"You admitted to the bar of the state of Georgia?"

"No, sir."

"You have a law degree, Ms. Childs?"

"No, sir."

"Then the next time you stand up and start shrieking in my courtroom, young lady, I'm gonna send you to jail. How's that grab you?"

"I understand. But before the witness is excused, could I have a moment to confer with counsel?"

Deaks glared. "No, ma'am, you may not."

Quentin, however, saved the day. "Your honor, I just have one more question for the witness. One more. Then I promise I'm done."

"One?" Deaks squinted. His eyes were huge slits behind his thick glasses.

"One, y'honor." Quentin held up one finger.

Deaks thought about it. "Nope. The defense is done with this witness."

At that point Mike Friend stood up. "Your honor, I've got a couple questions for this witness, too. Surely my client will be permitted a chance to examine this witness, too!"

Deaks chewed the inside of his mouth. It obviously went against the grain, but he really had no choice. If he didn't let Friend question Bollard, the case would crash and burn on appeal. "Alright, Mr. Friend. But it's gonna be short and to the point. You read me?"

"Loud and clear, your honor." Mike Friend stood up, then paused and placed his legal pad in front of me as though he were organizing his thoughts. He raised his eyebrows questioningly at me. I grabbed a pen off the table and scrawled one sentence on his legal pad. "Forget the law!" I hissed under my breath. "Forget the jury. Think about *who he is*. Ask him *this*." I banged my index finger on the legal pad next to what I'd written.

Mike Friend stared at the legal pad. As far as I was concerned, Mike Friend was a legal technician, a guy who was better at filing motions and negotiating plea bargains than making arguments in court. But right now he was all that stood between Gunnar Brushwood and the electric chair. I just hoped he understood what I was getting at.

Finally he stood up and walked to the podium.

"Mr. Bollard," Mike Friend said. "Simple question. Do you love Georgia Burnett?"

The room was very quiet. Someone in the jury box shifted their weight and a chair squeaked. Bollard sat there looking around the room like he had suddenly found himself dropped into a strange place. He seemed cowed and uncertain for the first time since he'd been on the stand.

"I asked you a question," Friend said. "Before all the world. Do you love Georgia Burnett?"

Bollard's lower lip pushed outward slightly and a tiny muscle trembled in his cheek. "You don't understand," he said finally, his voice hushed.

"What don't I understand?" Ratkin's lawyer said softly.

"*Nobody* understands."

Again there was silence.

"I asked you a simple question," Friend said. "You're answering with a riddle. Help me out here. Do you love Georgia Burnett?"

Bollard sighed then, a deep wracking sigh, and his face collapsed. "You don't know what it's like!" he said. "Nobody knows what it's like to have the kind of connection that I had to her. Love? That word is inadequate to describe it." His voice began to rise. "I *was* her. She *was* me. We were joined in the stars and the planets! We were yin and yang. You want to call that love, mate? Words fail, mate! Words fail in the face of a power like this." Tears were suddenly streaming down his face.

"So you loved her?"

"Yes! Chroist, yes! I loved her more than . . . oh god, oh god, oh god."

Bollard put his face in his hands, and his shoulders began to heave.

"This is all very touching, your honor," Gorin Maples said. "But it's not the slightest bit relevant."

"I'm almost done," Mike Friend said.

"One more question, and that's it," Deaks said.

Bollard looked up slowly, his face streaked with tears.

"Mr. Bollard, did you kill Georgia Burnett?"

"No!" Bollard looked aghast. "I could never, never do something like that!"

Mike Friend's face fell. For five minutes we had been watching this man fall apart, hoping against hope his passion might lead him to fess up. But it hadn't and he hadn't. That was that.

"Thank you, Mr. Bollard," the judge said.

"But I know who did!" Bollard shouted. "I saw it happen."

Everyone froze for a moment. The courtroom was so silent it seemed as though every one of us had stopped breathing.

Quentin made a tiny, frantic, pushing motion with his

right hand, urging Mike Friend to ask the obvious follow-up.

"Who?" Friend said. "Who killed Georgia Burnett?"

Bollard stood up in the witness box and pointed his finger angrily into the crowd. "That's who did it!" Two eyes stared back at him, wide with apparent surprise. "That's your bleddy murderer!"

Then Bollard called out the killer's name.

CHAPTER 41

I **T TOOK TWENTY-FIVE** minutes, but finally Quentin and Friend came back, both looking very smug. "He's gonna allow Bollard's answer to stay in the record," Quentin said softly. "We don't get any further follow-up, though. After this he goes into cross-examination. Should be interesting. Maples doesn't have any choice but to crucify him."

Reasonable doubt. Surely we had reasonable doubt. For a moment I felt elated. But then the elation quickly passed. Even if Gunnar walked on reasonable doubt, he'd become an untouchable, an O. J. Simpson, walking around for the rest of his life with people whispering that he had gotten away with murder.

And there was still the fingerprint on the baseball bat. How could they make that fingerprint go away?

When the bailiffs brought Bollard back, he looked like a different man from the smirking joker who'd walked onto the stand that morning. He was solemn, chastened, empty.

The jury filed in soberly.

The room was very quiet for a moment, then the bailiff announced Judge Deaks's return.

"Be seated," Deaks said. "Mr. District Attorney, does the state have any questions for this witness?"

"Yes, your Honor, I do." Maples swaggered to the podium. "Mr. Bollard, you made some very serious charges earlier today, did you not?"

"Yes, I did."

"You have pointed your finger at a person in open court. You have spoken their name. You have accused them of the worst crime a human being can commit. Do you still hold to that claim?"

"Yes, I do."

Maples smiled condescendingly, then said in a dismissive voice "Well, sir, can you *prove* any of this?"

Bollard blinked. "Sure," he said offhandedly.

The courtroom was silent for a moment. Gorin Maples then made the classic lawyer's mistake: he asked a question that he didn't know the answer to. "And how might you do that, Mr. Bollard?"

Bollard leaned forward and spoke distinctly into the microphone. "I've got it on tape." Then he lifted one hand. In it was clutched a small black rectangle of plastic. From where I sat, it looked like an eight-millimeter videotape.

The room erupted.

Maples blinked and then said, "Ah, Judge, I request a brief sidebar."

CHAPTER 42

THIS TIME AFTER the jury was sent out, the judge said, "Alright, folks, I want to see counsel and Mr. Bollard in chambers."

Quentin rose to a crouch. "If I may, I'd like to bring my investigators in. They both have some expertise in videotape surveillance and analysis. Mr. Cherry here is former Deputy Special-Agent-in-Charge of the FBI in Atlanta and—"

"Sure, sure, whatever. . . ." Deaks said vaguely. He seemed to lack his usual decisiveness.

We filed back to Deaks's large, plain office. Someone from the Rome Police Department was called to set up a VCR so that it would play Bollard's eight-millimeter tape, and some old man—a courthouse hanger-on—was made busy bringing in chairs so that everyone would have a place to sit, a court reporter included. It all took about half an hour.

"Before we see this tape," Deaks said finally, "I want to have a brief evidentiary hearing. Madam Court Reporter, would you swear Mr. Bollard in?"

The court reporter did as she was told.

"You say you've videotaped the murder, Mr. Bollard?" Judge Deaks said.

"Yeah."

"How'd that come about?"

Bollard looked uneasy. "I think I'd better take the fifth."

"Off the record," Deaks snapped. The court reporter took her hands off the steno machine. "Now, boy, this fifth amendment bullshit ain't gonna float right now. If you been withholding real, bona fide, exculpatory evidence, evidence that caused two men to be improperly charged in this matter, then you're damn sure in trouble already. So don't give me no fifth amendment, you understand me?"

Bollard looked at him calmly. "You want to know how I got this tape, you give me immunity. No charge for trespassing, no charge for perjury, no charge for obstruction of justice, nothing."

"Oh-ho!" Deaks said. "All of a sudden we got us a jailhouse lawyer."

Bollard said, "You got a bollocksed up case here, Judge. Without sufficient foundation for this tape, this case will hang around your neck like a bleddy millstone and you'll end up a judicial laughing stock. If you want this tape in the clear from an evidentiary perspective, then I get immunity. Here and now."

Deaks looked slightly taken aback by this display of legal acumen. He turned to the DA. "Gorin?"

Maples looked pugnaciously at Bollard. "I'm fairly happy with the state's case. I don't necessarily have any interest in the tape coming into evidence."

"You may recall," Deaks said, "that your oath of office requires that you serve in the interest of justice, not just as a prosecutorial advocate."

Maples shook his head. "No, your honor, until I know what's on that tape—"

"Goddammit, boy, I said give him his goddamn immunity right this goddamn minute," Deaks barked.

Maples's fuzzy blond mustache twitched. "Well, heck, you don't have to get all . . ." The DA sighed noisily, turned to Bollard. "Alright. *If* this tape is what you say it is, then you got your immunity."

"Total transactional immunity. Anything connected to this case, you can't charge me."

Maples hesitated. "Okay, yeah. Total transactional immunity."

Bollard nodded. "Done."

"Back on the record," Deaks said. "Now, Mr. Bollard, how'd you get this tape?"

"Well," Bollard said. "It's like Mr. Senior here was saying. I was kind of . . . ah, I was sort of camping out under Georgia's house."

"Why's that?"

Bollard looked at Deaks like he was a fool. "I had to learn enough about her so that when I finally approached her, she would understand."

"Understand what?"

"That we were meant to be together. Forever. Soul mates. Like that, see?"

"Uh-*huh*. So you're living under the house. Then what?"

"Well, I kind of, what I did is I installed some video cameras. Little ones. In the walls."

Suddenly I remembered being under the house. When I had discovered Bollard's hidey-hole, I had noticed a coaxial cable dangling from the joist, the kind used for carrying video signals. I had assumed he was tapping into the cable TV. Obviously I'd been wrong.

"I had some monitoring equipment down there, see?" Bollard continued. "VCR, TV monitor, routers, stuff like that. That way I could watch her go from room to room." His voice suddenly took on a silky, frightening quality. I felt chill bumps on my back. "I could watch her eat. Watch her sleep. Watch her dress." He smiled fondly.

"So you recorded this stuff?" Deaks said.

"Sure. Had an eight-millimeter deck, studio quality. That way I could play things back when she wasn't at home. Keep the connection with her, you know."

Deaks looked at Bollard like he was giving off a stink. "So tell me about the day of the murder."

Bollard's face sagged. "I was watching her in her room. Must have been around noon." He smiled sadly. "She sleeps late, you know, because she has an artist's temperament. Got up, took a shower. Such a lovely, sweet body. She was walking around naked. Then . . ." Bollard touched his eyes, then put his face in his hand. "Watch it," he said, his muffled voice breaking. "You'll see."

Deaks nodded at the Rome Police officer who was running the video equipment.

The TV winked on, showing an empty, sun-drenched room—Georgia's bedroom. A digital counter in the bottom left corner of the screen gave the date and time—DEC 9 12:21 P.M. After a moment, a naked woman came out of the right hand side of the screen, from the direction of the bathroom. It was Georgia Burnett. Her hair was wet, and she was rubbing herself with a towel. Bollard was right, she *was* lovely. Though I couldn't help taking catty notice of the fact that her breasts were a bit too perky—presumably from the implants that Virginia had mentioned.

As she was toweling off, she looked up suddenly, as though she had heard a noise coming from the direction of her door.

"Is there any audio here, Mr. Bollard?" Deaks asked.

"No. I hadn't gotten around to installing microphones yet." Bollard didn't sound the least bit ashamed.

From the expression on her face, it appeared that Georgia was puzzled but not frightened. Then her lips moved and her face showed recognition, as though she were talking to someone on the other side of the door.

Georgia engaged in a brief conversation with the person outside the door, frowned, then retreated out of view. For at least a minute the screen was blank.

"There's a walk-in closet over there, Judge," I said, pointing in the direction she'd disappeared.

Suddenly the door to the left of the screen opened, distorted by the wide-angle effect of the lens, and a figure entered the room. Despite the distortion of the lens, and despite the fact that a large fawn-colored Stetson covered the face, it was obviously a woman: underneath the Western-cut shirt and the jeans were breasts and feminine hips. As the woman moved across the room under the camera, a long, red braid became visible dangling from the rear of the hat. She wore cowboy boots.

"Marla Jeter," Bollard said simply.

Then Jeter, too, disappeared out of the right side of the screen in the direction of the walk-in closet. For a long time nothing moved.

"I could hear them yelling," Bollard said. "All the way down in the basement."

"What were they saying?"

"I couldn't make it out exactly. Something about a baby. Something about Georgia wanting to stay married. It was hard to tell."

The screen remained empty of motion. The digital counter changed to 12:39, then 12:40, then 12:41.

"I saw them in bed together, Georgia and Marla," Bollard said, in a low, harsh voice. "I saw the disgusting, vile bleddy things that they did. But I could tell Georgia didn't enjoy it. Marla had some kind of sick spell over her, took advantage of her because she had a bad marriage." Bollard looked at Ratkin with anger in his eyes. "You, mate, you never loved her either. She was just a possession to you. Just a toy."

Ratkin's face was white, glued to the screen.

Suddenly there was an eruption of motion. Georgia burst into the bedroom again, mouth open in a noiseless scream. Jeter was behind her, pursuing with Jeremy Ratkin's aluminum baseball bat in her hands—the same Spaulding that had been found in the trunk of Gunnar's car.

It was all over in seconds. Jeter—her back to the camera—raised the bat and struck. Georgia fell, twisting into a ball, as Jeter hit her again several times. On the fourth or fifth stroke of the bat, Georgia's body relaxed. Jeter kept hitting her, then finally stopped and stood staring down at the body. I wanted to know what the expression was on her face, but it remained hidden because she was facing away from the camera lens. What would move a person to do something like that? I wanted some sort of clue, some sort of understanding that would help me dislodge the sensation of horror that had grabbed my stomach. But I suppose no amount of reason ever makes a thing like this add up.

Ratkin's face was white, trembling, glued to the screen.

So that was it. There had been an affair. Georgia announced her pregnancy, told Jeter that the affair was over, that she was going to devote herself to the child, that she was rededicating herself to her marriage. Whatever. And Jeter had snapped.

On the screen, Marla suddenly stiffened as though she'd heard something. With the bat still in her hand, she turned and hurried out of the room.

The counter in the bottom corner read 12:28.

"Seven minutes," Quentin said. "She hears Gunnar ringing from the front gate, she runs back to the staff house, maybe throws the bat behind a bush, goes inside and tells Ben Pryor she's been in the bathroom. Next she buzzes Gunnar through the gate. When she sees Gunnar walk off behind the house to look for Georgia, she tells Pryor that she's going into the kitchen to get some pizza or whatever, she trots outside, drops the bat in the trunk of Gunnar's car, and she's back at the card table in thirty seconds."

"Shut the TV off," Deaks said. Then he turned to Gorin Maples. "Well, Mr. District Attorney?"

Maples looked down at the floor, thinking, then suddenly turned to the police officer who had set up the video equipment. "Sergeant, go arrest that woman."

As the cop headed for the door, Judge Deaks called

to him, "Hold on, Sarge. What you gonna tell him to charge her with?"

The policeman looked at him blankly.

"Gorin," Deaks said, "you gave Marla Jeter transactional immunity. You can't touch her."

Maples looked a little pale. "Well, dadgum it, I got to charge her with something, Judge!"

Judge Deaks winked at the policeman. "Charge her with perjury, Sarge. We'll figure something out eventually."

After the policeman went away, Maples sighed heavily. "It was that doggone fingerprint!" he said, turning to look at Gunnar. "How in the heck did that fingerprint get on the bat, Mr. Brushwood?"

"I've thought and thought and thought," Gunnar said, staring into the air with a puzzled expression on his face. "You know what? I still got no earthly idea."

After a few minutes the policeman came back and said, "About Miz Jeter, sir? She's gone."

Chapter 43

OUR CELEBRATION LASTED well into the night. Jeremy Ratkin didn't stick around long, but Mike Friend did: he turned out to be a decent guy once he got a couple of drinks in him. Gunnar kept hugging me and telling me how I'd saved his life, how he loved me like I was his own daughter. He told me that I had to come back and work at Peachtree Investigations again, that everything would be like the good old days.

Around one in the morning, Quentin—who had made significant progress into a bottle of MacCallan single malt—hit on me in a fatherly sort of way. Gunnar overheard his advances, got offended on my behalf, and punched him in the nose. After the bleeding was stanched, Quentin and Gunnar started singing military songs together. Apparently they'd both served in the Special Forces back in Vietnam, though not at the same time. It was all very special and masculine.

And when it was all over I ended up in bed with Barrington Cherry. I suppose it had been inevitable.

● ● ●

I was awakened at 8:30 the next morning by the insistent, annoying, shrill tone of the buzzer to the downstairs door.

I got up slowly, stumbled over to the intercom. "What?" I said irritably.

"FedEx," a voice said.

I buzzed the Federal Express courier in, told him to take the elevator up. Wrapping myself in a sheet, I went over to the elevator and signed for the small box, then sent the FedEx guy on his way.

"What is it?" Barrington said sleepily.

"Those jerks in Australia finally got off their duffs and sent us the records on Bollard."

"A day late and a dollar short," Barrington said.

As I started to open the box, a loop of the sheet I'd been holding around myself fell to the floor, exposing the better part of my torso.

"Oh my my my," Barrington said. "I think you better come here." Barrington's inviting brown body lay stretched out on the bed.

I laughed, let the rest of the sheet fall to the floor. Covering as much of my body as I could with the unopened FedEx package, I made a pretend show of modesty, sashayed back to the bed, letting strategic bits of myself peep out at him from behind the package. "Oh, deah," I said in my best *Gone With the Wind* accent. "I seem to have mislaid my gahments, dahling."

"Here, let me mislay this for you, too." Barrington took the FedEx package from my hands and tossed it across the room. The package hit the floor with a resounding boom, then slid under my dresser. And that was the last I thought about Ian Bollard for a very long time.

AMONG HORSES

CHAPTER 44

THE NEXT DAY a team from the Georgia Bureau of Investigation and the Floyd County Police Department served a warrant on the apartment where Marla Jeter had been living. Among the evidence found there was something that the GBI described as a "latex wand" with an impression of Gunnar Brushwood's fingerprint imbedded in the tip. The TV reporters called it a rubber finger.

How Marla got the rubber finger remains an unsolved mystery. A few months later, though, Gunnar ran into a fingerprint expert at a convention who said that if you had the right equipment—a computer-controlled micromilling machine of the sort used to make parts for computer disk drives and similar precision machinery—you could use the scanned digital image of a fingerprint to carve a steel die that would contain a "negative" of the original fingerprint. This steel die could then be used as a mold in which to cast a rubber finger. You could then use the rubber finger or latex wand or whatever you wanted to call it to leave fingerprints . . . anywhere, anytime. It was, according to the expert, a technique used occasionally by the CIA. He'd never heard of its use in a civilian case before.

Marla Jeter has not been seen since.

I got a card in the mail once, though, from some swanky resort in the little central American country of Belize. The picture showed lots of banana trees and some cute guys sitting around a very blue swimming pool. Scrawled on the back were the words, "I didn't do it." It was signed, *Marla*.

CHAPTER 45

FROM TIME TO time I go into what I like to call a Temporary Vegetative State. When TVS hits, I put on an old blue cotton nightgown, dial the tube to some idiot sitcom, turn the sound down to a barely audible buzz, and start reading a copy of *People* magazine. It's comforting to me, God knows why, to get lost in the details of other people's lives.

About nine months after the trial, I got in one of my TVS moods and sat around my loft one night with the latest copy of *People*. Imagine my surprise to flip the magazine open to page sixty-seven and find a multi-page spread showing Jeremy Ratkin and his pretty young wife, Leesa, relaxing out behind their four hundred-acre horse farm in Rome, Georgia. Country radio sucks so bad these days that I've pretty much stopped listening to it, so I didn't recognize the cutie—but according to the magazine, she was the Hot New Thing-of-the-Week in country music.

The next page showed a candid moment from their recent wedding—white dress, cleavage, rice arcing through the air. I stared for a long time.

If you had to describe her, Ratkin's new wife would have sounded a lot like Georgia: vivacious, cute, and yet fundamentally undistinctive, as though the camera lens was just the slightest bit out of focus. A little blonder and a decade younger, yeah, but basically carved from the same block of plaster as Georgia. The story also mentioned that Leesa was recording for ArchRival Records—which Jeremy, the article further explained, had just sold to some big, German entertainment conglomerate for an undisclosed amount. To top it all off, *Billboard* had listed Leesa's album at number one on both the pop *and* country charts.

Notwithstanding all this recent good luck, Ratkin's face looked gloomy and sobered in all the pictures. He had, after all, experienced a terrible blow from Dame Fortune—and not so long ago. The article quoted Leesa at great length talking about Ratkin's "bravery" and "staunchness" in the face of what she quaintly called his "misfortunes." I smelled the breath of Gill Merrit in every word she said.

The whole thing gave me an itch. I tried to watch the sitcom, tried to get absorbed in the latest poop on Tom Cruise—but I couldn't do it. Finally I picked up my phone and called a friend of mine, Honey Chanteuse (yes, as far as I know, that's her real name, and, no, she's not a drag queen), who is the biggest country music fanatic in the known universe.

"Honey," I said. "Have you heard of Leesa DuVall?"

"Baby!" Honey sounded aghast, her deep whiskey voice full of surprise. "Surely you know about Leesa Du*Vall*?"

"Not really."

Honey clucked sadly. "Shoot, her first album came out about three months ago. Big, *big* hoopla. Immense publicity campaign. I bet her record company spent a million dollars promoting it."

"Is it any good?"

"If you like Garth Brooks, you'll love Leesa DuVall."

"That bad, huh?"

"It's slick, has a lot of neat little guitar hooks, it's

produced by Keith Stegall, has all the best session guys on it, songs by all the top songwriters . . . all the required elements. Her video's getting good rotation, too—and not just on country networks, either. It's on VH-1 till you fixing to throw up every time you see it."

"Second question, Honey. Do you happen to know when ArchRival got sold to that German company?"

"Oh, that was only a couple months ago. I would say it was about a month after Leesa's record hit number one. Hey, and you want to hear mondo irony? The record Leesa knocked off the number one slot was Georgia Burnett's."

"So Georgia's last record was big, too?"

"Oh, yeah. Huge. ArchRival milked the publicity about her murder to death." Honey laughed her big, cynical laugh. "Pun intended."

"Huh." I started toting up how much time had elapsed on my fingers. "Do you know how long it takes to make a record?"

"My understanding, country records usually go into development at least a year before release. The studio work doesn't take all that long, but you've got to find the right songs, shape your publicity campaign, set up your album tour, all that stuff."

"So Jeremy Ratkin must have been working with Leesa DuVall well before Georgia died."

Honey didn't respond for a minute. "Baby, are you just talking . . . or are you *saying* something?"

"Thinking out loud, Honey, that's all."

About the time I got off the phone, I heard the elevator grinding up to my loft. Barrington stepped out. I might mention that we had moved in together about three months after the trial. He also rejoined the FBI after having gotten magnificently bored after about a month of working as a freelance PI. Doing car accident investigations and errant husband stakeouts were not his thing. He had to take a pay cut and he lost two rungs of civil service rank . . . but at least he's happy.

I might *further* mention that, while it's still a little early to tell, it's possible that he's The One. I've been wrong on that score so many times, that I'm withholding judgment until the goo-goo eyes phase wears off. But I've got my fingers crossed.

"Hey, sweetheart!" I said.

Barrington studied me for a moment. "What?" he said finally.

"*What* what?"

"It's 11:30 at night and—except for that ugly-ass robe—you look like you're ready to run a footrace."

"What's wrong with this robe?" I said.

Barrington was smart enough not to take the bait. He stretched leisurely. "I've been on stakeout for sixteen hours. Mercy mercy mercy, I need some sleep."

I stood there bouncing up and down on my toes. I guess he was right: the Temporary Vegetative State seemed to have suddenly worn off.

"So look," I said. "Think you could check on something for me?"

Barrington sat down on the edge of the bed, pulled off his shirt. I noticed he'd gained a few pounds since we'd moved in together. But then, hell, so had I. That's a good sign, too, I hear: you meet The One, you gain weight.

"Like when?" Barrington said.

"Uh . . ." I said.

Barrington looked up at me with his exhausted eyes, then sighed deeply and pulled his shirt back on. He knows that there are times when I turn into a force of nature, and it's a testimony to his good nature that he's willing to accommodate himself to that.

Like I say, he might well be a keeper. He really might.

While he was gone doing the late-night errand I had sent him on, something occurred to me. Let me preface this by saying that I make no claims to housekeeper stardom.

I don't clean the tub, for instance, until it takes on a sort of petri dish quality. I don't do dishes until I run out of plates. Oh, yeah, and I don't sweep under furniture—not even when my mother comes to visit.

So when I got down on my belly and looked under the chest of drawers, the FedEx package that had been sent to me by the Australian police was lying right there nestled among the bumper crop of dust bunnies where Barrington had thrown it back in January.

I pulled the package out, cracked it open, leafed through it for a while. After a minute, I had to sit down on the bed. Suddenly my legs didn't want to hold me up anymore.

Half an hour later the door of the freight elevator clattered open and Barrington stood there shaking his head. He went over to the kitchen table and set down two pieces of paper. I stood next to him and studied them, comparing the papers with each other. They were computerized forensic enhancements of automobile tire tracks with FBI document control numbers stamped in the top right corner.

"Identical," I said.

"I can't believe I didn't see it," Barrington said. "I just can't believe it."

"Wait," I said. "It gets better."

I threw a photograph of Ian Bollard on the table, a photograph that I got from the Australian police file.

Barrington looked at the picture for a while. "Looks like they forgot to turn on the light," he said finally.

CHAPTER 46

WHEN I DROVE out to meet Chief Robard and give him all of the information I had eventually turned up, I was surprised to see Ben Pryor standing in the front office of the Floyd County Police Department. The big man was wearing the uniform of a Floyd County policeman.

"Since when did this happen, Ben?" I said, pointing at the badge. "I'd have thought small town law enforcement would be a little dull after being bodyguard to the stars."

"They were hiring, so I applied for the job," he said. He shrugged, smiled gently. "I like the country around here. Being a bodyguard means living in the city most of the time. Never much took to city life." He looked away from me so I wouldn't see it; but he was too late. His eyes had suddenly welled up with tears. "Besides, I feel Georgia every day, like her life is bearing down on me. If I'd done my job right, she'd be alive today. I don't want that responsibility anymore."

"I could see how that would be." I patted his large arm. "Is the chief around?"

"Sure." Pryor wiped his eyes on his sleeve. "Let me

go snag him for you." The big officer walked off down the hall.

After a while Chief Robard came out. His hair was sweaty and pressed down in a ring around his head from wearing a hat. "Sunny Childs. To what do I owe the pleasure?"

"Could we sit down in your office for a minute?" I said. "It's about Georgia Burnett."

The Chief looked slightly puzzled, but led me on back to his office. He still had the two-by-four on his credenza with the gold spike in it and the words NAIL THE BASTARD carved in the side. I sat down, then the chief sat down and spread his hands in silent invitation.

"Let me ask you a question," I said. "When you brought Ian Bollard in the day before he testified, you didn't charge him or book him or anything, right?"

"No. We were just holding him as a recalcitrant material witness under subpoena."

"So you never booked him, never fingerprinted him?"

The chief didn't answer my question. "What you driving at, Ms. Childs?"

"Well, I just took a peek at Ian Bollard's criminal records from Australia. Take a look at this picture."

I slid a photograph of a man across the chief's desk. The man in the picture had pitch black skin, thick red-speckled lips, a shock of curly black hair. The chief stared at the picture.

"And who is this, Miss Childs?"

"Racially speaking," I said, "the man you're looking at is a native Australian. I'm not sure if it's the politically correct terminology, but another way of putting it, Ian Bollard is an Aboriginal."

"I don't follow you."

"I'm saying the guy in this picture is the real Ian Bollard."

"Then who . . ."

"The guy who testified in court? There's no telling."

The chief's knee started jiggling up and down, until

finally his foot was tapping softly on the floor of his office.

"Something else," I said. "When we came up to investigate the kidnapping last year, I found a guy camped out on Georgia's property. The guy we believed to be Bollard. Presumably the same guy who slept under Georgia's house. I mean he admitted to it on the stand, right? Anyway, when I found the guy up there on the hill, he ran away, hopped in a black Toyota Land Cruiser and drove away. At that time, my forensic guy—you may recall he was a fellow named Roy Nidlett—took a cast of the Toyota's tire tracks.

"Later on, Georgia's kidnapper abandoned his vehicle at the MARTA station over near Perimeter Mall. The FBI took a print of its tire track and put it on their computer. I've had Roy Nidlett compare their computer print against a computer enhancement of the cast he took up at Georgia's house. It's his firm opinion that they were one and the same vehicle."

I set the two images of the tire tracks on his desk. Nidlett had circled and numbered various unique characteristics of the tires with a red pen, demonstrating clearly that they were not just the same brand, but the same actual tires.

The chief looked at the two pieces of paper. "I don't see the significance of that."

"When the FBI took over the kidnapping investigation, they eventually concluded that the whole thing was a setup. I'm sure they made you aware of this."

"Sure. That's why we were immediately suspicious of Ratkin when Georgia was murdered."

"Off the record I'll tell you this. Ratkin admitted to me—in a sort of hypothetical way—that the kidnapping was bogus. But the other thing he said to me was that the guy in the Land Cruiser at the MARTA station was *not* Bollard. What he claimed to me was that after I had found that Bollard had been squatting on their farm, he changed his plan, had his henchmen—whoever they might have been—go out and buy a black Land Cruiser with the idea in mind of throwing blame for the kidnapping on this creep who had been stalking his wife. He figured it would add a little vérité to this cooked-up kidnapping."

The chief looked at me for a moment, then said, "But if he went out and bought a different truck, the tires would be different."

"But they weren't," I said. "Same tires, same truck. Therefore the guy we thought was Bollard, was actually working for Ratkin from the very beginning."

"So not only was the kidnapping faked, but the whole stalker thing was fake. So he was probably never living under the house at all."

"And if the stalking was fake, then what does that tell you about the videotape?"

The chief's face took on a gray cast. "Oh my God," he said. "Her face."

"We saw the hat, the boots, the jeans, the long red pigtail." I smiled thinly. "But the one thing we never saw on that tape was her face."

We sat silently for a while. I looked out the door, saw Ben Pryor walk by.

"So I'm guessing you've got a theory," the chief said.

I nodded. "Here's what I think happened. I think Ratkin was behind everything. *Every*thing. As you recall from the trial, he was in financial trouble. He needed money to get his company back on its feet. Now those of us who knew the kidnapping was fake, we assumed that he had done it for the publicity, that he'd done it with Georgia's connivance.

"But here's another way of looking at it. Ratkin's marriage to Georgia is shaky. His financial situation is shaky. Right? I'm guessing he asks her for some money to prop up ArchRival Records and she says no. So he figures, screw it, I'll get your money anyway. He hires some guy to be a 'stalker.' I'm going to call him John Doe. In order to make the stalker thing look good, he searches for a viable suspect, somebody that his bogus stalker can impersonate. Now they don't want him to be American because it would be too easy to locate people who knew him, photographs, files, etc., etc. So he probably hires a PI to run a search on the Interpol computer for a celebrity stalker from another country. Who pops up? Ian Bollard. They pull a copy of his fingerprints from the Australian crime computer and they hire some clever machinist to create rubber fingerprints like we found in Marla Jeter's room.

"So John Doe follows Georgia around for a couple of months. Ratkin tells Marla to hire a PI to trace John Doe. Meanwhile John Doe is wandering around with these rubber fingers leaving Ian Bollard's prints in hotel rooms, on water glasses, and so on. Eventually the PIs that are tracking him manage to get the prints. There's no match. But that's okay. Ratkin doesn't want Bollard's identity to show up until the kidnapping—which is what the whole Bollard identity was aimed at to begin with.

"Anyway, the tour's over, John Doe goes up in the woods, sets up his supposedly creepy little stalker hangout. He tramples some brush, maybe he leaves Ian Bollard's fingerprints here and there, craps in the latrine, throws empty potato chip bags on the ground, fills up a tent with pictures of Georgia that he's torn out of magazines. Then on the appointed day John Doe—and probably some accomplices—show up and kidnap Georgia."

"Yeah, but if he wanted money . . . didn't she have her money in some kind of trust? So he couldn't get his hands on it?"

I smiled. "From the very first moment I met Ratkin, I didn't like the guy. He just didn't seem sufficiently cut up about his wife's kidnapping. Let me tell you an odd little story. The one time I noticed him get real emotional was when he started calling his bankers. I can remember seeing him dial up a number, and it was kind of funny, he said, 'This is Jeremy Ratkin, Georgia's husband.' Think about it: if it was *his* banker, how come he identified himself as 'Georgia's husband?' That implies that the very first call he made was to *her* banker, not his. Anyway, I remember watching him. He talked for a while, then suddenly he looked like somebody had whacked him in the neck with a hatchet. At that point he looked up and asked us to leave the room. I could see him through the window and after that he made several more calls. At the time, I didn't think anything of it. But in retrospect, I think I know what happened. Celeste Williams testified that she established the trust during the summer. But ten to one Ratkin didn't find out that it existed until he placed that call to her bank. That's why he got so freaked out: it wasn't until he's right there in the middle of the kidnapping that he finds out he can't get his hands on her money."

The chief blinked. "I'll be dog," he said. "He was trying to siphon off all her money." He smiled grimly. "Man, don't you know he felt like seven kinds of fool once he found out he couldn't touch her dough."

I nodded. "But by that time, he's already riding the tiger. He has to keep holding on or he gets chewed up. I mean, if he bails out at this point, it'll be obvious the thing was bogus. So to keep up the charade, he's got to transfer what little money he *does* have into these overseas accounts . . . which undoubtedly were his in the first place. Has to chisel the supposed kidnapper down from five million to one point seven. Has to go through the whole exercise. Setting up this fake kidnapping probably cost him a mint. And he got nothing out of it."

"So in order to salvage something from the wreckage," the chief chimed in, "he turns the whole thing into a publicity stunt."

"Complete with fake gunfight. It sells a lot of records. Which helps him out. But apparently it's not enough to bail him out completely. Anyway, at this point, he's in the hole for whatever the kidnapping setup cost him— which is probably a lot—and he's still got his face against the glass wall, staring at Georgia's money."

"And meanwhile, she's apparently having an affair and talking to all her friends about whether or not she should leave him."

"Right," I said. "So that's probably when he cooks up the scheme to kill her."

From outside the room I heard a squeaking noise, like somebody was leaning against the wall. The chief stood up, peered out into the hall, then closed the door. "Thought I heard somebody out there," he said. He sat back down. "Here's the thing, though. If he set up the killing, how come he did it so he'd look like he was involved?"

"Think about it this way: once he decides to do it, he knows damn good and well that he's going to be the prime suspect. First, the husband's always a suspect. Second, he knew that all the law enforcement people involved in the kidnapping investigation were suspicious about it, that they believed it was bogus. So once he gets that far, he knows they'll find out about his financial troubles. If he sets himself up with an unshakeable alibi, he knows they'll conclude that this was a murder for hire."

The chief picked up the two by four with the gold-painted nail hammered into it, started slapping the piece of wood against the palm of his hand. "So why go through the hassle of this huge trial?" he said finally. "It must have cost him a mint in legal fees. If he controls Bollard, and Bollard's got the tape, why not cough it up at the get-go?"

The chief shook his head skeptically, still slapping his NAIL THE BASTARD plank softly against his hand.

"Look, here's where the profound arrogance of this guy comes in," I said. "He probably figures, hell, this is going to be another O. J. trial no matter what. Media circus. Why not ride the tiger again? Play it out to the very last second."

"Aside from being risky, it seems awful damn baroque, Sunny. Seems like something only a writer could imagine."

"Exactly."

Robard frowned. "I don't follow."

"You know the first thing Jeremy Ratkin did when he got out of college? He told me he drove down to L.A. and started writing screenplays. Music producing only came after he more or less washed out as a screenwriter. Point is, this is how the man thinks: He believes he can orchestrate reality, make it up from whole cloth. That's the arrogance I was talking about. He came right out and told me that he scripted the kidnapping just like it was a movie. He thinks life is a movie, and he's the screenwriter and the director and the producer all rolled into one.

"So once you make that leap, once you start thinking of this whole thing as a suspense movie, hey, why not go all the way? He's loving this shit. It would be too boring to have the whole story end in the middle of Act One, right? Hell no, he's got to have the big courtroom showdown, the wrongfully accused defendant, the media circus. It's right out of John Grisham." I smiled. "And, of course, what would a big courtroom drama be without the last-minute witness who saves the day?"

"Bollard."

"Sure. And it makes sense from a practical standpoint, too. Since Bollard, in a sense, doesn't exist, he had to keep him off the radar screen until the trial."

The chief frowned. "Yeah, but Sunny how did he know you'd find Bollard?"

"That whole candlelight vigil bit? It was basically his idea. He suggested it in the vaguest form, then I took the bait. Hell, once I got rolling on it, I practically thought it was my idea. But it wasn't, not really."

He waved his NAIL THE BASTARD plank in the air. "I still say it's all too risky and too complicated."

"On the contrary, it's the only way. First, he had to find a fall guy. And what kind of moron would agree to that? So he pays Marla off, sets it up so that she gets transactional immunity. Remember in the trial how Marla had said that Ratkin sent his own lawyer over to represent her, and how he made her hold out for transactional immunity. That way she could take the blame, but she couldn't be prosecuted for the crime. He probably paid her a zillion dollars, which she's now living off of down in Belize or wherever.

"But that's not the main reason, Chief. The main problem is that he knew that videotape of the murder would never hold up under scrutiny. Neither would Bollard. If Bollard had showed up at the very beginning, y'all would have dug around for ten minutes and found out that the whole Bollard scenario was bogus, that the real Bollard's an Aboriginal guy who's still knocking around down in Australia somewhere.

"No," I went on, "it had to be set up so that Bollard would arrive at the eleventh hour, once it was too late for you guys to do any sort of real investigation to punch holes in it. I mean once that tape showed up in the middle of trial, that's all she wrote. Case dismissed. And planting the rubber finger in Marla's apartment, that was the icing on the cake, see? That crashed the one supposedly unimpeachable piece of forensic evidence that the state's entire case had relied on, thereby allaying any residual suspicions you guys might have had about Ratkin."

The chief leaned back in his chair, blew out a long breath. "So there wasn't no lesbian affair, huh? He *paid* Marla to do it."

I shook my head. "Nope. That wasn't Marla on the tape."

"What? You're saying Marla didn't do it either?"

"We never saw her face, remember? Because of the high angle of the camera. All we see is a tall thin woman, a long red braid, a big hat."

"That still don't answer my question. Who was she?"

"He," I said. "It was a he."

The chief looked at me solemnly.

"Through a, uh, contact in the FBI," I said, "I was able to persuade the Georgia Bureau of Investigation to send me an inventory of the items in Marla's apartment after she had skipped town. Among them were a bunch of videotapes. My FBI contact was able to convince the GBI to let him review a couple of them. You got a VCR?"

The chief said, "I'll be damn. She made a copy of the surveillance tape that she gave to Ratkin, didn't she?"

"Sure she did," I said. "It was supposed to be her insurance policy. I guess when the crunch came, she didn't have time to get her hands on it. Or maybe she made several copies."

The chief got on the phone and said, "Hey there, Ben. You mind rolling that VCR in here?"

A couple minutes later Ben Pryor rolled a video rig into the office on a trolley. I put the tape in, started the machine.

On the screen, a picture of the entry to Georgia's driveway appeared, the shot obviously taken from a camera mounted next to the gate. To the right side of the screen was the empty patrol booth and the short stainless steel pole with gate code touch pad and inter-com built into it.

After a few seconds, a car appeared at the gate, an old red Dodge Omni, the driver's side door painted with gray primer. On top of the car was a plastic triangle with the Domino's logo on it. A thin arm slid out of the window, pressed the button for the intercom. After a moment the gate opened and the car drove in. Because the surveillance tape was shot at one frame per second, the video had a jerky, fast-motion quality.

"The pizza man," I said. "The pizza man did it."

The chief looked at me through narrowed eyes.

I hit the rewind button, froze the shot where the arm came out of the car. It was hard to see, but the face of the driver was barely visible. Blond hair, thin face, a long blade of a nose.

"Meet John Doe," I said.

Chief Robard squinted at the screen for a long time, then his NAIL THE BASTARD plank came down, *whack,* on his desk. "I'll be goddamn. I interviewed that pizza delivery man myself. Dismissed him out of hand. When he came back a month later with all that black hair and that black beard, dark contact lenses, a suntan, hell, I didn't even recognize him. But still, how . . ."

I pointed at a fawn-colored splotch on the back seat. "Right there is a big tan Stetson. Hard to tell, but I guarantee you it's the same model that Marla Jeter wore."

"Yeah but . . ."

"Marla Jeter was a tall, thin woman. John Doe, the guy that claimed to be Ian Bollard, is a slim man. He puts on a pair of women's pants, with butt pads and hip pads built in. He slides a pair of falsies under his shirt. He hangs a long red braid out the back of the hat. We know how meticulous Ratkin is. John Doe probably practiced walking through that room fifty times, got every angle memorized so he knows how to hold his head in a way that will keep his face hidden under that hat and out of view. Presto, he's Marla Jeter."

"Even if the whole case weren't ridiculously complicated, and too far fetched, we still couldn't even prosecute Ratkin," the chief said.

"Double jeopardy."

The Chief nodded. He looked utterly defeated. "I guess we can go after John Doe," he said.

"Except that you have no idea who he is. You don't have his fingerprints. You don't even know if he's Australian or not. He could be an American guy who's faking the accent. He could be anything."

The chief made an inarticulate noise of disgust.

"Let's face facts, Chief. Jeremy Ratkin just got away with murder."

The chief stared moodily at the legend on the side of the two-by-four in his hand.

• • •

We talked for a while and then the chief stood up to usher me out of the office. The VCR trolley was in his way.

"Ben?" the chief called out the door of his office. "Deputy Pryor? How about getting this video equipment out of here?"

There was no answer.

"Ben? Hey, Ben!"

The chief poked his head out the door and looked around.

"Well, dadgummit, where'd that boy go?"

Suddenly I had a queasy feeling.

"Chief," I said. "Does Ratkin still own the farm out there?"

"Sure."

"I don't suppose you'd know if he's out there today or not?"

The chief frowned. "Matter fact, this new honey of his, she's a horsey type just like Georgia. It was in the paper this morning: they're throwing some kind of equine shindig out there today."

"Better get your car, Chief," I said.

CHAPTER 47

I HAVE NEVER driven as fast in an American sedan as we did driving out to the farm where Georgia Burnett had died. The police chief was trying to look grim and bothered, but I could see he was loving it, the speed and the urgency and the fear. Lot of cops are that way.

There was an off-duty Rome policeman working the gate at the farm. When the chief screeched to a halt, the cop peered in the window with a nervous look on his face.

"Something I should be worried about, Chief?" the cop drawled.

"Why?"

"One of your boys just drove in."

"Son of a bitch," the chief said. "You better open the gate, son."

"Uh, *now*, sir?" the policeman said.

The chief gave him a hard look.

"Sorry, sir." The Rome cop went back to his guard booth and the gate doors began to open.

We drove pell-mell down the gravel drive, pulled up in front of the mansion. There were a lot of cars parked there already. Range Rovers, Suburbans, some Caddies, a Bentley, the usual wheels of the horsey set. I didn't see Ben Pryor's cruiser, but there was a cloud of dust on the dirt track leading around to the stables.

I pointed. The chief grunted, wheeled around past a couple of pretty women in jodphurs and tight blue coats, headed down toward the barns.

Coming into view was a large red-and-white striped tent that had been set up on the lawn behind the big house. Horse people milled around eating off paper plates and drinking out of crystal champagne glasses.

"Whole nother world, ain't it?" the chief said.

"No, Chief, it's the same one you and I live in."

The chief looked at me funny, but what I meant was, in this world it was still about love and respect and trying to find things to do in life that didn't make you feel dirty when you went to bed. The rest was just tinsel.

Ben Pryor's cruiser was parked next to some horse trailers, the door hanging open.

The chief pulled up behind it, stopped in a roiling cloud of dust. I jumped out of the car and started running over toward the striped tent. Jeremy Ratkin was standing among the knot of people eating cold pasta off a paper plate. He turned, met my eye, set down his food.

"Do you mind my asking what you're doing here?" he said, wiping a small fragment of lobster off the corner of his mouth with the tip of one finger.

"Where's Ben Pryor?" I said.

"Who? Oh, that security guy." He shook his head. "Why would *he* be here?"

It was my turn to look puzzled. "I thought he came here to kill you."

Jeremy Ratkin's looked vaguely irritated. "What are talking about?"

"He knows what you did," I said. "He knows you hired that guy, the one who claimed he was Ian Bollard. He knows you had Georgia killed."

Ratkin's face remained impassive. He looked around to see if anybody had heard us. "You mind keeping your voice down. I have guests."

"Hey, fuck you," I said.

"Anyway, what's that got to do with him killing me?"

I laughed a little. "He was in love with your wife. *He* was the one she was having an affair with. *He* was the one she was probably going to leave you for."

Jeremy Ratkin laughed loudly. "Dream on," he said. "Georgia leaving *me* for a security guard?"

I gestured broadly with my hands, taking in the house, the pastures, the horsey people. "This was all you had to give her, you arrogant prick. And you'd already given it. You had nothing else left that she needed."

Ratkin trained his dark, disdainful gaze on me, but didn't say anything.

I poked him with my finger just to the left of his sternum. "Right here," I said. "You are empty as a dry ditch. Ben Pryor is not. It's that simple."

I turned and left him standing there, then headed down to the stables. Ben Pryor wasn't there either. But I found him a minute later.

He was out in the middle of the pasture behind the barn. Running across the green expanse, Pryor limped a little from the old football injury, and his arms were spread like wings. Around him moved a whirling mass of beautiful horses—bays, roans, Appaloosas, and a regal white mare that I recognized as Georgia's horse. Eyes rolling, nostrils dilated, their iridescent flanks streamed with sweat in the bright sunshine.

I climbed over the fence and ran toward him. When I got closer I could see that his eyes were red and his face was wet with tears. He was smiling, though, too—furious and sad at the same time.

"I thought you came here to kill Ratkin," I said, gasping a little for breath.

Ben Pryor kept trotting along, arms spread, driving the horses in crazy, wheeling circles. I jogged with him. He looked a little puzzled, then he laughed strangely. "I just came for the horses," he said. "These are all *her* horses. That man doesn't deserve them."

"What, you gonna steal them, Ben? Drive them out

one of the gates and into the woods? I mean, seriously?"

Ben's big arms shrugged. "Guess I had some kind of vague notion like that. Once I got here, though, it just didn't make no sense."

Around us was only grass and the plosive thud of hooves. Horses are dumb as hell, but they've got a kind of emotional sensitivity most people don't have. They pick up on things. And so, I think, they were joining Ben Pryor in whatever he was feeling, his horror and sadness at finding out that the man who killed the woman he loved was going to walk away without paying any sort of price.

I spread my arms, too, then and abandoned myself to Ben Pryor's confused passion as he herded the horses around and around the pasture. I felt a strange sense of freedom, a giddy sense of leaving something behind— those human desires for things you can't put your finger on, things like Right and Truth and Justice and Retribution.

It was about that time that we heard the shots, two of them, almost simultaneous.

I ran back toward the stables, gasping and wheezing by then. Ben Pryor gimped along at my heel. And behind him came the horses, whinnying and snorting. As we reached the stable, I heard two more shots.

I rounded the corner and saw a man lying on the ground in the middle of the long barn. Standing over the figure on the ground was Chief Ray Robard, a black nine-millimeter clutched in one white-knuckled hand.

I ran through the barn toward them, not stopping until I saw the long-nosed face of the man on the ground. It was John Doe, Ian Bollard, Robert Smith—whatever his name really was. In his hand was a cut-down shotgun with duct tape wrapped around the grip.

"I found him mucking out a stall in here," the chief said. His eyes were bright with fury and adrenaline. "He must have thought I was going to arrest him. This time he knew it would stick, so he drew on me. I had to shoot him."

There was only one visible wound in the dead man's body, a small hole in his cheek. I couldn't see because of the way he was lying, but it seemed likely there was not much left of the back of his head. I wondered who the hell he really was, what his name was, where he came from. I supposed we'd find his real identity soon enough.

"I heard four shots," I said.

The chief nodded to his left, looking at something over my shoulder. I turned then and saw Jeremy Ratkin. He was leaned up against the open gate of one of the horse stalls, blood dripping off his neck and onto the straw-covered floor. As best I could tell, he'd been shot once in the neck and once dead center in the chest. As always, his eyes were alert and calculating, full of a hard, cold intensity. But in the few moments I watched him, that fierce intensity drained slowly out of his black eyes. When it was gone, he fell down on his face and didn't move a lick. All around us horses were stamping and whickering nervously.

"Ratkin, too?" I said. "*Ratkin* drew on you?" I couldn't really picture Jeremy Ratkin pointing a gun at anyone. That was the sort of thing he hired other people to do.

The chief was looking around him like he was a little confused about something. I noticed then that there was blood running down his hip, staining the side of his khaki uniform trousers. John Doe, whoever he was, must have caught the chief in his side, right above the pelvis, with a blast from the shotgun.

The chief bent down stiffly, pulled a small revolver out of a holster around his own ankle, and began walking slowly toward Ratkin's limp, prone body.

"I asked you a question, Chief. They *both* tried to shoot you?"

The chief glanced at me, wiped his prints off the little

revolver with his brown necktie, then tossed the gun in the straw next to Ratkin's motionless right hand.

"Hey! Chief! *Both* of them?"

"Both," Chief Ray Robard said softly. His face was getting pale, and I had a hunch he was about to go into shock. He looked at me and smiled. "That's my story, and I'm sticking to it."

I must have made a face of disgust because Ray Robard said, "What, Sunny? You gonna dispute me?"

I stared at him for a few moments, then looked down at the gun lying next to Ratkin's right hand. "I believe, Chief," I said, "that Ratkin is left handed. You might want to kick that little throw-down over to the other side of his body."

Then I turned and walked away, back to where Ben Pryor and the horses were waiting. Outside the barn the beautiful, dumb animals stamped and snorted in nervous confusion. The things that had happened in that barn—and in the house behind it—they were way too complicated for any horse to ever understand.

"Five minutes," I said to Ben Pryor. "For just five minutes I'd like to be one of them."

"Yeah," he said, wiping at one eye with the back of one hand. "Me, too."